JIHADI
Black Widow

By Rik Thistle

ACKNOWLEDGMENTS

Thanks to my family and friends who have helped with ideas and criticisms of this story. You know who you are! Without their support, the Jihadi series would not have been written. I have used some of their names either first or last, as a tribute to their friendship and help throughout the process. Hope you enjoy this story.

Rik Thistle

For all the United States of America military men and women past and present who put their lives on the line every day to protect our way of life and freedom.

ji·had·i
ji ' hädē/
noun
A person involved in a jihad; an Islamic militant.

Qur'an 3.151

"Soon shall We cast terror into the hearts of the Unbelievers,

for that they joined companions with Allah, for which He had

sent no authority"

Jihadi Black Widow

Copyright ©2018 by Thistle Literary LLC

Thistle Literary LLC. Edition April, 2018

For information about special discounts for bulk purchases, please contact the author at rikthistleauthor@gmail.com

Manufactured in the United States of America

10 9 8 7 6 5 4 3 2 1

ISBN 978-0-692-10114-8

Chapter 1

Quetta Afghanistan - July 5th

Nimr Yazdi was one of the most trusted of Hamza bin Ladin, the current leader of al-Qaeda, the son of Osama bin Ladin. He is the linchpin between the terrorist group and The Republic of Iran. His role was key in the plot to develop and deliver a hybrid virus that would have killed 90% of the world's population, but would have left the Iranian population unscathed when the scientist who developed the flu/ebola virus gene spliced out a Persian gene. It was called Red Death and was developed to be the ultimate ethnic cleanser and lead to Muslim domination of the world. But Nimr made a major mistake. He trusted his boyhood friend who had moved to America and worked for the CIA. When Mailis al-Din came to him in the middle of the operation, he should have known better. He should have killed him when he had the chance. But instead he brought him into the secret al-Qaeda facility and gave him the opportunity to fulfill his deadly mission. Now a large number of the al-Qaeda leadership is dead. Mailis had tricked them all and killed most of them. But not him. Nimr was fighting for his life. He wants revenge on America and this gives him the strength and the will to survive.

After Mailis shot him in the shoulder inside the al-Qaeda sanctuary, Nimr ducked under the table while the shooting continued. When he looked up, he could see Mailis standing over him with absolute hatred in his boyhood friend's eyes. Then all he saw was the muzzle of the AK-47. As Nimr was sure he was going be to shot in the head, he began to pray. As Mailis pulled the trigger, all Nimr could think of was how he had multiple opportunities to kill him. The explosion of the AK-47 deafened him and knocked him back and to the side. Somehow the bullet grazed his head. He heard some continued shooting, but it seemed to be in a distance. Suddenly in a moment of clarity, he knew that he had to get out. Where he was would be a death trap shortly, the U.S. military probably followed Mailis and if they weren't here now, they would be soon.

While Mailis fought his way to the main elevator, Nimr knew there was a secret elevator that led to the adjoining building and up on the surface. He crawled out of the conference room and turned right heading for the cafeteria. It was total chaos. People shot, running for cover and yelling for help.

Nimr could feel the blood from his shoulder wound dripping down his back and he was having problems moving his left hand. His vision continued to fade in and out. After several minutes, he reached the elevator and with a shaking hand keyed in the code.

The doors opened as he held the Russian PPM pistol at the ready. The U.S. military could be right outside the elevator, but he knew he had to get out quickly. His intention is to kill whoever he encountered and track down Mailis, if he escaped. Assuming the U.S. military is not already targeting them with a cruise missile or a bunker buster bomb; they will shortly. The elevator slowly made its way to the surface and just as the doors opened and he stepped out, Nimr could feel the first missile hit. The ground shook, and then a huge explosion rocked the area. The U.S. Military had just hit the main warehouse and the housing unit three stories down. He got out of the elevator just in time. The underground explosion collapsed the structure and flames and smoke billowed out. The building he is in is also destroyed by the blast. Nimr is buried by parts of the building roof, but is saved by a beam that fell and created a pocket of protection. The second blast confirmed for Nimr that everyone underground was dead. He lay still for several minutes waiting for another missile, but he only hears silence. Amid the destruction, Nimr passes out.

After several hours, Nimr wakes to total darkness and total silence. He is thirsty and his shoulder is numb. He reaches up and pulls a piece of roofing off his head. As he looks up he can see some sunlight, but with a cloud of smoke still hanging over the area. After another ten minutes, Nimr begins to pull debris off himself and climb upward.

Every movement causes incredible pain in his shoulder. After several hours, Nimr crawls out of the destroyed building and collapses next to a smoking car. He lays there for several minutes to catch his breath. Nimr sees that this is the car he and Mailis used for their escape. Then he remembers that in the back of the car that brought him to the facility were several bottles of water. He pulls himself up to the car door and peers inside. There on the floor are three bottles of water. Nimr tries to pull the door open but it is mangled and still hot and won't open. He slowly moves around the car tries the passenger door and it opens using his robe to cover his hand. Climbing inside, he maneuvers himself so that he can reach the bottles with his good hand. Sitting in the passenger seat, Nimr guzzles one of the bottles of water. As he lies back with his eyes closed, he has to decide whether to stay where he is and hope that the authorities come to investigate or try to walk out to the main road. Nimr knows he has lost a lot of blood and is getting weaker by the minute. Making up his mind, he stuffs the remaining bottles of water into his pockets and climbs out of the car. He decides to leave the gun as it won't be much help now.

Walking slowly, he makes his way to the main gate and sees the bodies of the guards, each with a bullet hole in their foreheads. Nimr knows now that Mailis led the U.S. military to the al-Qaeda site and is the reason for all this death and destruction.

Hopefully Mailis was killed in the missile attack, but if he survived Nimr swears to Allah, that he will kill him.

Overwhelming hatred fuels his body with energy as he begins to walk slowly to the main road. After two hours, he struggles to the highway and sits. He finishes his last bottle of water and waits. It is now late afternoon and the sun is starting to set. Suddenly he sees a truck coming his way. Nimr slowly and painfully rises and waves his good arm for the driver to stop. The truck slows, and then stops. Nimr struggles to walk and then collapses beside the truck. The driver gets out and sees all the blood. He doesn't want to get into the middle of a gang fight, but he can't leave this man to bleed to death. The driver gets a medical kit from his truck and bandages Nimr's shoulder and head. After giving Nimr some additional water he helps him into the passenger seat.

As the driver starts the vehicle, Nimr says with difficulty, "if you can drive me to Islamabad, Hamza bin Ladin will give you a large reward for saving my life." The truck driver smiles and decides to alter his route to head north to Islamabad.

Nimr sits back and closes his eyes trying to block out the pain. He concentrates on what he needs to do next. "Can you turn on the radio?"

The truck driver nods and pushes the radio knob. The radio blasts some music. Nimr tunes the radio to a news channel.

What Nimr doesn't hear causes him to wonder if his uncle's plan was successful. There is no mention of worldwide sickness. If Mailis was able to alert the U.S. military to their plans, then perhaps they were able to stop the Iranian virus, he thinks. Instead of the world dealing with a doomsday hybrid virus, the Great Satan dodged a world changing event. The anger he had suppressed now returns. Nimr pledges to himself and Allah that if he survives, he will bring pain, humiliation and death to America. He smiles knowing that the West will think he is dead and he'll be able to implement a new plan that is forming in his head.

Chapter 2

Los Angles, California - July 14th

Mark Aldin is standing silently at the grave of his son, Paul. The service is over and everyone has left the cemetery. He knows he can't stand here forever, but he just doesn't want to let go.

Over the past couple of weeks, Paul's heroism has been broadcasted on every medium in the United States and around the world. Mark's son was one of the victims of an al-Qaeda suicide bomber that killed or wounded over 400 people in Jordan. But what Paul did is what everyone is talking about. The bomber walked into a hotel ballroom in Jordan full of kids dancing. But before he could get into the middle of the room, Paul saw him for what he was and pulled him down. Unfortunately the suicide bomber's handler saw what had happened, and triggered the bomb. What Paul did unselfishly saved hundreds of lives.

After his son's death, Mark using his Arabic name of Mailis tracked down the handler who was also the key link between al-Qaeda and Iran. To Mark's surprise, that man was Mark's boyhood friend, Nimr Yazdi. When the CIA discovered that Iran had developed a deadly hybrid virus by combining the flu and Ebola viruses, the fate of the world was in Mark's hands.

Mark discovered the list of Iranians agents who were tasked with releasing the virus around the world. After transmitting the Iranian agents' burner phones to the CIA, each team was captured or killed ending the virus threat. At the same time, Mark who had befriended Nimr Yazdi, infiltrated the secret al-Qaeda underground site. He killed Yazdi, and then escaped with U.S. Special Operators who destroyed the facility decimating the terrorist group. Mark's heroism would only be known to a few key insiders within the CIA and the President, and that is fine with Mark.

Mark can sense someone standing behind him. He knows he is a target by al-Qaeda and wonders if this is the time they get their revenge. His hand moves slowly to the Sig Sauer on his hip under his coat. "Mark, I am so sorry." he hears. Mark knows the voice and smiles. As he turns he sees Michelle Samaha, his CIA handler. She moves forward and they embrace.

"Thank you Michelle. I didn't see you during the service."

"I was in the back. I didn't want to intrude."

Mark smiles. "Thanks for coming."

Michelle breaks the embrace and looks up into Mark's sad face. She wonders how he will ever get beyond his grief. They stand for several minutes in silence looking down on the fresh dirt of the grave. Then Mark turns and they walk away. As they reach their cars, Mark turns and smiles. "How long will you be here?"

Michelle is the Assistant Director of Middle Eastern Affairs for the CIA and has worked with Mark for the past two years. As a team, they were instrumental in stopping the worst terrorist attack in history. "I'll be here as long as you need someone to talk with. Are you going to the reception?" Michelle says.

Mark is suppose to go back to the reception at his former house after the funeral service, but can't face his ex-wife again. Sitting at the grave site next to her was one of the most emotionally draining moments of his life. She still blames him for allowing their son Paul to travel to Jordan for a graduation gift, leading to his murder by the terrorists. Jennifer will blame him for the rest of her life and has turned most of their friends and family against him. Even his daughter Mary blames him for her brother's death. She barely acknowledged him during the service. Mark knows how devastating the loss of her brother is to her. She looked up to him as her older brother, but also as her guide into adulthood. Paul seemed to always do the right thing, say the right thing. Now he is gone and her life will never be the same. Mark breaks out of his private thoughts and replies. "No, I just can't."

Michelle can see tears forming in Mark's eyes and wants to hold him, but stops herself.

"How about lunch then?" You can leave your car and we'll come back after you've had something to eat.

Mark nods and gets into Michelle's rental. "I saw a restaurant just a couple of blocks down, would that be ok?"

Mark says, "Yeah, that's the AMMO at the Hammer."

Michelle smiles, "Well it sounds like my type of place."

Mark smiles back, "its good normal food and has a courtyard. It shouldn't be too crowded at this time."

After a short drive up Wilshire Drive, Michelle parks and they walk into the restaurant. There are several open tables and they find one under an umbrella. It's a warm day, but with a gentle breeze. They order and Mark tells her about the Hammer.

"This restaurant is attached to the Hammer Museum. It was built by Dr. Armand Hammer to house his collection of fine art. It was finished in November, 1990, Dr. Hammer died just three weeks after the opening." The food arrives and they start in silence.

"Oh, that is too bad." Says Michelle between bites of her tuna salad sandwich.

14

"UCLA operates the museum now. It contains hundreds of priceless art. Monet, Degas, Van Gogh and a Rembrandt if I remember correctly. Would you like to walk through?"

Michelle is surprised that Mark would like art, but then again he consistently surprises her. "Sure, I'd love to."

After they finish their meals and pay the check, they stroll into the museum. It's free and Michelle picks up a brochure. As they make their way through the various rooms, Mark points out key paintings and seems to have the history of each at his command. They stop in front of two paintings. "This is a Moreau. *King David* painted in 1878, the other is *Salome Dancing Before Herod* painted in 1876. They are two of my favorites." They stand side by side admiring the painting. "The detail on the king's crown and also on the lamp are amazing. I would come over here between classes sometimes and just stand for hours looking at the smallest details."

Michelle smiles. "They are beautiful."

Mark then leads her to another part of the Hammer. "I want you to see Van Gogh's *Hospital at Saint-Remy*." They stop in front of a wild painting with vivid colors and a building in the background. "Vincent Van Gogh voluntarily committed himself to a mental hospital in Saint-Remy in the south of France. This was six years after he cut off his ear."

Michelle had read some about Van Gogh but like most people, didn't know many details.

"He felt it was a wonderful place and he rented two rooms, one of which was his studio. During his time at Saint-Remy he painted many of his best works including this painting and *Starry Night*, his most famous." Mark pauses and stares at the painting.

"It reminds me that even in the worst of times, something beautiful can be created."

Michelle turns to him. There are tears running down her cheeks. She wants to hold him, hold him tightly but she tells herself to stop. "Mark, something good will come out of your tragedy. I know it will."

Mark smiles and wipes a tear from her cheek, "I think so too. Let's head back to the car."

After a short walk, they get into Michelle's car and she starts the car but doesn't put it in drive. "Mark, the President would like you to come back to Washington D.C. with me to get an award from the CIA for your heroism and helping to stop the spread of the virus. It would be at the CIA headquarters with no outsiders." That is fine with Mark as he wasn't looking for medals or kudos. Michelle continues, "Also, I have been appointed the Director of a new division within the CIA. I'd like you to be on my team."

Mark is surprised and is silent for a minute. It would be hard to move to the East coast, harder still to leave UCLA, Mark thinks.

Michelle waits while he considers the offer. "Just come to Washington with me and meet the President. Hear what he has to say. Then make your decision."

"What kind of new organization are you heading up?"

Michelle knows that until Mark is on the team and a full time employee of the CIA she can't tell him everything, but she also knows he will be a key member and that he still has his top secret clearance. Michelle decides to tell him all that she can. "The President asked me to head up a Super Black division that will be strictly off the books. Funding will come from another CIA black project. No Congressional oversight."

Mark looks confused. "What's the mission?"

Michelle smiles. "The President is done with the current rules of engagement. He wants an organization that can identify, track and kill as many terrorists as possible. Go on the offense instead of being on the defense."

Mark nods and smiles. "Sounds like something I could get behind."

Michelle lights up. "I knew you'd be interested. But there is one more thing."

"What's that?"

"The President has signed a secret Executive Order authorizing this group to operate anywhere in the world, including the United States."

Mark nods. "Unfortunately ISIS, al-Qaeda, Hamas, Iran and others will be coming for us. They already are. We really have no idea how many cells are currently in the United States.

It could be hundreds. Unfortunately the general Muslim community is not stepping up and publically condemning radical Islam. What is happening to the Coptic Christians in Egypt is a disgrace. Hamas and the Muslim Brotherhood are systematically killing Christians and Muslims much as they did when I was a boy."

Michelle looks into his eyes. "That is why I need you. The country needs you."

Mark looks down at his hands. "Who else is on the team?"

"Jonathan Bardsley is the Head of Analysis; he has a team to five key analysts. I brought in a dozen senior agents including Ducky," referring to Tom Duckworth one of Mark's U.S. Navy SEAL teammates. "Plus I have one ace in the hole. It's a kid we discovered who is a savant in internet analysis. He can trace anything and anybody. We got him from the Justice Department. He's highly motivated and will be with us for at least ten years."

Mark looks puzzled. "He is under contract for ten years? How can you guarantee that?"

Michelle smiles. "Well, he had a choice of working for us for ten years or doing twenty years in a Federal Corrections facility. He was caught moving almost a hundred million dollars from one of the major U.S. banks to an off-shore account in the Caymans. He was then transferring the money to various refugee and philanthropic causes. A modern day Robin Hood, I guess. Doing it for fun."

Mark counters, "So if he is so smart, how did he get caught?"

Michelle smiles, and then continues. "He has a certain addiction that was his undoing."

"What? Drugs, women, porn?"

"M&Ms"

Mark looks totally confused. "S&M? Bondage, that sort of thing?"

Michelle laughs. "No, the little chocolate candies."

"How did M&Ms get him caught?"

Michelle looks out the windshield and replies. "He was holed up in his college dorm room at MIT using the University computer system to communicate with multiple servers around the world. He was using the remote servers to break into and steal a small percentage of each of the banks' international transactions, but which totaled almost a hundred million dollars in just a few months. The IRS noticed money being funneled into a particular Cayman account that was divided up into three major charities, but couldn't trace the electronic transactions. Then one Saturday night our savant had a munchies attack and went to the dorm's cafeteria to get something to eat. Fortunately for us, he left his door unlocked and another student went into his room to ask him if he wanted to go to a Frat party and discovered what he was doing on his laptop. He called the police, who called the FBI and within four hours conducted a raid and discovered him transferring several millions of dollars while eating M&Ms."

Mark laughs. "Wow. Good for us."

"After the FBI understood his level of internet expertise, the FBI Director spoke with the Director of National Intelligence and they worked a plea bargain. For his freedom, he will work for us for the next ten years to help us track terrorists, their money and their communications. I believe he will be a key part of our success."

Mark is silent for several seconds, then replies. "Ok, count me in."

Michelle starts the car to take Mark back to the cemetery. "Great, do what you need to do here and we'll get a plane to get you to Langley next week for the ceremony at the CIA and then we'll get to work."

Chapter 3

Washington DC - July 14th

The President's eyes light up every time he sees his grandchildren. Oliver, Filip, Samuel and William are ten, eight, six and four but they seem to be able to say or do something that delights "*Poppy*" each time. They race around the Oval Office with the youthful exuberance that comes from being free of worry and full of energy. The new President is just six months into his first term, but already he has faced several daunting tests. First was a well coordinated al-Qaeda attack on Detroit and Minneapolis that resulted in over 250 murdered. The suicide attacks in Paris and in Jordan were even worse. In addition to those killed in the Middle East was the son of Dr. Mark Aldin, a part-time CIA contractor who is now agreed to work for the super secret Ultra Black organization that is now being set up to proactively fight the terrorists on their own turf.

William Kellan Baker was able, with the help of Mark Aldin and Michelle Samaha, to stop Iran from releasing a hybrid virus that would have decimated the world's population. He has reflected on how different the world would be now if they had not been able to intercept the twelve briefcases and destroy the virus.

The four boys are starting to slow down so the President decides to let them in on a secret of the Oval Office. "Boys, come over here." The President is standing next to his chair and behind the Resolute desk that many Presidents have used as their primary desk. "Look under the desk and let me know what you see."

The boys are curious and kneel down and peer under the desk. "Boys, if you climb under the desk, you can slide a secret front panel and climb out." The boys are immediately intrigued. Oliver climbs under first then slides the panel and climbs out to the delight of his brother. Then Filip does the same, then Samuel and finally Will. They repeat the process five or six times while the President and his daughter laugh out loud. Finally the President calls a halt in the game and moves the Presidential chair in the way.

"Claire, I appreciate you bringing the boys over. I need the comic relief after all that has happened the past several months. So I understand you and Oliver and Filip are planning a trip to Italy in two weeks. Where are you going to go?

The President's daughter smiles. "Yes, we are going to visit a college roommate in Rome, and then we head to Siena, Florence, Pisa and finally to Lake Como. I haven't seen Diane in almost fifteen years. As I think you remember, we were roommates at Colorado. Then she went to University of Virginia and is working for the State Department in Rome."

The President nods. "I remember Diane. A red head? An infectious laugh?

Claire nods. "Yep, she was the life of the party. She still is, I hear. Coming with a ten year old and an eight year old will be a big shock to her. I wish Andrew could come along, but he is trying to close a big deal and can't get away. Plus Andrew will have to take care of both Samuel and William." Referring to her husband and the President's son-in-law who is the President of a mid-sized commercial development company in Denver, and a super dad.

"Well, I want to beef up the Secret Service protection while you are in Italy."

"Dad, having two Secret Service agents with us all the time is more than enough. I think it actually brings more attention to us, than if we were just walking around Rome by ourselves."

The President shakes his head. "No, you have to have some level of protection. I'd like to add two more agents. Just for your time in Italy."

Claire sits in one of the chairs while the kids wrestle on the Presidential rug. "No, I want this to be a real vacation and we can't do that with FOUR agents trailing us. Please dad! We feel comfortable with Agent Kim and Agent Bale. Don't add two more people the kids have to get used to. We'll be fine.

The President looks over to the four young boys wrestling in a playful manner. "It's just very dangerous now. Always has been, but especially in today's world with ISIS, al-Qaeda and a dozen other terrorist groups."

The President's daughter rises. "I understand Daddy, but we will keep a low profile and I am sure Diane knows where to go and where not to go. She has lived in Italy for over six years and she has the State Department Intel there about what is happening."

President Baker moves to hug his daughter. "Ok, we'll go with just the two agents. Just be careful."

Claire collects the boys and they head back to their Washington D.C. hotel looking forward to a vacation in beautiful Italy unaware that she is being tracked by the most dangerous terrorist group in the world.

Chapter 4

White Sands Missile Range - July 14th
New Mexico

General Joseph Skyhar enters the High Energy Laser Systems Test Facility (HELSTF) conference room and all of the officers stand. "Please be seated. Are we ready for the demonstration?

A Colonel remains standing. "Yes Sir! What you will see is our latest version of our High Energy Laser (HEL) Weapon. It is mobile on a specially built truck that allows the HEL system to be moved to intercept incoming threats or to destroy tanks, planes or buildings. We have been able to intercept up to a dozen incoming missiles and have been able to destroy a tank from two kilometers."

The General rises. "OK, let's see the demonstration."

The group exits the conference room and then the building into the searing heat. It's 97 degrees Fahrenheit with a slight breeze. The group enters a series of jeeps and is driven to a specific test range location. There is a viewing stand set up for the invitees and as each member leaves the jeep, they are handed binoculars. The General and his staff move to the shaded stands and wait for the demonstration to begin.

The Colonel sits next to the General and tells him that the demonstration will start shortly.

Within a minute, a large truck with a turret on top moves to an area near the stands. It is impressive. It is large with the Army desert camouflage paint and multiple mirrors and sensors inside the turret. It swings to the west.

"General, look out with your binoculars to 10 o'clock. You will see a tank sitting on that ridge."

The General raises his binoculars, as does all of the staff. In the distance, the General can see a tank.

"That tank is approximate 2 Klicks away. Within seconds, the HEL system can acquire the target, then fire the tactical high energy laser and destroy the target." The Colonel gives the signal.

Within seconds the HEL mobile system emits a soft whine, then fires. While the General watches, the tank explodes.

The Colonel sees a smile spread across the Generals face.

"Damn" he says.

The Colonel says, "we have a remotely controlled jet which will make an attack on our position. It will be in a terrain hugging approach. At more than two miles, the HEL system will engage and shoot it down. The cost of an inexpensive surface-to-air missile is $100,000. The laser can shoot at a cost of $10. Also, the laser can pick up a dozen targets and get those shots off within 30 seconds."

The General looks over at him. "What happens if the laser misses?"

"The HEL system will fire another shot until the target is destroyed. But 92% of the time, it takes just one shot to be successful. Also if the jet releases a missile, the system will target the missile first, then the jet."

The Colonel nods to his assistant and she tells the drone pilot to bring the jet in. After a minute the group sees a small dot on the horizon, coming in low and fast. Suddenly the HEL system whine can be heard then the jet explodes and tumbles into the desert.

The General stands as do most of the other visitors. "Holy Crap!"

Suddenly three dots come over the horizon. The General looks at the Colonel with surprise on his face.

"Watch this," says the Colonel.

The HEL system acquires the first jet and fires. It cartwheels and explodes in the distance. The other jets suddenly take evasive actions. One dips to within 50 feet of the desert floor, the other pulls up and swings wide to make another approach. The HEL system tracks the lower flying jet, and then shoots. It immediate re-acquires the third jet and fires. The laser ignites the fuel line of the second jet. The third loses its wing and both jets explode and crash.

The General has a huge smile on his face. "Colonel, well done. Very impressive. How many of these systems do we currently have? How many can we build in the next six months?"

The Colonel replies. "We have four prototype systems built, a demo system plus some spares. Lockheed Martin can build at a rate of six per month, perhaps more if we have the funding."

"Believe me Colonel, you will get the funding. I am going to brief the President."

The General and his staff leave the facility and board a jet for a flight back to Washington D.C. wanting to inform the President of this new and effective weapon.

Chapter 5

CIA Headquarters - July 21st
Langley, VA

Mark and Michelle are sitting in a CIA conference room. She is smiling while Mark tries to straighten his tie. Michelle rises and moves to stand in front of Mark. "Let me fix that for you."

Mark relents and allows Michelle to pull his Winsor knot tight and she straightens his collar. She can sense that Mark is nervous. He has been pacing for the past half an hour waiting for the President to arrive at Langley to present Mark with the CIA citation. Mark can smell Michelle's perfume and sense her sensuality being so close to him. "Thanks Michelle. Why don't these conference rooms have a mirror?"

Michelle laughs. "Maybe because at the CIA, most agents don't want to look at themselves too closely."

Mark nods knowing what she means.

Suddenly an aide to the DNI opens the door and lets them know that the ceremony is ready. The pair follows the aide to the iconic lobby where several hundred chairs have been set up in front of a small stage that contains six chairs and a podium. Three chairs on one side of the podium, three on the other. Mark and Michelle walk up the stairs to the podium, joining Tom "Ducky" Duckworth. On the podium already is the Director of National Intelligence Andy Cobb, the Director of the CIA Cameron Anderson and the President of the United States. As they shake hands with each other, the President moves to the podium.

"A month ago we learned that the Iranians in conjunction with al-Qaeda planned multiple terrorist attacks, two of which were here in the United States. Additionally, the Iranians developed a doomsday virus that potentially could have killed 90% of the world's population to allow the Jihadis to rule the world." The President motions towards Mark. "Dr. Mark Aldin was a part-time CIA contractor who accurately translated al-Qaeda documents that revealed both plots. Without his translation, America and indeed the rest of the world would have been devastated. As all of you know, his son Paul was killed in the suicide bomber attack in Jordan. Mark could have attended to his family during this time of sorrow. But instead he tracked down the key linchpin between Iran and al-Qaeda, discovered the cellular phone numbers of the twelve terrorists carrying the briefcases with the virus and got that information to his CIA handler. Then Mark allowed himself to be kidnapped to a secret al-Qaeda facility in Pakistan where our military were able to follow him and destroy hundreds of al-Qaeda leaders. Dr. Mark Aldin risked his life and went above and beyond with courage to quite frankly save America. I am proud to award him the CIA Distinguished Intelligence Cross.

With that, the crowd stands and claps loudly. Mark stands while the President places the gold cross around his neck. Mark shakes the President's hand, then the DNI and then the Director of the CIA. As Mark sits, the DNI rises and takes the President's place at the podium.

"Michelle Samaha and Tom Duckworth were instrumental in the success of our two operations, guiding Dr. Aldin and taking direct responsibility for tracking Dr. Aldin and calling in the Special Operators to destroy the al-Qaeda facility. For their valor and courage, I am happy to award them both the CIA Medal of Merit."

After the ceremony Mark, Michelle and Tom are shaking hands and chatting with many of the CIA top management. Andy Cobb moves across the room to talk with Michelle and Mark. "Congratulations Mark and Michelle. You both deserve the adulations. We are very grateful for your service. I think your next assignments will be just as critical." He says with a smile.

"Thank you sir." Michelle says. "We are excited about the opportunity."

Mark shakes the DNI's hand. "We are ready to take the fight to the terrorists."

The DNI smiles, "I have a time critical assignment that I'd like to speak with you both about this afternoon. Come to my office at 3 pm."

Both Michelle and Mark reply in the affirmative and Andy Cobb moves off to speak with the Director of the CIA. The President comes over and shakes Michelle's and Mark's hands. "Congratulations. But you know that these awards are called *Jock Strap Medals.*" Michelle smiles knowing the joke, Mark is puzzled.

"Jock strap medals?" asks Mark.

The President replies with a smile. "These awards around you neck will never see the light of day. With the classification level of your operations, the medals can not be displayed or even acknowledged publically. So the Agency has specially-built lockers for each employee who is awarded a medal, where they can store the medal and any other awards."

Mark laughs. "Damn, I was planning to send the award to my dad for him to wear during his poker nights."

Michelle knows the rules and had already mentally put the award away and smiles at Mark's joke.

The President lowers his voice. "DNI Cobb informed me of a top secret operation that he is planning and you both will be involved in. Good luck."

"Thank you Mr. President. We are scheduled to meet with the DNI this afternoon."

The President nods and then moves away with his secret service agents in tow.

Michelle turns to Mark. "We should get back to the office, then over to the DNI office. Let's go."

Both Mark and Michelle give their medals to a CIA administrator who will place them in their personalized lockers, then leave the CIA headquarters for the half hour drive back to the Ultra Black site.

As they get into Michelle's car, she turns to Mark. "I know you've made the right decision to join our team. We will make a significant difference and save lives here at home."

Mark smiles. "I hope so. I am excited to see what I can do to help."

"First I'd like you to meet our latest recruit. The internet whiz kid who I believe could be a very valuable asset to help us find and destroy the al-Qaeda leadership."

Chapter 6

Bihsud, Afghanistan - July 22nd

Hamza bin Laden is sitting quietly beside the bed of Nimr Yazdi. The patient has been in the safe house for the past couple of weeks recovering from the U.S. military bombing of the secret al-Qaeda facility in Quetta. Hamza is amazed his friend was able to escape, but sad that so many committed Jihadis died. After escaping, Nimr fled to Islamabad trying to find bin Laden. He made his way to one of the safe houses and was taken in. After a week of being tended to by an al-Qaeda doctor, Nimr was transported secretly at night from Islamabad to Binsud across the border into Afghanistan. The doctor told Hamza that the patient was lucky to be alive. With two gun shots and some second degree burns from the explosion, he should be dead. Instead with the grace of Allah, Nimr not only survived but was able to find his way to Hamza.

"How are you feeling, my friend?" Says bin Laden.

The patient opens his eyes and smiles. "I am much better today and I will be stronger tomorrow."

Hamza nods and gives Nimr a glass of water. "The Americans were able to stop the virus. Then they bombed the

Iranian research facility and killed Dr. Rahimi. How they found out about the virus and how it was being distributed is a mystery."

Nimr stays silent. Trying to decide whether to tell Hamza about how his boyhood friend that he allowed into the al-Qaeda facility and was able to not only kill many of the al-Qaeda leadership, but probably was responsible for stopping the virus. Nimr wants revenge on Mailis Nasir al-Din and the American President.

"Rest now and we can talk more tomorrow."

Nimr sits up in the bed slightly and says, "We must talk now. You said you have a plan to make America pay for what it has done."

Hamza takes the water from Nimr and places it on a night table beside the bed. "Yes, we have a person in the new American administration, and they have given us some critical information."

Nimr tries to sit up straighter and winces with the pain of his shoulder. "What information?"

"The American President is very family oriented. He has a wife, three daughters and five grandchildren. Our contact has informed us that the President's daughter and two of his grandchildren are planning a vacation in Italy for later this month.

We have a very strong organization there and we are planning to abduct them and hold them for ransom."

Nimr furrows his brow. "Why not just kill them with a bomb?"

"Because they are worth a lot more alive, than dead. Over the past couple of years the Americans have shutdown our ability to raise significant amounts of money. ISIS was giving us millions of Euros a year from their black market oil sales. But ISIS is in retreat in Iraq and Syria and in no position to help us. We have gotten funding from friends in Saudi Arabia, Qatar and the UAE. But it's not enough for us to coordinate large attacks on the west. If we can capture the President's daughter and grandchildren, we can ask for almost anything for freeing them."

Nimr sees the logic, but knows it will be extremely difficult to abduct relatives of the President. "Doesn't the family get Secret Service protection?"

Hamza smiles. "Yes of course. But our contact is in the U.S. State Department and can give us information about their schedule. She has recently come to Islam and has been secretly plotting to help us. She has passed us information on the President's movements and some other classified information which we have passed on to our friends, but yesterday we received a message from her about the Italian vacation.

I decided that if we can put the plan into action, it is an opportunity we can not miss."

Nimr smiles, "Of course, but it will take a flawless plan."

"That is why I want you to head up the planning and execution of the operation. You have been to Italy and you know the Americans as well as anyone we have. If you are feeling better, I'd like you to meet with two of my key people to start the plan. Within a few weeks we hope to have the President's full attention."

After Hamza leaves the room, Nimr lays back and tries to focus his mind on how he could implement the plan. In one of the corners he sees a spider spinning his web. Nimr smiles, it is a sign from Allah that he will be successful in setting a trap for the American president.

Chapter 7

CIA Ultra Black Site – July 27th

Tysons Corners, VA

The commercial building is just one among thirty that are spaced throughout the sixty acre site. Many American and international corporations that work closely with the United States Federal government are headquartered in this small community, just thirteen miles from the CIA. Billions of dollars flow from various U.S. departments to these companies, especially from the Department of Defense. Large military contractors such as Booz Allen Hamilton, MITRE Corporation, SAIC, SpaceNet, BAE Systems and Northrop Grumman are just a few of the key companies that have office buildings in the business park. One nondescript building at the back corner of the park has 100,000 square feet of office space, but has some unusual security measures. The company name on the building is SkyNet Software Services. S-Cubed for short. But it's a shell corporation for an ultra black organization funded by the CIA.

Michelle Samaha pulls her car into a reserved spot and smiles. Everything has happened so fast. Just a few years ago she was a mid-level CIA intelligence analyst, then promoted to

Assistant Director of Middle Eastern Affairs. Because of how she handled the al-Qaeda suicide bombers and the Iranian virus attempt, she was selected by the President to be the Director of an Ultra Black CIA organization charged with taking the fight to the terrorists. The current President campaigned on going after the various terrorist groups, but then the United States was hit with two suicide bomber attacks. One in Minneapolis and the other in Detroit, combined they killed almost two hundred fifty people. Michelle will be running the show and will be responsible for America's secret counter-terrorism payback.

Looking at the building, the average person would not see anything different from the other thirty buildings in the commercial office park, but this building is very special. It is classified as a Facility Security Level (FSL) V building, with special-use design criteria that merits a degree of protection above that specified as a FSL Level IV. The outside has discreet stanchions or bollards at standoff distances that will stop a truck loaded with explosives from coming too close to the building. Large trees were planted that not only obscure the building, but would stop a truck or car bomb from being driven near. The glass has special glazing to reduce shattered glass injuries in the event a bomb was detonated near the building. All of the doors have coded locks with a badge and retinal scanning. There are hundreds of cameras outside and inside the building with artificial intelligence software that track and log all vehicles and people outside in a five hundred meter area. The lobby area has discreet armed guards posing at receptionists. There are always two armed people who were former Special Operators in the lobby, with just off the lobby area a room where four other Special Operators who monitor the cameras looking for threats. Due to the nature of their operations, the Ultra Black site needed to be totally secured and the Federal government has insured that it will be. The building design is classified Top Secret. What isn't shown on the drawings is that there is one level below the main building.

Michelle enters the lobby and uses her badge to step through the secure turnstile while at the same time a face recognition program verifies twelve facial features in milliseconds. "Good morning Kevin." Michelle says to the main guard. He smiles but quickly returns to his stoic demeanor. Michelle takes the elevator up to her third floor office. As she approaches her office she sees two people in her conference room.

"Good morning Mark and Tom! I am happy to see that you both made it."

Mark gives Michelle a hug and offers her a cup of coffee. "Thanks I need this. We have our first assignment. I've asked Jonathan Bardsley to join us. He has the operational details." The three exchange their weekend activities and talk about the amazing building and staff.

"Mark, are you settled in yet?"

Mark shakes his head. "I found a small furnished apartment about ten minutes from here on a month-to-month basis. Minimalistic, but comfortable. If you guys know of anything better, let me know. I'm having my Porsche shipped out so I should have a car next week. In the meantime, I'm getting used to Uber. Other than that, not much else to report."

Michelle smiles. "Glad your move was smooth. We appreciate you joining our team."

Tom "Ducky" Duckworth shakes his head. "If you need some advice on the top bars, clubs or pick up spots nearby, just let me know. I've been to all of them."

Mark laughs. "Well, if I can't figure it out on my own, I'll let you know. I might need a wing man."

"I'm here for you buddy."

At that Jonathan enters, he shakes hands with Mark. "Sorry for your loss Mark. I can't imagine how hard that was. Congratulations on the CIA award, you certainly deserved it."

Mark smiles. "Thanks Jonathan, without your help we never would have successfully stopped the virus attack."

Michelle steps into the conversation. "We all work well as a team. That is why the President gave us this responsibility. Jonathan, would you fill us in on the target and the initial plan to get to him."

Jonathan remains standing and refers to the white board. He puts a photo up on the board. "This is Muhammad Ibrahim Bayunoni. He is designated as a key lieutenant of Hamza bin Ladin. Over the past five years he has steadily risen in the al-Qaeda leadership. He is forty-six years old, born in Pakistan and educated in Saudi Arabia. He is married with two kids, a boy and a girl. He fought in Syria against the Americans and most recently with Assad. We believe he was instrumental in the use of chemical weapons, mostly Sarin, against the Syrian people in Ghouta in 2013, Aleppo in 2016 and Khan Shaykhun in 2017."

Mark sits up and says. "While I was a SEAL, in 1999 we investigated WMDs in Syria and found hundreds of shells loaded with Sarin. I guess the past three administrations didn't think it was important enough to take them out."

Jonathan nods. "Yeah, it's sad that they used gas on their own people. But Bayunoni was in the middle of all of it. What we suspect is that he brought some of the shells back with him to Pakistan and al-Qaeda currently is storing them for future use. We need to know where those WMDs are."

Ducky speaks up. "So we know where Bayunoni is located?"

Jonathan puts up another photo. "This is a drone photo of a compound in southern Islamabad. We believe he is living there. We have two teams there now trying to follow him in hopes he leads us to bin Ladin. Either way, we have authorization to take him."

Mark gets up and looks at the compound photo. "Looks like high walls all around, probably eight to ten feet high. No wire I can see. Maybe sensors? Probably better to try to take him outside the compound. Does he have a security team with him?"

Jonathan slaps up another photo onto the white board. "He usually travels with three guards. All well armed, probably former Syrian special forces. The first option is an IED along his route, but there will be civilian casualties. The boss has said no to that option." Referring to Michelle. "Second option is a sniper team that would disable the vehicle. Kill each person exiting. Low potential of civilian casualties but low chance to snatch the subject. Third option is to capture him in his compound, get him out of the country and to a black site for interrogation. That option is the most dangerous, but with the highest reward."

Mark looks at Ducky and then both nod at the same time and say in unison. "We like the third option."

Michelle closes her folder containing the full Intel report. "I thought you'd both agree. I'd like you two to come up with an operational plan. The number of people you'll need with you on the ground. The equipment and the Intel required. We will have no help from the Pakistani ISI."

Mark looks at Bardsley, then at Ducky. "Let's get to work and see if we can grab this guy and make him talk."

Chapter 8

Denver, CO - July 31st

Claire Sweeney has been packing for the past two days, not only her own clothes but those of both boys who have particular clothing requirements. One Captain America shirt is a must for Oliver, a Batman shirt is required for Filip. Three large suitcases are lined up by the front door. The boys have just finished breakfast. Their brother, Samuel is singing softly in the corner in his chair and the youngest, William is sitting next to his brother playing with his food. Named for his grandfather, he is the spitting image at four years old. Both of the younger boys are not going on this trip. Claire feels that the older boys will appreciate the vacation. Traveling with four young boys would make the trip exponentially more difficult. So Samuel, "Samko" as he is called, is going to a day soccer camp for this week, then a swim camp the following week and Will can expect to have plenty of playtimes with their nanny. David Sweeney is finishing his coffee and kissing each of the kids goodbye.

"Hope you guys have a great vacation. I wish I could come along with you." Says David.

"Hey Dad, did you know that the airplane will be traveling at over mach 1 or over 660 Miles Per Hour!"

David smiles. His second son is extremely bright and just loves airplanes. "That is right buddy, maybe someday you can fly a jet."

Filip's eyes brighten and his smile widens. "That would be so cool."

Claire comes down the stairs with a backpack. "Well, this is the last of it."

"Hey mom, did you get my Captain America shirt?" Asks Oliver. His is ten but has the sophistication of someone twenty years his senior. He is also very smart and extremely articulate. "Also my Messi soccer jersey?"

Claire nods. "Yes honey, I packed several soccer jerseys including your Surf Soccer t-shirts." Claire looks over at her husband. He smiles and puts his coffee cup in the sink.

Suddenly her cellular phone rings. "Hello?"

"Mrs. Sweeney, this is Julia Barstow. I am the Assistant Secretary of State. I will be coordinating your trip to Italy."

Clare switches ears as she tries to put Filip's jacket on. "Ok, but I am planning to meet with Diane Fusco who is a former college roommate and is posted in Rome with the State Department."

"I understand, but we need to know your schedule day by day for security purposes."

"Ok, our Secret Service agents have put together a schedule. I'll ask them to send it to you."

Julia replies, "Excellent. Have them fax it over to the State Department before you leave."

Claire sees Samuel finishing his breakfast. "Ok, I'll tell them. Thanks." With that she hangs up.

Her husband notes she is off the phone, and says. "The Secret Service SUV should be here by 8 am. I have to leave now to get Sammy to the soccer camp on time." Turning to his son he says. "Are you ready buddy?"

Samuel hops down and deposits his cereal bowl and spoon by the sink. "I have to get my soccer ball." The youngster speeds out of the kitchen and into the garage. Samko is tall and wiry for his age and extremely fast. He is one of the stars on his U6 team with the kids just learning to pass to each other rather than running together in a pack chasing a soccer ball.

"Ok, I have to go. Love you babe." The two parents share a long slow kiss. The boys know their parents love each other and them. It's a happy family.

David kisses each boy then grabs his briefcase. "Hope you guys have a great vacation. Be careful and be safe."

With that, David strides into the garage and sees Samko already buckled into his car seat. He starts his car and pulls out of the garage heading for the soccer fields, then on to the office.

Claire watches her husband leave the kitchen, and smiles. Being the President's daughter has its perks, but also has some major negatives. Lack of privacy is one; the other is being recognized in public places. "Come on boys get your jackets and let's go!" Claire puts on a big floppy hat and grabs her suitcase just as the doorbell rings. She swings the door open and sees Michael Bale, her primary protector. The Secret Service agent smiles, "Good morning Mrs. Sweeney."

"Good morning Michael. I can get my luggage, could you grab the boy's bags?"

"Sure thing." The agent grabs the two bags and easily carries them to the SUV. A second agent is waiting by the open back door. "Good morning Mrs. Sweeney."

"Hi Kari. Thanks for coming on the trip with us. I feel better about traveling with you guys."

Agent Lee smiles, "You have such a beautiful family, it's our job but we also enjoy being around you guys."

Clare then returns to the home for last minute instructions to her nanny who will be in charge of William when David is not home. Also, David's mom lives just five minutes away and is willing to help as needed.

With all the bags in the SUV, the Sweeney family pile in and buckle up. The Secret Service agents secure the doors and hop in. The vacation is underway and the excitement is evident among all of the passengers.

Chapter 9

Washington D.C. - August 2ⁿᵈ

Being one of the most outspoken critics of the new President has gotten her better tables at local restaurants but not much more power in the United States Congress. However, the press has eaten up her negative criticism of the President's policies and that has gotten her on CNN, MSNBC and even Fox, which has in turn increased her visibility nationwide. She is strongly against any military action against the Jihadists overseas despite the two terrorist attacks in Minneapolis and Detroit. Her district in California has thousands of Muslims and each she views as potential voter for her in the upcoming election. Representative Jackie Jones is meeting with several lobbyists from the environmental protection lobby and hopes they will help her win a third term. Not only does she support their agenda but will need the campaign funds that they will funnel her way.

"Good afternoon Congresswoman Jones, your party is already here." The maitre'd smiles and escorts the Congresswoman to her favorite table. It is in a back corner where she can see who is coming into the restaurant but limits the potential for someone to interrupt her meeting by coming past her table.

"Thank you Stephen."

After greeting her two guests, they review the menu and order drinks. During the discussion, Congresswoman Jones sees several other people from Congress and one Senator eating and chatting with someone they are trying to strong-arm or cajole. The Prime Rib is one of the most exclusive restaurants on K Street. It's close enough to the White House and Capital Building to be convenient, but far enough away to meet discreetly. It's an old school steakhouse where political deals are brokered and politicians are there to be seen.

"Congresswoman, we believe that the President's war on terror stance would lead to more conflict and therefore damage the world's environment, speeding up climate change and hurting or killing millions of people. We would ask you to vote no on H.R. 3113."

Jackie knows that the House Bill 3113 has bipartisan support and would give the President a wider range of power to combat terrorism. After the bombings several weeks ago, the Speaker of the House rushed a bill into Congress that he and the President believes is necessary to keep America safe.

Congresswoman Jones nods. "Yes, I think we need to rein in this President. He is an independent and has no political anchor. Like a sailboat, he will be pushed in one direction or another by events not by political ideology. That can be dangerous. Yes, the bombings in the Midwest were bad, but does that justify going to war as he has said against the Jihadis?"

The two lobbyists smile and nod. This is exactly what they wanted to hear.

"Another issue is the Delta Smelt in the Sacramento-San Joaquin Delta. There are developers who want to build commercial properties nearby. One of those developers is David Sweeney."

The Congresswoman looks up from her notes. "The son-in-law of President Baker?"

"Yes. His company is one of the sub-contractors who have proposed to build three apartment buildings and two office complexes on a ten acre site. They have met all of the current environmental requirements which has taken them nearly five years, but we would like you to introduce a new law prohibiting any building within one mile of the delta. That will effectively kill the deal."

The lunch arrives and Jackie and the lobbyists begin to eat their wonderful meal. As they are chatting about other environmental issues, the Congresswoman notices a man and woman enter. She doesn't recognize them but they are particular because of their dress. The man is obviously Middle Eastern; the woman has her head covered. They both are wearing overcoats even through it's in the mid 80s today. It isn't unusual to have many different countries and ethnicities at the Prime Rib, but their coats make them stand out.

"Another issue that we want to discuss is the rising ocean levels...."

Jackie was only half listening as she watches the couple speaking with Stephen. It was obvious that they did not have a reservation. Suddenly the man walks away from the podium. Jackie wished she was armed but she is anti-gun and therefore she is unarmed. Her guests are facing her and can't see the commotion behind them.

The maitre'd calls for the man to stop. Another man steps out of the kitchen and walks quickly to intercept him. Other diners start to notice the man too. He stops in the middle of the restaurant and Jackie suddenly understands what he is about to do. "Get down" she screams and slides under the table.

The man screams "Allahu Akbar!" At that moment a huge explosion rips through the restaurant. Within moments another blast destroys the front of the restaurant and killing anyone within fifty feet outside.

The dust, smoke and debris fill the now destroyed building. Jackie can hear some screams and crying over the ringing in her ears. The table had overturned and had protected the Congresswoman, but her two lunch companions were not that lucky. Both had been killed immediately by the high velocity ball bearings that were imbedded into the C4 on the suicide vest. She could feel blood soaking through her blouse. Jackie reaches down and feels the wetness. Suddenly she realizes that it isn't her blood. On top of the table is the body of one of the lobbyist. The top of his head had been blown off and it is his blood that is dripping onto her. She panics and begins to push against the table moving it slightly. Jackie sees a space between the table and the bench seating. She crawls out from under the table and hears the first responders starting to arrive. There are hundreds of people wounded and killed. A firefighter reaches down and pulls her to her feet. "Are you hurt?"

The Congresswoman, in shock, shakes her head. "I am ok, look for others that have been injured."

Some people are stumbling out of the building; others are being carried out by the firemen and police officers. Jackie moves to sit on the curb and begins to cry. A first responder puts a blanket over her. A nurse or doctor asks her if she is injured. She shakes her head. "I am ok."

Suddenly Jackie understands the true danger of terrorism first hand and decides that she will vote yes on H.R. 3113 and give the President those powers he needs to stop these bastards.

Chapter 10

S-Cubed – Tysons Corner, VA - August 2nd

Michelle is sitting in her office with her television on but the sound muted. Out of the corner of her eye she sees a smoking building. She turns to see that it is a building on fire. She turns up the volume and hears that there was a bombing at the Prime Rib in Washington D.C. Michelle had eaten there several times and sat in the bar a few of times when meeting girlfriends for a night out on the town. She keys her phone and calls Mark and Ducky.

"There has been a bombing in Washington D.C. Come on up."

She hears Mark's voice. "We just finished the first draft of our plan. We'll be right up."

Several minutes later, Mark, Ducky and Jonathan rush into Michelle's office. "Looks pretty bad. It was at the height of the lunch hour. The restaurant holds several hundred people I would guess. There are twenty-six confirmed dead."

They all watch the news coverage as the first responders pull bodies from the restaurant. The talking heads are describing the carnage, the number dead and that several Senators and Congress people were in the restaurant at the time of the bombing.

"Ok, let's get to work. What do you have in terms of an operational plan? Let's get to the conference room."

The four move the meeting to the adjoining conference room.

Mark moves to the white board and picks up a dry marker. "With this target, the only way to capture him without the potential of significant civilian casualties would be an assault at night of his compound. It would also give us a better opportunity to get away to a safe house or an Agency jet without interference by the ISI or the local police. During the day, traffic would be a problem with the getaway. Also, it is more likely that the target will be there late at night. So we would recommend surveillance to try to establish a pattern, then hit the compound when we have confirmation he is there. The take down should happen on a moonless night. That will happen in one week. I would recommend hitting the compound at 2 am. We would cut the power to the compound, use wall-climbers to breech the wall, suppressed weapons to take out the guards and any others who impede the operation. We should know where in the compound he is and keep him contained. The amount of time in and out should be six minutes or less. The number of operators should be eight total. "

Michelle stands. "Is eight operators enough?"

Mark nods. "If we have the right people, eight will work. More than that might attract attention."

"How are you going to get the target out of the country?" Asks Jonathan.

Ducky consults his notes. "If we can capture the target alive. We will drug him and get him to a van, which will then drive to the Indian border. At that point, we can cross the frontier at night and from there transport him to a black site for interrogation. Second option would be a CIA jet at Rawalakot airport. It is a local airport about 30 minutes from the compound. Its run by the Pakistan Civil Aviation Authority so no commercial traffic. Also no military. The only issue is that the runway is just 2,598 feet long."

"Ok, pick the best option and get to Bagram AFB to finalize the details. We should keep this tightly compartmentalized." Says the Director.

At that point a person walks into the conference room that looks like he is in high school, but he is huge. He's six foot six inches tall and quite rotund. He is wearing jeans and a shirt pulled out over his ample belly. But the most interesting thing about him is that he is wearing sandals. Mark does a double take, and then smiles.

"Gentlemen, I'd like to introduce you to Kelly Campos. He is working with Jonathan and is quite adroit at using the internet to ferret out information for our analysis.   Kelly, this is Mark Aldin and Tom Duckworth."

Mark stands and shakes Kelly's massive hand, Ducky does the same.

"Sorry for the intrusion but you'll want to see this."   Kelly pulls out a photo from a folder and hands it to Michelle. It shows two people just about to enter the Prime Rib restaurant.   "These are the bombers, I ran their images through the FACE system and they are Abbad Fakhoury and his wife Sabiha. The entered the U.S. in 2013 from Syria.   They worked at a Washington D.C. coffee shop.   They are, or were thirty-eight and thirty.   No children.   But the most interesting thing about them is that they have a direct tie to Muhammad Bayunoni."

Michelle looks up suddenly. "Really? How?"

Kelly looks over his notes. "Sabiha is Muhammad's sister. I believe she was sent to the U.S. specifically to coordinate a suicide bombing in here. I hacked into her computer which is amazingly still on. She bought the ball bearings online and had them delivered to their apartment just three days ago. Not sure how they obtained C4 but with some digging, I am sure I can track it down.   But the most incredible thing is that she was sending messages to her brother over the past four years. I might be able to use the same links to hack into his computer."

Mark is amazed at the maturity of this young man and his obvious technical skills.

"Ok, thanks Kelly. Let us know if you discover anything else."

With that, Kelly exits the conference room. All of the others sit there with smiles on their faces.

"I told you he would be a good addition. He's only been here two days." Says Michelle.

Mark nods his head. "Seems like he fits in just fine. We'll get going tomorrow to Afghanistan and coordinate from there. Here is a list of the other six special operators I'd like to use in this operation. While the guys on the ground in Islamabad do surveillance on Bayunoni, we'll do some training to get ready for the assault."

"Ok, this is our first operation, let's make sure it goes off without a hitch."

Mark laughs. "There is never an operation that goes perfectly. We just have to plan for every possible eventuality. We will have the best people available, the best equipment and a good plan. But you never know what might happen. If we can't capture him, we'll kill him."

With that, the group exits the conference room and kicks off one of the most ambitious operations since the killing of Osama bin Ladin May 2nd 2011.

Chapter 11

The Warehouse Bar – August 2nd
Las Cruces, New Mexico

Walter Cartwright is sitting on his favorite stool at the Warehouse Bar. It's bloody hot outside, but cool in here he thinks. He lifts the Bloody Mary to his lips and takes a long sip. He has been working in this hell hole for the past ten years and he still can't get used to the summer heat. To add to his misery is his divorce two years ago. His wife and kids suddenly had enough, and she moved out and back to England to live with her mother. What a bitch. Now he has to give her almost sixty percent of his salary, the U.S. government takes most of the rest. In England the magistrate ruled that the wife with three children was entitled to a majority of his income to "maintain" her lifestyle. What a joke. What he should do is buy her an industrial blast furnace and place it in her mother's home in Sussex. That would maintain her lifestyle there in England.

Walter takes a final gulp and signals the bartender for another drink. After graduating with a degree in Policing from the University of Northampton, he worked for the East Midlands police in administrative jobs for six years but dreamed of moving into a higher position. He got married and had kids, and then his brother-in-law got a job with the U.S. government and got him an interview. That same year he took a job with the U.S. Army Test & Evaluation Command (ATEC). He passed all the background checks and they moved to the United States. He had no idea what New Mexico was like, but it was a job in America. Now he knows. Bloody hot, bloody desolate. God he hates America.

The new drink arrives and the bartender takes away the used glass. Walter knows that his divorce is not the only issue he is dealing with. His trips to Las Vegas over the past several years to gamble has also put him in a hole. A big fucking hole.   His home is leveraged to the hilt and the majority of his salary goes to his wife. What kind of life is this? But he has a possible out. Walter was approached last year about giving a business type some low level information about White Sands projects. Nothing classified or anything like that, but some data that could help the businessman win a manufacturing contract. For the information, Walter was paid $10,000. Then the businessman wanted some project specifications. Another ten grand. Now he wants a drawing. He asked to meet him at the bar this afternoon. Walter works in the Test & Evaluation Command and has a Top Secret clearance and therefore could get the information easily. Today he has a thumb drive in his pocket that will be worth $20,000. He knows that some of the projects at White Sands were worth millions, but nothing he was giving up was really that valuable.

"Hi Wally, cheers!"

Walter hates that nickname, but tolerates it from Mr. Moneybags. He said his name was Bill but Walter knows better. Bill is Asian and Walter is pretty sure not many Asians were named Bill. He didn't want to know his name or what company he works for. Better not to know.

Taking a quick sip, Walter turns on his stool and shakes the man's hand. "Hi Bill, how are you?"

"Damn hot here. God, I don't know how you do it."

Walter lifts his drink and smiles. "This helps."

Bill motions to the bartender for the same drink. He is wearing a well tailored suit, a white shirt and polished shoes, but Walter thinks he is foreign. It's not his accent, but something about him. Maybe Chinese or Vietnamese, but it's so hard to tell them apart. Bill smiles and then slowly glances around the bar. Satisfied that nobody is within earshot, he turns to Walter. "Did you get the information I requested?"

Walter nods and pulls the thumb drive from his pocket and places it on the bar.

Bill moves his hand and cups the thumb drive. "The payment will be in your bank account this afternoon after I have verified the information."

Walter takes another sip and nods.

"I have another request and the payment goes way up on this one. We can pay up to one million to an account of your choosing."

Walter's eyes show his surprise. "A million?"

"Yeah, it's a big ask, so the payment should reflect that."

"So what is worth a million dollars?" he whispers.

Bill looks around, and then replies. "Our competitor has the High Energy Laser Weapon project. They have developed a direct energy High Energy Laser that we'd like to copy but make improvements so that we can win the next project go round."

Walter knows exactly what he is talking about. The Hephaestus Laser System is a tactical high energy laser that is mounted on a truck to make it mobile. Hephaestus was the Roman God of Fire. A successful test was completed just a few days ago. The Tactical High Energy Laser (THEL) is one of the most impressive weapons in the U.S. arsenal. "What do you need?"

The businessman takes a sip from his drink and lowers his voice. "For a million dollars we would like one of the THEL systems with the software."

Walter shows his surprise and almost chokes on his drink. "No way! That system is classified Top Secret and besides there would be no way to get it off the base."

"How many have been built and are on the base?"

Considering the question, he replies. "There are four systems on the base."

Bill nods. "Is the base scheduled to get any more?"

"No more coming until the Congress authorizes more money. But we have one demo system. The Advanced Systems & Development Directorate uses it for spares"

"Ok, if we could get a truck onto the base, could you open a door to the warehouse and we could take one of the operational units and you replace it with the demo system?"

Walter takes a sip of his drink considering the request. A million dollars would allow him to leave this hell hole and disappear. Two million would give him the *lifestyle* he has always wanted. He takes another sip of his drink. Finally he replies. "For three million I can get you inside the warehouse and we can move the demo system to where the operational unit is located. I'll have to disable the security cameras, but I can do that."

"I was authorized for one million, but let me call my boss and see if they will spring for another couple of million." With that, Bill pulls out his cellular phone and walks to a deserted section of the restaurant. After a few minutes he returns and smiles. "You drive a hard bargain but we can give you the additional two."

Walter nods. "Ok, but I want $500,000 in an off-shore account before Friday."

"Ok, give me the account information, the account number, the bank and we'll make the deposit on Thursday. Here is a cellular phone number to call with the information. Ok?"

Walter looks at the piece of paper and knows he is crossing a big red line, but to get out of his current situation and retire in style he needs to take a chance. "I'll get you the account information by then."

The businessman shakes his hand and leaves the bar. Walter takes a long swallow of his Bloody Mary, while he starts to think about how to get the company truck into the warehouse and how to substitute a demo THEL system for an operational system. It shouldn't be too hard. He is the Director of Security.

Chapter 12

Bihsud, Afghanistan - August 3rd

Nimr Yazdi is standing at the window of his room smoking a cigarette. He is lost in thought and doesn't hear his bedroom door open. "Nimr, good to see you up."

Nimr turns and smiles. "I was just thinking about how we can strike back at America."

Hamza bin Ladin moves into the room and sits in a chair. "Our contact in Washington DC has sent a message last night confirming that the President's daughter and two grandchildren will be leaving for their vacation in Italy tomorrow. She sent the itinerary and that there are only two Secret Service agents guarding them. If we can put together a plan quickly, we may be able to intercept them at the end of their trip."

Nimr moves slowly to the other chair and sits. "I have some contacts in Genoa, Italy. I would suggest that I contact them and see if we can quickly put together a plan."

Hamza smiles. "I am glad you are energized about this opportunity. I spoke with the doctor this morning and he said you have made remarkable progress. Will you be ok for the trip?"

"Absolutely. I feel much better and I would like to travel to Italy tomorrow once I've set up the meeting with my contacts there. While I was buried under that building in Quetta, I swore to Allah that I would put in motion an operation that would drive a stake into the heart of the American President."

"So what is your plan?"

Nimr steeples his hands in front of his face in thought. "We will capture the President's daughter and grandchildren in Northern Italy. Then we will take them to a safe house, then out of Italy in a shipping container to one of our affiliates in Africa. I will travel with them to insure security."

Hamza smiles. "We will get something from the President and the American government that would enable al-Qaeda to become the most influential Muslim organization, greatly expand our operations and enable us to continue to work closely with ISIS and other groups to create a caliphate. What I would propose is that we tell the President of the United States once we have his family, is that if he wants them back safely he would have to deliver to al-Qaeda one Billion dollars AND release a dozen of our brothers from GITMO."

Nimr smiles. "An excellent plan."

Hamza turns and paces the room considering the plan. "How confident are you with the people in Italy? I do not want to authorize an operation that will fail. That will hurt our recruiting and the morale of our people in the U.S. and Europe. We have multiple operations waiting to launch and I don't want to jeopardize them."

"Abu Moaz." Which is Hamza's nickname. "I am confident we will be successful. The key will be the drop off of the money. The plan would be to have the U.S. military drop several pallets of the money of a combination of both U.S. dollars and Euros from one of their transport planes into a place in Afghanistan of our choosing. The people on the ground can divide up the money and take it to multiple locations that you agree to. Then we can use the money to fund operations throughout the Middle East, Africa and the West."

Hamza bin Ladin smiles. "I have faith in you Nimr. You organize the operation in Italy and I'll put in place the right people in Afghanistan. Are you sure you feel well enough?"

Nimr is lost in thought and is staring at the spider that is sitting in the middle of his web waiting for his prey.

Nimr nods. "Allah will give me the strength. Allahu Akbar."

Hamza notices the spider and smiles. "You are like that black widow spider, Nimr. You are patient and plan carefully. I will use that name for you when we are referring to you so that the Americans won't know you are alive."

Nimr smiles. "I like that name."

"Ok, make ready for your trip. I will have a private jet ready for you tomorrow morning to take you to Milan. From there you can organize your team and make ready. I will ask our American contact for more detail on the families' itinerary."

"Hamza, I will not fail. On my life I swear allegiance to you and to al-Qaeda."

Hamza bin Ladin smiles. "Thank you my friend."

With that, the al-Qaeda leader leaves Nimr alone with his thoughts and dreams of revenge.

Chapter 13

Islamabad, Pakistan - August 3rd

Mark Aldin, Ducky Duckworth and two other Special Operators disembark from a United States Blackhawk helicopter at a private airport just outside Islamabad. A waiting blacked out van sits idling waiting for its passengers. At the wheel is a CIA case officer assigned to Pakistan.

Mark shakes the man's hand. "Khalid, how are you doing?"

The Pakistani smiles. "Welcome back to Pakistan Mark. I was very happy to hear that you are joining the Agency full-time."

"Well, with everything that has happened, I am convinced we can make a difference."

The CIA man claps Mark on the shoulder. "There are still many of us here that want to rid the Muslim world of these rabid dogs. Killing Muhammad Ibrahim Bayunoni will be a major step."

Mark smiles, "Well we are hoping to capture him and take him to a black site for rendition, but it will take a carefully thought out plan and execution."

Mark hops into the passenger seat while the rest of the team piles into the van. Khalid closes the driver door and looks over at Mark. "We have been tracking him over the past week.

He uses multiple vehicles, varies his time to leave his compound and he has not met with Hamza bin Ladin yet. But each night he returns and spends the night. He has eight guards during the day when he goes out. At night however, we believe he only has two or three guards. That would be the time to grab him."

Khalid puts the van in drive and starts out of the local airport as the Blackhawk returns to Bagram Air Base in Afghanistan. It's 4 am and most of the city is still at sleep. After driving for forty minutes, the van enters a garage and the men disembark. Each team member has a large black satchel which contains their weapons, ammunition and tactical body armor. They enter the safe house and find six other Special Operators already there. After introductions, the men take a bed and get some rest.

Mark, Ducky and Khalid sit at the kitchen table and pour over a map of the compound. "We believe Bayunoni sleeps in the Northwest bedroom with his wife. The kids sleep in two bedrooms on the opposite side of the house. The team did an infrared scan last night and it shows two guards downstairs that are stationary for the most part, plus one who moves around the compound. The plan would be to take out the outside guard initially, then enter the house and take out the two guards. At that point two Special Operators will mount the stairs and enter

Bayunoni's bedroom. We would prefer to snatch him, but if he has a weapon then the shoot to kill order is authorized." Mark looks at both men. "Any comments?"

Ducky looks up. "Sounds too easy. Are we sure there are only three guards? What about a camera system? Alarm system? Is there a basement?"

Khalid sits back. "We have only been watching him for a couple of weeks. Several times he did not return to the compound. But usually if he is out, he returns shortly after dusk and the rest of his security team leaves."

"What about our escape route, vehicles, timing?"

Khalid pulls out a notebook. "We have two SUVs with Pakistani stickers that will enable an ISI convoy to pass through any government blockage. We also have ISI documents for the team. That will scare the shit out of any normal police or army soldier who tries to stop the SUVs. Also all of you will be in Pakistani ISI military uniforms. The escape plan is that the two SUVs leave Bayunoni's compound by 2:30 am, you rendezvous with the Blackhawk at the Rawalakot airport by 3:30 am. By first light you will be into Afghan airspace, then to Bagram Air force base. Then the rendition guys can take Bayunoni into custody and start the interrogation process."

Mark nods. "Ok, let's plan for the snatch tonight at 2 am. Get some rest."

With that, the three stretch out on two couches and a floor mat to get some fitful sleep before the operation to capture one of Hamza bin Ladin's key aide.

Chapter 14

Florence, Italy - August 5th

After landing at the Florence airport; Claire, the two children and the Secret Service agents pass through the customs area easily, getting special treatment afforded the daughter of an American President.   The family and their protectors meet with the American Consulate based in Florence.   After some brief pleasantries, Secret Service Agent Bale gets the State Department SUV and waits by a private door off the main terminal. Claire and the kids load into the SUV while Agent Lee stands guard, her hand on her weapon. Standing thirty yards from the SUV, one of the al-Qaeda operatives loiters causally smoking a cigarette. He has identified the target and photographed the SUV license plate with his smart phone. He snuffs out his cigarette butt and walks away. After the family is inside, the driver puts the car in drive and they head for the Westin Excelsior hotel.

Arriving and taking the elevator up to the Fifth floor, Claire starts getting her children organized. "You boys put your bags in your bedroom, and then wash your hands."

"Ma'am, we are in the adjourning rooms.   Your suite has adjourning doors. I will be on one side and Agent Bale will be on the other side. We have asked the State Department to post a guard on your door from 10 pm until 7 am. If you have any issue, hit the panic button on your phone."

"Thank you Agent Lee, I am sure everything will be fine. I think we'd like to get something to eat, and then go to bed. I'll call for room service. How about you and Agent Bale?"

"We'll get something later. Thanks."

After ordering dinner for herself and the kids, Clare puts the kids to bed and then slides between the sheets and immediate falls asleep dreaming of all the activities planned for tomorrow.

At six in the morning, Agent Bale and Agent Lee meet in her room for breakfast and to discuss the security protocols for the day's events. Kari pulls out the itinerary and they review what is on the schedule.

"After breakfast the family will go to the Piazzale Michelangelo (Michelangelo Square) that was designed by Giuseppe Poggi in 1869 on a hill overlooking the south bank of the Arno River. Back then, Florence was the capital of Italy and was undergoing a "rebirth" or redevelopment. The square, dedicated to the Renaissance sculptor Michelangelo, has bronze copies of some of his marble works for which he is most famous. Mrs. Sweeney wanted to see the square and experience the view of Florence from its viewpoint. After that visit, they will head for the Basilica di Santa Maria Novella for a quick walk thru, then finally to Museo Nazionale del Bargello a former prison which is now an art museum." It will be a long day, but both Agents are confident in their ability to keep the family safe.

After the family has its breakfast, the Agents herd the kids to the elevator and wait until Claire locks the hotel door and reaches the waiting doors. When the doors open, Agent Bale exits and assesses the lobby. There are the normal collection of tourists and business people. None look threatening, so he motions for the family to exit. Strolling through the lobby Claire Sweeny has the feeling of being watched. She glances right, then left. Seeing nobody suspicious, she grabs Filips' hand and they exit the hotel into the waiting SUV. Another al-Qaeda operative sitting reading a local newspaper notes the President's daughters exit and calls his partner to follow the car.

As they travel the short distance to the Michelangelo Plaza, Claire gives the boys a history lesson. "Boys, the square we are going to visit first has some amazing views of the city and a real fort called Forte Belvedere." Suddenly the interest in the outing is increased with the mention of a fort.

"Is it a fort where they fought Indians?" Asks Filip.

"There aren't any Indians in Italy!" says Oliver.

Clare takes charge. "Boys, the fort was the largest built in Florence. It was built in the 1590s. A long, long time ago. It was used to protect the city."

Filip pouts, "But no Indians."

They all laugh as the SUV pulls into a private driveway near the top of the hill. After a fairly quick walk about and seeing the sweeping views of Florence, the group retreats to the SUV and a short drive over the Arno River where they arrive at the Basilica di Santa Maria Novella. It's a huge church built in 1279. Clare knows the boys will not be interested in the stained glass windows, the architecture or the history. But Clare was a history major in college and has always wanted to see this historic church. The interior is almost 100 meters long and is designed as a Latin cross that is divided into a nave and two aisles. It is magnificent and after a few pictures, they exit and return to the SUV. Again they don't see a small white car with two men watching them as they drive away.

"How about stopping nearby for lunch?" Asks Clare.

"We'll have to clear the restaurant first." Replies Agent Bale.

"Ok, but it should be fine. Just pick one at random."

The agent nods and then tells the driver to pull over in front of a small local restaurant. Agent Bale gets out and enters through the open door. After several minutes, he reappears and motions for the family to come in. They sit in the rear of the restaurant with the agents sitting at a separate table facing the door. Clare takes the time to talk with the boys about their next stop, the national museum of Bargello also knows as The Bargello.

"Did you know that the word "Bargello" means *fortified tower* in Latin?" Says Clare between bite of her sandwich. "The museum has works from Michelangelo, Vincenzo Gemito and Jacopo Sansovino.

Oliver speaks up "I studied Michelangelo. He did the Sistine Chapel and carved David."

Filip looks up. "He carved David? Did it hurt?"

Clare laughs and says, "No honey, he carved marble to look like David."

Two men enter the restaurant and both Agents tense. Agent Lee moves her hand slowly to cup the weapons handle. The two men speak Italian and are seated near the door. Agent Bale calls for the car and gets up and tells Clare that they should go. After paying the bill, the Agents take the family out the back door and safely into the waiting SUV.

After another short drive they arrive at The Bargello. There are hundreds of tourists milling around while the family and their protectors leave the SUV and enter the museum. They had hired a museum docent to explain the art and the history behind each piece. The boys are well behaved knowing how important this is to their mom. Plus Clare had promised ice cream after the museum if they didn't cause any problems.

During the hour visit they see the Madonna and Child by Michelangelo, his Bacchus and Vincenzo Gemito's Pescatore (fisherboy) one of Clare's favorites.   But after an hour the boys start to get antsy.   "Ok, Michael and Kari, we should probably get going."

"Ok Mrs. Sweeney. Let me check the rear exit and I'll call for the car."

The family waits with Agent Lee standing nearby.   The Agent hears the all clear in her earpiece and moves Clare and the boys towards the rear exit.   Moving through row upon row of boxes that the museum uses to receive and sent art to other museums.   Suddenly a man appears from behind a storage box. Agent Lee pulls her revolver and moves toward the man.

The man appears startled and says in Italian, "What are you doing back here?"

The docent who accompanied the family says to him. "They are with me, I am taking them out through the rear exit."

The man nods and moves away.   Agent Lee holsters her gun and quickly leads the family out of the museum and into the waiting SUV and the drive back to the hotel.

Chapter 15

Tysons Corner, Virginia - August 5th

Michelle walks into "The Cave" as Kelly Campos' SCIF is being called. The SCIF is a Sensitive Compartmented Information Facility in the basement of the building that has been built specifically to process sensitive information. Also the facility name is appropriate because he keeps the lighting to a very low level. Even though Kelly has only been in the facility for a week, he has made it his home, literally. He moved a King-sized bed in last week along with a coffee-maker and a large refrigerator. Food is delivered after passing through a series of company check points. Michelle gave permission to the unusual request because the young man needed a place to stay and didn't know anyone in this part of the country.

"Hi Kelly, how are things going?" Asked Michelle.

"Hi boss. Getting up to speed now and should have an update on Bayunoni later today. My understanding is that Mark's operation is scheduled to go active within the next couple of hours. I am tracking the chatter in Islamabad and especially any ISI communications."

"Ok, keep me informed of any updates. Anything else you need?"

"No, I am good." Kelly says while he pops a red M&M into his mouth.

Michelle smiles and heads for the door.

"Hold on! This is not good." Kelly says.

Michelle stops in her tracks and turns around. "What?"

"I just intercepted an ISI message about a possible foreign operation in Islamabad. They believe we have a team in Pakistan and they are searching for them now."

"Crap. I'll get a message to Mark. Let me know if you get anything else."

Michelle exits the SCIF and quickly heads up to her office to place a call to Mark to inform him of the potential threat. Reaching her floor she moves directly to Jonathan Bardsley's office. He is the communications officer for the organization and can reach anyone almost anytime.

"Can you call Mark on his secure phone?"

Jonathan picks up his secure satellite phone. "Absolutely. It's almost 1 am there. They should be getting ready for the snatch."

The call is made and Michelle hears Marks voice. "Yeah."

Michelle can tell that they are in a vehicle and that Mark is under stress.

"Mark, we have some chatter that ISI knows an American team is in country and they are currently looking for your team."

Michelle waits while Mark considers the information. "But they don't know where or what we are doing?"

"Yes, that is correct so far. Kelly is monitoring their internal communications. I will call you if anything else comes up. If the target isn't there or the situation changes, get out of there and we can reset at a later date."

She hears Ducky say they are at the compound. "We'll get it done. Gotta go."

Michelle hangs up the phone and looks at Jonathan. "Can we monitor them?"

Jonathan smiles, "Thought you wouldn't ask. I requested a satellite over the target both to give Mark more Intel, but also to allow us to watch the operation via the infrared camera."

A few switches are switched and suddenly the main monitor shows an aerial view of a city block. Its 2 am local time and it shows just a few hot spots on the monitor.

"Can you zoom in?"

Jonathan manipulates the control and after a short delay the camera zooms to show what looks like a dozen hot spots within the target compound. "Is this Intel being transmitted to Mark?"

"Yes, he knows. His team is in place and is staged. Looks like he is going to go in despite the numbers. It's up to him now."

Michelle and Jonathan watch as the team can be seen just half a block away and starting to move into position. Michelle swears softly, but can't take her eyes off the screen as the eight agents begin their assault.

Chapter 16

Islamabad, Pakistan - August 6th

The team of six Special Operators and two CIA agents has taken up their positions around the building. Each is dressed in Pakistani ISI uniforms. The compound is at least a half acre and totally enclosed by a ten foot wall. Inside is the main house, a garage and a separate small building. It's 2 am. Mark has an infrared camera and is scanning the front entrance. He keys his throat microphone. "Two guards at the front gate. Four guards inside the building. Four others in the building at the rear. Four including the target upstairs."

"Roger" The lead Special Operator says.

There are at least ten guards within the compound, a lot more than Intel suggested. Getting in and out without causing an alarm now seems impossible.

"They seem to know that an attack is coming, so maybe we should give them what they are expecting." Mark says to Ducky.

Ducky nods and turns to Mark. "What are you suggesting?"

Mark outlines a change in plan and Ducky leaves to circle around to re-orient the team.

After fifteen minutes, Ducky dressed in a native robe and headscarf walks past the front gate and places a shaped charge explosive on the metal door, then continues by. "Package has been delivered." Ducky says in a whisper on his microphone.

"Roger" Mark says.

"Bravo, ready?"

The Bravo team of four Special Operators are at the back wall. They have approached the wall slowly making progress in inches before stealthy placing their C-4 explosive against the common wall of the small building at the back of the property, using the pressure-sensitive adhesive tape to stick the C-4 to the wall. "Bravo ready."

The Kilo team of four Special Operators are moving to the front door, approaching from each side. Mark is behind one of the Special Operators, Ducky behind another. All are carrying HK-416 submachine guns with suppression. They are compact 9mm sub machine guns that are favorites of the Special Operator community. Each has a thirty round magazine locked and loaded with multiple magazines within easy reach. Additionally, each team member has their GPNVG (Ground Panoramic Night Vision Goggles) on their helmet which enables the operator to see in near pitch black environments. The eerie green vision gives the team a major advantage in close quarters combat.

Two Pakistani team members are in the vans one block down from the compound.

"On my command; cut the power, then hit the back first, and then the front door." Mark hears several Rogers and readies himself. As all the men check their weapons, Mark looks at his watch. "Lights off, Bravo, initiate."

As Mark says the words, the lights in the compound go out, and then an explosion rocks the neighborhood blowing a huge hole in the wall and into the adjoining building. The four terrorist inside the building are thrown to the floor, while the Bravo team Special Operators pour into the space with their weapons ready. The lead Operator double taps the first terrorist as he is reaching for his gun. Suddenly another explosion goes off at the front of the property. The terrorists start to shoot at the Operators, while each Ranger moves to clear the room.

As Mark and Ducky blow the front gate they quickly enter amid the smoke and confusion. Mark sees one of the guards swinging his AK-47 in his direction. He fires first and rolls into a shooting position. The guard drops and Mark looks towards the house. The other guards are now pouring out of the house looking for targets.

Ducky has taken a position behind a car and is scanning the house. Suddenly he sees an upper floor window opening and the muzzle flash of a sniper rife. Raising his HK-416, he sprays the open window and most of that area with fifteen rounds. The shooting stops from the window.

Mark picks off two guards, and then moves towards the house. An explosion rocks the guest house and he knows they are in the battle of their lives. He squeezes off several other shots, and then moves again covering for his team.

Ducky shoots a guard just as he is about to throw a grenade. He moves quickly to behind a low wall and mics "grenade." An explosion near the front door takes out two other guards. Ducky moves quickly firing towards the house. From his left side he sees Mark also approaching. One of the down guards raises up with his AK-47 pointed at Mark from behind. Suddenly a shot hits the guard in the chest. Mark glances behind him and sees that Ducky has his back. Amid the smoke and gun fire, Mark and Ducky race up the stairs and enter the dark house low and fast. Two shots hit high as Mark slides into the room. The Rangers have the advantage with their GPNVGs. The remaining terrorist is shooting wildly in the dark, while Mark takes him out with a precision double tap. Suddenly the shooting stops and the house is silent. Mark immediately rises and starts for the stairs with Ducky right behind him. He releases his magazine and slaps in a new one. They move quickly knowing the local police will be alerted by now and could be out front of the compound anytime.

Mark rounds a corner slowly crouched in a shooters stance. He sees an empty hallway but knows that Muhammad Ibrahim Bayunoni is only yards away in one of the bedrooms. Mark motions to Ducky to take the left side, Mark takes the right. As they approach the first bedroom, Ducky throws in a flash-bang. They both cover their ears, close their eyes and open their mouths. The explosion is deafening and the flash is intended to disorient the target. Ducky quickly enters the room scanning for Bayunoni. The room is empty. Mark moves to the bedroom on the right and does the same thing. Empty. The third and final bedroom at the end of the hall suddenly erupts with bullets raking the wall. Both men drop to the ground and inch their way forward. They don't want to kill the target, but if it's him or them, then it's him. Mark edges to the double doors and slowly pushes it open. Another blast of machine gun fire makes him hug the carpet. In the silence he can hear Bayunoni slapping in a new clip into his AK-47. Mark pulls the pin on the flash-bang and tosses the grenade into the room and covers his ears and closes his eyes. The explosion rocks the house as Mark and Ducky rush in. On the floor is the target reaching for the gun he dropped during the flash-bang. Mark kicks the gun away and pulls Bayunoni over onto his stomach while Ducky puts Flex-cuffs on his hands. The man's wife and children can be heard crying in the bathroom. In the distance they both hear sirens.

They raise Bayunoni to his knees, and then standing while at the same time put a black hood over his head. While the other Rangers collect as much paperwork and electronic devices from the house as they can, Mark and Ducky quickly march the target out the front gate and into a waiting car. "Taking the package to the front." Each of the other Rangers exits the compound and enters a second van. Two have been wounded and are attended to by a waiting medic. As the two vehicles pull away, Mark can see the flashing lights of the local police coming fast just three blocks away. The driver pulls away with his lights off and turns the first corner with the trailing van right behind. After five minutes of evasive driving, they slow down and head for the regional airport where an Agency plane will be waiting to take them out of Pakistan and to Bagram Air Base in Afghanistan. Mark pulls out his SAT phone and places a call to Jonathan Bardsley. "Package is secure. Will be wheels up in twenty minutes." Bardsley acknowledges. The first Ultra Black operation seems to be a success. The U.S. now is taking the fight to the terrorists.

Chapter 17

Washington D.C. - August 7th

The President of the United States is sitting behind his desk putting the final touches on a speech that he is planning to deliver this evening in a national address to the American people. It's the fourth re-write and he wants it to be perfect. He knows as a new President, he will only get one shot at telling his side of the *War on the Jihadis*. The press has been hounding him over the past month about the suicide attacks in Detroit and Minneapolis that shocked the nation. Two hundred sixty-six Americans killed and over three hundred wounded in the two attacks. But it could have been a lot worse. Had the terrorists been able to bring down the Detroit RENCEN, thousands would have died. Then there was the bio-terrorism that was just averted. Of course the American people don't know anything about that. It is a highly classified secret that only a dozen or so people have access to. It would make his life and his administrations a lot easier by letting the press know about the Red Death virus and how the CIA was able to kill all the Iranian couriers, stop its release and the crippling sanctions leveled against Iran. But that might be for the history books if it ever gets out.

"Mr. President, the Secretary of State is here to see you." The President's secretary announces, breaking into William Baker's thoughts.

"Yes, please send her in."

"Good morning Mr. President."

"Good morning Cindy, what have you got for me this morning?"

Cindy Decker is up bright and early and has a communications cable in her hand. "An hour ago there was an explosion at a compound in Islamabad. It was attacked by unknown *soldiers* who killed twelve Pakistanis and appeared to abduct a man. It was a well planned operation and the Pakistanis are pissed off."

The President smiles. "As well they should." He settles back in his chair and waits for the Secretary of State to continue.

"Mr. President, if this was one of our operations, I need to know ahead of time to alert the embassy and give our people a heads up."

"So they could do what? Maybe have a leak to the ISI that the U.S. government is about to launch an operation inside their country and haven't told them? Assuming it was one of ours. Cindy, as you know the State Department is tasked with diplomatic interface with our friends and foes. It's a tough job, but when we have to do something covert, the fewer people who know the better."

"I understand that Mr. President, but now I have a shit storm over there that our people are trying to clean up."

The President stands, "Cindy, there are any number of countries who operate in Pakistan. It could have been the Brits or maybe the Indians? Who was taken?"

Cindy Decker knows the President is playing her and she knows why. She is just there to try to be kept in the loop. "Muhammad Ibrahim Bayunoni is the word from our ISI friends."

The President smiles and walks the Secretary of State to the door. "Sounds like that would be a good catch. After all that just happened here and around the world, it would be good news to a nation that needs some good news."

The Secretary of State knows that it was an American operation and that she will have to clean up after the CIA once again. "I hope it will be worth it."

The President nods. "Well, it is one bad guy out of action and it will send a message to al-Qaeda."

As Cindy Decker is leaving the Oval Office, she turns and says "By the way, I spoke with Diane Fusco in Rome last night. She said that your daughter and grandsons arrived on time and they are out seeing the sights of Florence. She will travel up there later today and have breakfast with them tomorrow."

The President thanks the Secretary of State but is still worried. The EU is a dangerous place and his daughter and her kids would be an inviting target. He prays that the Secret Service agents are alert and ready for anything.

Chapter 18

White Sands AFB - August 8th

It's been a week since his meeting with Mr. Bill. Walter has given him that moniker as an inside joke based on the Saturday Night Live skit where a claymation named Mr. Bill would get hammered every Saturday Night and end up saying *Oh No, Mr. Bill.* Walter smiles at the irony. He will take the three million dollars, and then make sure Mr. Bill gets squashed. Walter has competed forging the paperwork necessary to *lose* one of the THEL systems. His plan is to substitute the demo system in the warehouse for one of the operational system that Bill's guys can take, and then be sitting on a tropical island long before the government discovers the switch. Walter has purchased a flawless fake passport in the name of Richard White and has deposited the $500,000 down payment in his Cayman Island account. All he has to do now is coordinate the pickup and he'll be ready to disappear.

Walter picks up his cellular phone and punches in a number to a burner phone.

"Bill, the paperwork has been completed and we are ready for the pick up."

At the other end *Bill* smiles. "Ok, I'll have a truck there tomorrow night at 9 pm. Fax me the paperwork." With that he clicks off.

Asshole, Walter thinks. He is giving him a multi-million dollar prototype and not even a thank you. He sits at his desk contemplating what he is about to do. His life tomorrow will change forever. "Fuck it" he says under his breath. Time to enjoy his life; get some sand between his toes, drink tropical cocktails and hook up with some local ladies. Just two more things to do.

Walter gets up and wanders into the warehouse looking for his right hand man, Chuck Hayward. Chuck is a Technical Sergeant in the U.S. Army. He grew up in Oregon, son of a minister who wanted to see the world. He joined the Army out of high school and never looked back. Now twelve years later he is managing a warehouse with many top secret projects. The most exciting is the THEL. He was out on the range when the Tactical High Energy Laser was demonstrated. He had seen it in action before during its initial tests, but this time hitting multiple targets within seconds, was extremely impressive.

Walter walks into the massive warehouse and down the row upon row of spare parts, weapons systems and cases of ammunition. He passes dozens of enlisted personnel checking equipment out, receiving new inventory and cleaning used machines. Walter sees his number one, Technical Sergeant Chuck

Hayward and changes direction approaching him directly. "Chuck, I have a special pick up tomorrow night. The Navy pukes want to borrow the THEL Demo system for a shipboard test."

"Boss, I am scheduled for vacation time starting tonight at 17:00."

"Damn, forgot about that. No problem. I'll stick around to receive their paperwork and make sure the squids get the system. Who will be on duty tomorrow night?"

Chuck breathes a breath of relief. His girlfriend would kill him if he had to cancel their vacation. She doesn't know it but while sipping a tropical drink on Maui, he was going to propose to her. "Thanks boss. Staff Sergeant Susie Davies is my second. I will inform her of the pickup."

"Ok. I'm going to head to lunch. Hope you have a good vacation."

Chuck knows about Walter heading off to lunch. Three to four hours of drinking at the Warehouse Bar, available by phone only if there is a huge issue. Otherwise the Boss is incognito. How this idiot keeps his job is beyond him. But Chuck is just following orders. The military is like that sometimes. Incompetence rises to the top in some organizations. He just doesn't want to be around when the shit hits the fan as Walter makes some kind of major mistake. Chuck smiles as he has applied for a position similar to his current job at Edwards AFB in

California. It has the Air Force Flight Test Center (AFFTC) that conducts leading edge research, development and evaluation of aerospace systems and should be a good change of pace. He can't wait to get out of New Mexico.

Chapter 19

Tysons Corner, VA — August 8th

Kelly Campos is monitoring the operation in Islamabad while Michelle is watching over his shoulder. Over the past hour the team has moved into place and informed headquarters that there are at least twice as many guards in the target compound. Michelle is in direct contact with Mark while she watches the body cams.

"The package is secure." Michelle hears Mark's voice. She breathes a sigh of relief.

"Roger. Pick up is ready when you get there." Michelle says referring to their ride out of the country.

Kelly checks his monitor. "CIA jet is fueled and ready for the team and the package. It was tight for the Falcon to land on that short a runway, but they made it." He says to Michelle.

She knows that the Air Branch of the CIA Special Activities Division (SAD) uses the Dassault Falcon 50 for covert insertion and extraction of CIA personnel.

Michelle has another issue to speak with Mark about but wants him to be totally focused until they are out of Pakistani airspace. She knows that there are still multiple threats that could upset their plans.

Suddenly Kelly sits up and starts typing. "We have a problem. The ISI has sent out an alert for a van and they are setting up roadblocks at key intersections. But they didn't mention a color."

Michelle keys her microphone, "Mark , ISI has sent out an alert, roadblocks being set up."

"Roger" is Mark's tense reply.

Kelly brings up a map of the city of Islamabad. He overlays a real-time satellite image. "We can identify the ISI vehicles by the numbers on their roof. I think I can steer the team through the net. Tell Mark to head North on M1 to N75."

"Mark take N75 North, then a rural road to the airport."

"Roger".

Kelly does some additional typing then asks Michelle, "the plane is at Rawalakot airport. It's just 30 minutes out. No roadblocks yet."

The pair watch as the vans travel out of Islamabad and up the N75 highway. Kelly keys his mic.

"Crap. Mark they are setting up a roadblock just south of the airport."

"Roger. If we get into a firefight, tell the plane we will be coming in hot."

Michelle knows the CIA has a Dassault Falcon jet ready to go. But will not be able to avoid Pakistani military jets if they have to make a break for it.

Kelly types an encrypted message to the pilot.

*   *   *

Mark and his team are racing up N75, and then turn off onto the rural highway. At 70 MPH they are flying past many of the other cars and trucks on the road. Ahead Mark sees flashing lights of the roadblock ahead. They slow. Mark turns and tells the men to ready for a firefight. They cover their captive who is bound and gagged with a blanket over him. Each man clicks off their weapon safety and tenses for a fight.

As they slow for the line of cars, Mark makes a decision. "Pull around the cars and drive up to the soldiers." The driver pulls out of line and drives forward flashing his lights. The soldiers turn and point their AK-47s at the van. The vans stop and Mark hops out and strides purposely toward the roadblock. Mark is in an ISI Colonel uniform. He salutes the Sergeant in charge and in perfect Arabic says. "My team is part of the Internal Wing and we have been directed by Lt. General Naveed Mukhtar to secure the airport."

The Sergeant notes the Colonel rank insignia. He snaps to attention. "Sir, I need to confirm with headquarters."

Mark sneers. "Sergeant, if I am delayed implementing my orders I will make sure you find yourself on the front lines of the Kashmir facing the Indian troops. Move your truck and let my team through."

The Sergeant knows life on the front lines is hard and he wants no part of that. "Yes sir." He turns to his troops. "Let the Colonel through!"

Mark turns and strides back to the van. At that point, the caravan moves forward and through the roadblock. As they speed towards the airport, Mark places a call to S-Cubed. "We are through the roadblock, will be to the pick up point in five minutes."

Michelle and Kelly both breathe a breath of relief. "Roger."

The vans pull onto the commercial terminal tarmac and pulls next to the CIA jet. The stairs drop down and each man pulls his weapons sack from the van and races up the stairs and into the jet. The package is carried up and placed on the floor in the back. Mark and Ducky watch the perimeter for any approaching Pakistani military or airport police.

"Ok, leave the vans and let's get out of here." Mark says as they move to the stairway. The pilots have the jet warmed up and ready for take off. Mark follows Ducky up and into the cabin. He pulls the door closed and seals it. "Let's roll" he yells to the pilots.

Immediately he feels the jet starting to taxi as the pilots pull to the end of the deserted runway. Because it's a local airport, there are no planes or personnel out and about at this hour. Mark and the others sit and fasten their safety belts and look out the windows looking for flashing lights indicating the ISI has discovered their ruse. A few minutes later, Mark feels the jet revving their engines, then the release of the brakes and the jet rollout. As they lift off the ground, Mark starts to relax a bit. He knows that until they reach Afghan airspace they still could be shot down, but the pilot is a thirty year U.S. Air Force veteran and knows how to evade if necessary.

Within twenty minutes the jet flies into Afghan airspace and the pilot receives a communication from Bagram Air Force Base indicating that they are tracking him and gives the pilot the vectors to bring the jet to the air field.

Mark gets on the secure SAT phone and calls Michelle. "We are clear and should be landing at Bagram in about an hour." He can hear the relief in Michelle's voice.

"Excellent. Glad the operation went well."

There is a pause then Michelle speaks again. "I just got some information that you'll want to hear. Your sister is alive and living in Tehran. She is married to Captain Sajad Aziz, the son of General Hamid Aziz."

Mark swears softly. When Mark was just a ten year old boy, his mother and younger sister were abducted by the Muslim Brotherhood as they lived in Syria. They were sold to an Iranian businessman and lived in Tehran. His mother died of cancer just a few years ago, but what happened to his sister was a mystery. Until now. Mark knows that General Aziz is the head of the Republican Guard, the most powerful military organization within Iran. Saarah married to the son of that asshole.

"She has no children. Doesn't seem to get out much, but has been involved in a children's charity locally. We have an agent there that has had eyes on her over the past several weeks."

Mark takes a deep breath. "Ok, can you send me any information you have to Bagram. I'd like to try to get into Iran to get her out."

Michelle knew this would be his response. "No Mark, you need a plan and you need support. Come back to the States and let's put together a team and reach out to other organizations for help.

Mark shakes his head and replies. "This needs to be my operation. Nobody else in-country. If this goes south, I don't want to be responsible for anyone else getting caught or killed."

Michelle knows how stubborn Mark could be, but if he fails, not only will his life be in jeopardy, but her whole operation could be compromised. "Mark, I have to insist that you return to the U.S. and we will work out a successful plan together. If you get caught or killed in Iran this could be very damaging to the country and the President. We have waited this long. Let's do this right."

There is a long pause, and then Mark says. "You are right. I want to get her out, but she can wait another few weeks. Thanks Michelle."

Michelle smiles and looks at Kelly. "We will start now to put together some ideas and we'll discuss them when you get back. Talk with you then."

Mark clicks off the SAT phone and puts it back into his sack. Ducky looks over at Mark, "Good news?"

Stretching out his long legs, Mark closes his eyes. "Yeah, seems that everything is starting to come together."

The jet starts to dip toward Bagram Air Force base bringing Mark closer to freeing his sister and dealing out justice to her captor.

Chapter 20

Florence, Italy - August 9th

The boys are up and reading their books in the common room between their bedrooms. They are early risers and have learned to wait for their parents to get up before they can start running around the house. They both have brought many books on their iPads and are sitting in the comfortable chairs reading by the early morning sunlight.

Agents Lee and Bale enter the common room and smile seeing the boys quiet and reading their iPads. "Hi boys, how did you sleep?"

Oliver pipes up. "I slept ok, but Filip snores."

"No I don't."

"You do." Says the older brother.

The agents sit and start to read the local English language newspaper. After twenty minutes Claire emerges from her bedroom looking rested. She walks over to the boys and touches each of them on their heads while they read.

"Thanks boys for keeping quiet." Claire moves to a table and pours a cup of coffee. She looks to the two agents, "how did you guys sleep?"

Both agents nod. "I was able to get to sleep by 2 am, but that is normal for me." Said Agent Bale.

"I hit the pillow hard and slept like a baby." Agent Lee says.

"Great, what is on the schedule for today?"

At that point they hear a knock on the door. Both agents quickly rise and pull their guns. Agent Bale approaches the door and looks through the eye piece. He sees a tall red headed woman.

"It's Diane Fusco, State Department and best friend of Claire Sweeney," announces the red head. The agents sees her flash her State Department credential and her brilliant smile.

Claire hears her friend's voice through the door and shouts, "Hi Diane." As the agent pulls the door open.

The two women embrace. Claire laughs, "God, how long has it been?"

Diane laughs too. "Twelve years maybe?"

"At least. Thanks for coming up to Florence." Diane hears two boys giggling. "I would guess that this is Oliver and this is Filip."

Oliver steps forward as he was taught and smiles and shakes her hand. "I am Oliver." Then his brother does the same thing.

Diane looks at Claire. "Oh, they are beautiful. Very gentlemanly."

After introductions to the two Secret Service agents the women sit on the couch and plan the day.

"Well, we saw the major highlights of Florence yesterday. We were thinking of driving over to Pisa today, then up to Genoa for a day, then over to the Lake Como area for three days. Then home."

Diane nods. "Great trip. Maybe next trip you can bring David and come to Rome. It is such an amazing city. But not really for children."

"Well, let's pack up. We have room service coming and after that we can get on the road to Pisa!"

The boys go into their room to pack as does Claire. While the family is out of the room, Diane turns to the agents. "I didn't want to alarm Claire or the boys, but we received some Intel last night that there was some chatter about an attack on the first family."

Both Agents nod and quietly say, "We are nervous about only two of us being assigned to the family on an international trip. Normally we would have a minimum of four Agents."

Diane looks pensive. "I asked our Intel group to alert us if anything more turns up."

The three sit quietly for a minute. "Well, we will make the trip as safe as possible. We don't have armored vehicles. I don't feel good about the trip. But if we keep moving, then unless they know our itinerary it will be tough to target us."

"I'll call the Embassy and ask if they will contact the local police for extra back up."

"No don't do that. Local police might leak that the family is in their city to the newspapers or others. I'd prefer that we sneak in under the radar and get out before they know the family was there."

"Ok, I'll be with the family for the rest of the trip, but I'll have to check in with the Embassy."

The agents rise. "Ok, but try to keep your whereabouts to as few people as possible."

At this point, the boys come out of their bedroom wheeling their suitcases. Shortly thereafter, Claire comes out with hers.

The room service arrives and after checking out the wheeled table, everyone sits and enjoys a wonderful Italian breakfast. After finishing, the group leaves the hotel to their waiting car. The agents leapfrog each other from the elevator, to a back door, and then out into the car. The transfer goes without a hitch as the car leaves the hotel and onto the SGC Firenze-Pisa-Livorno highway on the one hour drive to Pisa and the continuation of their holiday.

Chapter 21

Tyson Corners, VA - August 10th

After dropping off Muhammad Ibrahim Bayunoni to a rendition site in Afghanistan, the team hops on an Agency jet for the long trip back to Washington D.C. Mark, Ducky and six of the Special Operators stretch out and relax after the intense fire fight and flight out of Pakistan. The other two operators who were wounded are staying in Afghanistan until they can be flown to Germany for medical care.

The flight of fifteen hours with the extended range jet is comfortable and allows the passengers to get a good long sleep and enabling them to arrive at Dulles Airport rested and refreshed. Each have taken a shower and changed into clean clothes and have a hardy breakfast, all before landing.

Upon leaving the jet Mark and Ducky bade the other Special Operators thanks for their support and head for a waiting car to take them to S-Cubed.

Arriving at the Ultra-black site, Mark and Ducky check in and Mark immediately walks down to Michelle's office.

"Hi Mark. Congratulations on the successful snatch."

Mark smiles. "It was a bit more exciting than we wanted, but everything worked out well. Two Special Operators were wounded, but one was a through and through to the shoulder, the other was a leg wound, but both should be fine."

Michelle stands and hesitates between a handshake and hug. Mark solves the issue by sitting on the couch. "So I guess that you want the INTEL on your sister."

"Yes, that is all I could think of on the flight back. What do you have?"

Michelle leans against her desk and grabs a folder. I asked the CIA SAD (Special Activities Division) to do a deep dive on your sister. The President authorized the operation and the SAD team reached out to their Iranian agents to find her. It wasn't too hard once we focused on her." Michelle flips the page of her report. "Saarah Nasir Al-Din, as you know was purchased by Javad Tousi. He lived with your mother and sister over the past thirty some years. Your mother died of cancer three years ago. Saarah was raped by Tousi and had two abortions that were reported. At 30, your sister married a Captain of the Republican Guards, Sajad Aziz. He is the son of General Hamid Aziz, who we believe helped to coordinate the Red Death virus attack on the West. Saarah and Sajad live in an upscale neighborhood in Tehran. They have no children."

Mark knows all this and is getting impatient. "So where is she? Let's put together a plan to get into Iran and then get her out."

111

Michelle puts the folder down. "What if she is happy, what if she doesn't want to leave Iran?"

Mark shakes his head. "I can't believe that. Of course it will be hard, but right now she has no choice."

Michelle sighs. "Ok, but I think we should try to get her a secret note asking her if she would like to meet with you. One of our agents could slip her the note and a method for her to reply yes or no without putting her at risk."

Mark closes his eyes and massages his temples. He knows this is the sensible route. Least risk for everyone involved. But damn, he wants to get his sister out. Mark lets out a long breath. "Ok, let's get a note to her and see what she says."

Michelle nods. She makes a note in her notebook. "We'll get a simple note to Saarah as soon as we can. Then make sure she can reply discreetly, yes or no."

Mark looks up and nods.

"Ok, I'll set it up," says Michelle.

*   *   *

Two days later, the Mossad agent within Iran receives the note and drives the six miles to a children's school where Saarah Aziz volunteers her time several days a week teaching children English. He is sitting across from the school now watching

112

hundreds of school age children file into the school. He has a photo of Saarah and is carefully scrutinizing each adult approaching. Suddenly he sees her. She gets out of a Mercedes Benz, closes the door and walks slowly towards the school entrance. The agent gets out of his car and follows. Saarah stops to chat with a parent with a child. Then takes the child's hand and leads her into the school, the agent just steps behind.

Saarah stops to let the girl enter her classroom. At that point, the agent bumps into her and says "excuse me" in Farsi. He then puts the note in her hand. Saarah looks startled, having a man she doesn't know touch her hand. She looks down at the piece of paper she is holding.

Softly the Agent says, "Your brother Mailis wants you to read this in private." At that, the Agent turns and walks out of the school.

Saarah's heart seems to stop at the mention of her brother's name. What is happening? She stands still for several seconds, and then Saarah looks around to see if any of the teachers noticed the note exchange. Everything is the normal controlled chaos. With her heart racing, she walks to the women's lavatory. Once inside, she moves to one of the stalls and sits. With trembling hands she unfolds the note written in Arabic.

Saarah, I am sending you this note to discreetly make contact with you. I am doing well and living in America. Would you like to meet? I may be able to get you out of Iran, but it would be dangerous. Consider this carefully. If you wish to meet, wear a red scarf within the next two days when you travel to the school. I will then be back in touch with you within a few weeks. If not, I understand. Destroy this note for your own protection. Love, Mailis

Saarah starts to cry softly. Her brother is not only alive but might be able to get her out of Iran. Her mind is reeling. She takes a deep breath and wipes her eyes. Her hands are shaking. Saarah rereads the note.

She hears the bathroom door open. "Saarah are you ok?"

Saarah almost drops the note but catches it at the last second. "Yes, I am ok. I'll be back in the class shortly." She considers keeping the note, but if anyone discovered it, she could be considered a spy and go to jail or even be executed. Her husband because of his position in the Republican Guard might be able to shield her, but perhaps he would not. She makes her decision and tears the note into small pieces and flushes them in the toilet.

After a few minutes she exits the stall and washes her hands. Saarah looks up into the mirror and breaks into a smile. She has to guard against showing too much emotion. Go about your day, stay calm, she thinks to herself. Taking a deep breath, Saarah exits the bathroom and heads for her classroom.

Chapter 22

Pisa, Italy - August 10th

Clare, her boys and her best friend, Diane look out the car window at the downtown of Pisa. They pass the Piazza dei Miracoli on their way to their hotel. Clare points out the leaning tower of Pisa and then the Duomo. "After we check into the hotel, we can go for a walk and check out some of the cool sites", she says to the boys.

Agent Bale is sitting in the front passenger seat. He is armed with his SIG Sauer P229, but also has a 9mm Heckler & Koch MP5 submachine gun in a specially designed holster built for the Suburban vehicle. The side and back windows are tinted and treated to reduce shattering in the event of an explosion. Agent Lee is sitting in the middle section by the driver side door. She also has similar weapons at her disposal. The driver is on loan from the Embassy and is an expert in avoid and evasion techniques.

Clare and Oliver are sitting next to Agent Kim,

Diane and Filip are in the third row in the back. All are taking in the beautiful buildings, and then pull in front of the Grand Hotel Duomo. It's a four star hotel with a beautiful orange façade.

Agent Bale exits the vehicle first and scans for any threats. Agent Kim then steps out of her door looking across the street, her hand on her weapon. Agent Bale then walks up the green steps to the hotel door. He enters, then comes out and signals an all clear. At that point Agent Kim moves to the passenger door and opens it for the President's daughter, children and her friend. They step down onto the pavement and walk quickly into the hotel lobby.

After checking in, the family and guards take the elevator up to the top floor. Agent Bale steps out his hand on his weapon. He scans right, then left making sure the hallway is empty. He spots a maid's cart outside a room. He turns to his charges. "Wait in the elevator." The agent moves quickly and checks out the cart, then the maid who is in one of the rooms turning down the sheets.

Agent Lee is watching with her hand on her weapon, then she receives an all clear and she herds the family to their rooms.

Clare pulls her luggage into her bedroom while the boys do the same into theirs. Diane spots some flowers sent by Clare's husband and coos about what a catch David is. Clare comes out and picks a card off the bouquet and reads it. *Hope you and the boys are having a great vacation. It's lonely here! Have fun and take lots of pics! Love Always, David.*

Diane smiles. "What beautiful flowers. I wish my boyfriend would do the same, but he is an Italian and only thinks of …" Not completing the sentence as Oliver and Filip enter the room. The women laugh.

"How about going for a walk? And maybe get some ice cream?"

The boys scream "Yes!" and head for the door.

Agent Lee is standing by the door and stops them. "Hold on, we have to do this my way."

The boys stop and look back at mom. "We have to be safe and sticking with Agent Bale and Agent Lee is very important."

With that, the group exits the suite and heads for the elevator. Reversing the security protocol down the elevator then into the Suburban even through the Piazza dei Miracoli was only a few blocks away.

The Agents are very nervous with the family exiting the vehicle and walking among the tourists on the wide expanse of beautifully manicured lawns. Agent Lee is in front, Agent Bale behind the family.

As they approach the Duomo, a woman approaches. "Buongiorno Clare, my name is Rosalia but everyone calls me Rosa", then she switches to English. "I am excited to show you the Duomo, the Museo Nazionale di San Matteo and of course the leaning tower."

Clare smiles and extends her hand to the docent. "Buongiorno. These are my sons, Oliver and Filip and my best friend Diane." Handshakes are exchanged, and then as they walk up the Duomo stairs, Rosa begins her guiding of the Pisa treasures.

"The Duomo was started in 1064 but it took several hundred of years complete. In 1380 the elliptical dome was added. An interesting fact is that the cathedral was paid for with spoils from a 1063 naval battle that the Pisans fought against an Arab fleet off Palermo. To mark the victory, and to symbolize Pisa's military domination, the cathedral was Europe's largest when it was completed."

The group approaches three pairs of huge 16th Century bronze doors.

Her attention is drawn back to the guide. "There are three pairs of 16th Century bronze doors into the main entrance. Each has Biblical scenes that illustrate the immaculate conception of the Virgin Mary, the birth of the Christ, the crucifixion of Christ and the ministry of Christ." The group marvels at the quality of the bronze artwork. "Also, boys can you spot the rhino?" Suddenly the boys are interested and look intently at the doors.

After about five minutes Oliver shouts, "there it is!" pointing to one of the doors. The rhino is green with age but beautifully detailed showing its armor around its belly and its horn from its nose.

Everyone smiles and enters the Duomo to see the magnificent cathedral. After a quick walk-thru, the group walks to the leaning tower. Rosa takes a picture of the group in front of the tower with each of them leaning the 4 degrees to simulate the tower's lean.

"The tower was started in 1173 but because of poor soil, the bell tower began to lean. Construction was stopped but then began again trying to correct the issue. The bell tower is freestanding and is 186 feet tall. In 1990 the tower was stabilized. We can't all go inside since young children are not allowed."

Oliver and Filip are just as happy. They want to complete the tour and get to the ice cream shop.

The group continues to the Museo Nazionale di San Mateo with an amazing collection of 12th Century paintings and sculptures. Several state police are standing nearby holding their H&K MP5 submachine guns. Clare notices several men walking a distance away. They are bearded and seem to be shadowing them. She doesn't want to be paranoid, but suddenly she is getting nervous. Her intuition is kicking in. The group enters the

Museum and quickly walks through admiring the artwork.

After a quick tour she softly speaks to Agent Lee and they decide to exit through a back door. After thanking Rosa for her historical guiding, the group leaves the building just as their Suburban rolls up. Agent Lee moves to the vehicle door and opens it while Agent Bale scans the area. Within fifteen seconds, the boys, Diane and Clare are in the car and the door closed. After another fifteen seconds, both agents are also in the car and they move out.

Clare peers out of the windows looking for the two men, but she doesn't see them. She relaxes and turns to the boys. "Guys, how about getting a banana split with chocolate sauce at the hotel?"

The boys let out a yell of approval as the car pulls to the back of the hotel and everyone piles out and they head for the suite. The boys do a rock-paper-scissors to be able to place the room service call.

Clare and Diane sit on the couch with a glass of wine talking and relaxing. Tomorrow they travel to Lake Como and a few days of just fun and sun.

Chapter 23

Tyson Corners, VA - August 11th

Michelle and Mark are sitting in the conference room pouring over several maps of Iran.   Several cups of coffee sit cold and untouched.

"I think there are two options.   One is to just fly into Tehran with a Russian passport and pose as a businessman. My Russian is passable and probably much better than most Iranians. Plus I would just mix in some Persian or Farsi. It would work. The second option would be to use a boat and I could swim into a beach town and travel to Tehran that way."

Michelle considers Mark's options. "The second option would be more dangerous. You could be spotted swimming into shore; you would need transportation, then getting to Tehran without being stopped.   The first option is more direct and gives you the option to use your language skills if you need them. What you could do is fly into Russia as a German or French tourist, then fly from Rostov to Tehran and land as a Russian businessman. We can doctor the passports to have the correct visas."

Mark considers the advantages and dangers of both. "I think you are right. The direct approach would be best. It would also give me an opportunity to move about the city freely."

As they are considering all the angles, Kelly Campos saunters in. "Hi boss, just got a secure message that Saarah Nasir al-Din Aziz wore a red head scarf to school today."

Mark looks up with a huge smile on his face. "Then we are on. We have to get a message to my sister that we acknowledge and will be back in touch with her."

Michelle nods. "Kelly, we'll craft a short message that you can send to our contact today."

Mark returns his attention to the Iranian map. "The issue will be getting Saarah out of Iran. We'll have to produce a passport for her, Russian?"

Michelle considers the situation. "She can't speak Russian. What about a medical issue that prevents her from speaking? An accident that has her jaw wired? Traveling to Germany for medical treatment? The Iranian officials will understand that."

Mark looks up from the map. "I think that would work. Saarah traveling as my wife? Fiancée? What if immigration checks on her entry?"

At this point Kelly Campos speaks up. "I can hack their immigration system and show her entering the country at the same time you do.   Plus I can place an accident report with the local police."

Mark smiles. "Kelly, I will owe you as many M&Ms as you want."

Kelly smiles but before he leaves, he snaps his fingers. "I forgot to tell you something. I intercepted a message from Hamza bin Ladin. He said that the Black Widow was in place and ready for its meal."

Everyone gives Campos a blank stare. "Ok, I didn't know what that meant either. I'll do some checking."   Kelly then saunters out of the conference room and back to the SKIF.

Michelle stands. "Ok, I will put together a short message to your sister. We'll get the passports ready and you'll need to get some "Russian" clothes for yourself and for Saarah. You know this will be off the books and there is really no backup once you are in Iran."

Mark stands also and folds up the maps. "Yeah, I totally understand. This is my Op. If I am captured, no negotiations, no ransom... agreed?"

Michelle looks at Mark, "Agreed, but it won't come to that."

With that, Michelle returns to her office and Mark heads for his office to write down more details for the travel schedule, where to stay and the timing. He hopes he can leave tomorrow and be in Iran within two or three days and rescue his sister.

Chapter 24

White Sands AFB - August 11th

Walter Cartwright closes and locks the door to his condo for the last time. He smiles knowing he will not be coming back. He has pulled out most of what money he has in his bank account; he has sold his car and packed a bag with some clothes. Yesterday he made a reservation for a flight from Dallas to Mexico City as Richard White for tomorrow morning. Then he plans to take a bus to the Mexico – Belize border. Then into Belize on a bus where he will enter the country and live like a king. Walter smiles.

"Walter... you wanted to see me?" This breaks Walter out of his daydream. He looks up and sees E-5 Staff Sergeant Susie Davies standing at attention before his desk. Even though he is a civilian contractor for the U.S. Army, the base personnel treat him like a commander.

"Yes, tonight the U.S. Navy will send a truck to pick up the HEL demo systems to place on one of their ships for a fit analysis."

Staff Sergeant Susie Davies is only 31 years old and has quickly risen through the ranks over the past ten years of her service after graduation from Miami of Ohio University with an engineering degree. She is smart, dedicated and committed to the U.S. Army. "Yes sir. Do you have the paperwork?"

Walter pulls a file folder from his desk and hands it to Sergeant Davies. "The demo system is crated and identified as US41-HEL. The Navy pukes should he here around 9 pm. Help them load the crate and get their signoff."

Susie accepts the file and reviews the paperwork. She hates that this government contractor disparages the Navy personnel. He is fat, not that bright and she doesn't know how he got this job. But it's not her job to question the top command. Everything seems to be in order. "Yes sir. I'll make sure they get the demo system."

With that she leaves his office and Walter sits back in his chair dreaming about the beaches of Belize.

Chapter 25

Florence, Italy - August 12th

Agents Bale and Lee herd the Sweeney family plus one into the black Suburban and tap the driver on the shoulder for him to proceed. It is tight quarters with four adults and two children in the middle and back sections of the SUV. Both agents are in the middle section with Diane; the boys are in the back with Clare.

During the drive out of Florence, the driver John Rossi takes the normal route North out towards Milan. It's a beautiful day, sunny and warm. As the SUV drives along the expressway, Clare asks the driver if there is a more scenic way north.

"Clare, I think we should stick to the highway. More traffic, but safer." Says Kari Lee.

"I know but I'd like the boys to see the countryside and we are a couple of hours ahead of schedule."

Agent Lee consults her iPad Google maps to see what route might be both scenic but also keep on the schedule. After a few minutes, she finds a road that looks like it would work.

"John, take the next exit and head West on A11 toward Massa rather than taking A1 towards Bologna, at La Spezia lets head North on A15."

127

The driver complies and the SUV heads along the coast, showing the boys the beautiful Mediterranean Sea and pointing out the ships on the Ligurian Sea. The SUV settles into a quiet drive, the boys playing video games on their iPads while occasionally checking out the scenery, while Clare and Diane talking about mutual friends and their families.

Suddenly the SUV skids to a sudden stop with two white vans stopping in front of them completely blocking the highway. Agent Bale looks back and sees another van coming too fast to stop. "Get down" he yells just as the van crashes into the SUV.

Before any of them can react, five black clad figures pour out of the white van in front and one fires a shot through the windshield and instantly kills the driver. Both Agents Bale and Lee pull their guns. A second explosion hits the front windshield blowing it into the front seat. Then suddenly a tear-gas canister is thrown into the SUV. Within seconds the SUV fills with the gas that causes each of the occupants' eyes to water with a burning sensation, difficulty breathing and a panic sensation of smothering. Agent Bale opens the side door and is immediately hit with the butt of an AK-47. As he slides to the ground unconscious, his weapon is retrieved and his head is hooded and hands zip tied behind him.

"Do not resist or everyone dies, including the children," A voice in English shouts into the van. Clare has pulled both the boys to her and is scrambling to get out, coughing and blinded by the gas. As they exit, they have a black hood placed over their heads and their hands are tied behind them. Diane stumbles out and is quickly hooded. Finally Agent Lee comes out with her hands up. She is subdued and a hood placed over her head and her hands zip tied. It is all over in less than two minutes. All of the hostages are loaded into the lead white van and it takes off. Two of the terrorists shoot at the cars stopped behind their van. The people who were standing outside their cars watching, scatter and dive for cover. Then the terrorists pour gasoline on the van behind them and set it on fire. With that, as they hop into their waiting, van they toss a grenade into the black SUV and speed away. Suddenly the SUV explodes sending shrapnel all over the road and setting the SUV on fire, blocking the road.

As the terrorists speed away in the two vans, the highway is shutdown with smoke, fire and death. The first step in the al-Qaeda plan to humiliate and make America pay has been successful.

Chapter 26

Washington DC - August 12th

The President is sitting in the Roosevelt Room near the Oval Office, meeting with a group of business leaders talking about jobs, increasing economic opportunity in inner cities and increasing exports.

Suddenly the chief of staff rushes into the meeting. The President can see the panic on his friend's face. Randy Smith leans down and whispers into the President's ear.

The President stays calm, recalling President George W Bush's calm demeanor when he was told about the terrorist 9/11 attack on New York City while being filmed in a elementary school. He nods and Randy steps away.

"I am sorry Ladies and Gentlemen, but I have a potential emergency that I have to address right now. Mr. Vice President, would you please take over the meeting?" With that, the President stands and follows Randy Smith out of the Roosevelt room into a corridor to the Oval Office. As they enter the iconic room the President turns when his Chief of Staff closes the door.

"How could this happen? Were they hurt? What do we know?"

The Chief of Staff can see the anguish on the President's face. "Twenty minutes ago a report came in that there was an accident on a highway South of Florence, multiple cars involved, and a fire. Then just five minutes ago we heard from the State Department that the car involved was from their vehicle pool and was assigned to Clare."

The President slumps onto the couch near the Presidential desk. "Oh my God."

The Chief of Staff continues, "The local police arrived and determined it was a terrorist attack. Three white vans, six black clad attackers with AK-47s. When they investigated they found a male body in the front seat of the SUV. The vehicle had been blown apart by an explosive device and there was the smell of tear gas. They determined it was a State Department SUV, they called it in as a kidnapping. But it seems that all of the other occupants got out alive."

The President sits forward. "So what do we do?"

"We have the Italian police and counter-terrorism personnel on high alert. They have about an hour head start, but we are confident we can keep them contained to a 200 mile radius between Florence, Genoa and Milan."

"Is it al-Qaeda?" Asks the President.

Randy Smith sits across from the President. "We don't know yet. They do operate in Italy, but there are several Italian terrorist groups also that we should consider. We are setting up the situation room now to gather information and coordinate the search."

The President stands. "I have to contact David Sweeney."

"I will ask Marlene to find him and put him on the line for you."

"Thank you Randy. I'll meet you in the Situation Room shortly. I need to call my wife too."

"Mr. President, we have to assume it was al-Qaeda and that they will either use Clare and the kids for propaganda or they want something for them."

"Let's hope it's a ransom situation. It's something we can deal with. Let's keep this totally black, only key personnel read in. Also, contact Michelle Samaha and her group. They could be useful if we find out where they are being held."

"Yes Sir."

The President moves to his desk and places a call to his wife, then speaks with David Sweeney about his wife and children.

"David, I just received a message that Clare and the boys have been kidnapped in Italy. I want you to know that the full force of the American government will be used to get them back safely." The President can tell David is in shock.

"Please don't say anything to anyone else. If this gets out, it could hamper our efforts to negotiate. David, I am so sorry.

But we'll get them back alive."

The President hangs up hoping he can fulfill that promise but knowing that his daughter and grandsons lives hang in the balance.

Chapter 27

Genoa, Italy - August 12th

The two white vans pull into a large warehouse and the terrorists hop out. They are jubilant, shouting and congratulating each other on their successful mission.

"Quiet, control yourselves," yells Nimr Yazdi in Arabic. "Take the prisoners to the safe room and give them water to clean their faces."

The terrorists take each of the six prisoners and lead them single file to a room built especially for this operation. It has only one reinforced door, no windows but a small ventilation system, completely sealed with one light bulb.

Clare heard the shouting but doesn't understand Arabic and was unsure what it means. She is worried about her boys, but knows better than to speak. Already she was slapped when she tried to talk with her sons. She knows that the kidnapping has been done by Arabs, but maybe they don't know who they are. That is her main hope, that they are only local criminals trying to ransom them for money. That is something her father can deal with.

As they are led into the room, each has the hood removed from their heads. She can see both boys standing stoically, their faces streaked with tears from the gas. As soon as the zip ties are cut from her hands, she goes to the boys. Clare pulls them close and all three start to cry softly. Diane comes to them and puts her arms about them.

A water basin is placed in the center of the room and is filled with water. Two towels are laid down on the concrete floor and the terrorist leave the room and lock the door.

"Clare, wash your face and the boys. Each of us should clean up and get ready for the questioning. I am not sure they know who we are. We should keep to a story that you are American tourists on holiday." Says Agent Kim. "You hired us for protection because you are rich Americans."

Agent Bale nods, and then adds. "Hopefully they have a ransom number and we can have them deal with the State Department. They may separate us to see if our stories are consistent. Resist separating the boys from Clare."

Suddenly the door opens and three armed terrorists enter the room and a man who is the leader. The armed men take up position on either side of the door and the other removes the water basin and towels. The leader moves to the center of the room with a limp and smiles.

"Would you please sit down on the floor?" The man says in English. "My name is Nimr Yazdi and I am a servant of Allah. We would like each of your names and your positions with the American government."

Diane stands and states. "My name is Diane Fusco and I work for the U.S. State Department in Rome." Moving her hand towards Diane and the boys, "they are American tourists from Colorado and are of no consequence. I would suggest that..."

"Sit down. Enough lies." Nimr turns to Clare who is holding both boys in her lap. "You are Clare Sweeney, the daughter of President Baker. The boys are your children and the grandchildren of the United States President. That is all I need to know. You others are expendable if you do not behave. We will treat you with respect, give you food and keep you safe. What we expect from you is compliance with our demands. If you cause any trouble, you will be bound and the hood will come back. We intend to ransom all of you within the next several days. Stay calm and both of us will get what we want."

With that, the terrorist exits the room and the door is locked.

Clare looks at Diane. "Oh my God, he knows who we are."

Agent Kim looks around the room seeing if she can see any cameras or listening devices.

"Stay calm. They need you healthy. Just don't say much. Answer their questions, but ask them about their intentions. They may separate us, so just stay strong."

Clare pulls both boys to her. She can tell they are scared, but she wants to comfort them. "Boys, you have to keep your eyes and ears open. Do not say anything unless I tell you its ok. Poppy will get us out of this mess. Ok?"

Both boys nod and look up as the door is opened again. The man who spoke earlier enters the room and smiles, after him enters two men carrying a case of water and some bread and cheese. "Please have something to eat and drink. Clare, we'd like you to record a message to your father letting him know you are well, the boys are well and your security team is safe. Then I will negotiate for your release."

Clare stands. "The release must include all of us together. What are you asking for?"

Nimr smiles. "Over the past ten years your government has captured many of our brothers and put them in the prison on Cuba.   There are fifty-five of our soldiers detained at Guantanamo Bay.   We are only asking for twelve of them to be released for your safe return."

Clare looks over at Diane. Diane looks away unwilling to meet Clare's eyes knowing the U.S. Government would never swap twelve known terrorists. "We will have to discuss this, alone."

Nimr smiles again. "Of course, you have five minutes." With that, he and the guards exit the room.

The kids each grab a roll and a water bottle.

Clare, Diane, Agent Kim and Agent Bale move to a corner of the room and stand in a closed circle.

Diane speaks first in a whisper. "They want you to do the video for propaganda purposes. But it will give the government some clues, and they will know you and the boys are alive. That is worth doing the video."

Clare considers her friends council. "What if they edit the video, make is say something against my father or the government?"

"Could happen, but I think our people in Washington would know if it's been doctored. Do you know Morse code?" Asked Diane.

"Morse code?"

"You could use your fingers or blinking to send a secret message."

Clare smiles. "I know it from my Girl Scout days, but it was decades ago. I'll try."

Diane takes Clare's hands in hers. "Don't just do the video, negotiate with him to get something."

They all eat something while Clare practices Morse code blinking out a simple message.

Just then the door opens and Nimr walks in with his guards. "Well Ms. Sweeney, will you do the video?"

Clare steps up to Nimr towering over him at 5'10". "I would like two things in exchange. First, I would like pillows and blankets for us to sleep on. Secondly, I would like to talk on a phone to my husband to assure him that his children and I are ok.

Nimr considers the request. The pillows and blankets are no problem; the phone however could be traced. "I will agree to the pillows and blankets, but not the phone."

Clare looks at Diane, then to Agent Kim. "Ok, but only a short video and I want to read the script before I record it."

Nimr smiles. "Of course." With that he barks some orders to the guards and they bring in a blanket and a pillow for each person. "Please eat the rest of your food. I will bring you the script in an hour." With that, Nimr and the guards leave the room.

They all eat the rolls and drink the water not knowing when they might get any more.

Agent Kim begins working with Clare to craft a simple Morse code while they try to figure out how to deliver it during the video taping.

"The problem is that we are not really sure where we are. We could be anywhere within 100 miles of Pisa." Says Clare.

"I have to go to the bathroom." Filip says to his mom.

Agent Kim speaks first. "Yes, there is no bathroom here. They will have to take us out one at a time to use the bathroom. That will give us an opportunity to see where we are."

Diane shakes her head. "I am sure they will put the hood on us each time we leave the room."

"Well, let's test it. Clare walks over to the door and bangs on it. "My son needs to go to the bathroom."

Clare kneels in front of her young son. "Filip, if they don't put the hood on you. Look around and try to remember everything you can about the building, ok?"

Filip nods. Then Oliver speaks up. "What if I go with him? Then we'll have four eyes looking for clues!"

Clare smiles. "Excellent idea."

Just then the door opens and a guard motions for one to go with him to the bathroom. He has a hood in his hand.

Clare stands. "Both my sons have to go to the bathroom," motioning to both boys. The guard looks puzzled, then gets the idea and leads both boys out the door without putting the hood on either of their heads indicating that Clare could not follow.

Agent Kim then starts the Morse code lesson with both Clare and Diane in the event one or both of them are asked to do a video together.

Suddenly, they hear a gun shot. Clare screams and rushes to the door. It's locked of course and she pounds on the door. "What is happening? Where are my boys?"

After a few minutes the door is opened and Oliver and Filip run into their mother's arms. "What happened? Why the gun shot?"

Nimr enters the room. "The guard failed to hood your boys when he took them to the bathroom. For that failure, he paid the ultimate price. Your boys were in the bathroom and didn't see our punishment of him."

Nimr hands the one page script to Clare. "This is the script you will read. There will be no deviations. I will hold a gun to the head of your Agent Kim and if you fail to read the script as written. She will die. Is that clear?"

Clare looks down at the script, "what if I refuse?"

Nimr's hand moves quickly slapping Clare across the face and knocking her to the ground. "You will read the script, one way or another."

Diane holds onto the boys as they try to race to their mother's defense. Clare wipes some blood from a cut on her lip.

Nimr smiles and tells her that she has ten minutes to read the script over, and then they will begin the video taping.

Chapter 28

White Sands, NM - August 12th

Sergeant Susie Davies is sitting at her desk completing some paperwork. It's almost 21:00 when she sees two Navy officers walking towards her office. She pulls out the folder for the HEL system transfer.

One of the Navy officer's name is Chao a Lieutenant, the other is James a Warrant Officer. They both enter her office and salute. Susie stands and returns their salute. "Gentlemen, I have the paperwork for the HEL demo system. Can I see your identification and your paperwork?"

The two Navy personnel show her their IDs and then give Susie their paperwork.

"Everything seems to be in order. Where is the system?" Asks Lieutenant Chao.

Susie examines the Navy paperwork and something doesn't look right. She frowns. "Who is your commander? Should he have signed the order?"

Lt. Chao sides up next to Staff Sergeant Davies. "Oh yeah, the old man was back in Washington D.C. and his second, Lieutenant Commander McDonald had to sign."

Susie nods and makes a note on her paperwork, and then she leads them out into the warehouse and to where the crate is waiting. While they are walking, Susie notes that both the Navy officers are armed.

"Do you usually have your side arms for a pickup?"

Lieutenant Chao smiles. "This is a valuable piece of equipment. Just want to be on the safe side."

They motion for the Navy truck to enter the warehouse. The crate is large, standing at least ten feet high and thirty feet wide. A large Hyster Forklift slides into position and slips its rails under the crate. It lifts it easily and transports it to the Navy truck.

Staff Sergeant Davies looks over the truck; it doesn't look like any military truck she has seen. She starts to walk around the truck and notices the driver standing several feet away smoking. He is wearing an ensign uniform, but his name tag is askew.

"Ensign, your name tag is crooked."

The sailor looks at her and continues to smoke his cigarette.

Staff Sergeant Davies walks up to the man. He drops his cigarette and snuffs it out with his boot.

"Ensign, this is a no smoking facility."

The man looks down at her and sneers, "Yes ma'am."

At that point Lieutenant Chao moves between the two and smiles. "Sorry Staff Sergeant.   Williams, would you secure the crate and get the truck started while I finalize the paperwork."

With that Susie and Chao walk back to her office.

"What's up with that Ensign?"

"Sorry about that, he is a problem. I apologize."

The two sign each other's paperwork. Lt. Chao salutes Staff Sergeant Davies. "Thank you for your cooperation." The truck moves out of the warehouse and sits idling. Susie nods and puts the paperwork in her folder.

As the Navy officer leaves her office, Susie calls after him. "Lieutenant, I'd like to examine the crate. I want to make sure it is what it's supposed to be."

Chao frowns. "We are already late, that will take twenty minutes to open it up."

"I am sorry, but I should have inspected the crate before it was loaded."

They walk to the back of the truck.

As they approach the truck's tailgate, Chao moves behind Davies. He looks around, then pulls his revolver and hits the Staff Sergeant in the back of her head, dropping her to the pavement.

"Get her quickly into the cab of the truck." Chao says to his Ensign.

The Warrant Officer and the Ensign pick Davies up and place her in the back section of the truck, then bind her hands and gag her.

The truck is then fired up and the Navy personnel leave the U.S. Army base using the forged paperwork, transporting a U.S. Army Staff Sergeant and a fully functional HEL system.

Chapter 29

Washington D.C. - August 13th

Mark Aldin and Michelle Samaha have been working fifteen hour days developing a plan for Mark to enter Iran, rescue his sister and get out alive. Ducky and Jonathan join the meeting.

"Did you receive the passport, visa and other supporting documentation?" Asks Jonathan.

"Yes, excellent job. I've seen many Russian passports and I can't tell that it's a forgery. Even the cover is distressed, the ink is faded on the older stamps and the analysts used the old nomenclature for the USSR."

Michelle smiles. "They are the best in the business."

Mark studies the map one more time. "Let's go over the complete plan from entry to exit just one more time."

Michelle knows the plan as well has Mark, but understands that it's his life on the line and he wants to make sure they have every contingency covered.

"We fly you into Ukraine, and then slip you into Russia using the Ukrainian Zbroyni Syly Ukranyiny (ZSU) military. I am sure we can get a recommendation from the Joint Chiefs."

Mark shakes his head. "I wouldn't trust my life to

someone I don't know personally. I know a guy I trust who is with the Alpha Group there in Ukraine. He and I had special forces training together here in the States when I was a SEAL, and I've kept in touch with him over the years."

Michelle nods. "Ok, it's your OP. As long as you trust him."

Mark taps the map. "He is stationed in Mariupol. I'll contact him and I can fly into Ukraine on my fake Canadian passport and he can help me get into Russia."

Ducky, Michelle and Jonathan all agree that this phase of the plan will work

"Once I am into Russia, I'll spend a day getting ready, and then fly from Moscow into Iran using my false passport. Assuming I get in, then I'll go to an international hotel and make contact with Ethan Gallin who has been in Iran working for Mossad for the past ten years."

"Was he the one who killed Dr. Rahimi?" Asks Ducky.

"Yes, we believe he was the one who found Dr. Rahimi and had eyes on him prior to his death. So we assume it was him who took him out. I wish it was a bit more violent." Laments Mark.

Michelle smiles. "Ok, we get a note to Saarah with the date and time to "abduct" her. She can change clothes in the van on the way to the airport. I would recommend that you drive to Imam Khomeini International Airport. It is less than an hour from Saarah's school. She can leave her home, drive to the school, then tell them she is not feeling well and leave. At that point, you can pick her up nearby in the van. You drive to the airport; you'll have luggage and your passports and visas to travel to Germany. Saarah will have to have a surgical bandage over her jaw so that she can not talk."

"Yes, I can apply that to her face. The issue is her passport photo. Ethan can get a photo printer and take a photo of her in the van and glue it into the passport. It isn't exactly what I'd like, but it's the best we can do." Says Mark. "Then we just walk into the airport like any couple, go through customs and get on the plane for Germany."

Michelle considers the plan. "Ok, I think it will work. You and Saarah will be out of the country by the time anyone discovers she is missing. I think she should be listed as your wife. That will allow your outrage if they question your situation. Also, we should develop a doctor's letter recommending her travel to Germany for surgery."

Mark nods. "I'll ask Kelly to make the reservations for both of us coming into Iran and the reservations for us leaving. Also, the accident report of Saarah being hurt in a car accident needs to be in place. It should work."

The group stands for several minutes silently working through the plan in their minds. Finally Michelle says. "I agree, but what is Plan B in the event you can't get to the airport or things go south at the airport?"

Mark shrugs. "At the airport at passport control if they question the passports, then we will be screwed. They will take us into a secure room for questioning and who knows how it might go. Saarah would be in real jeopardy. They might bring in a doctor to examine her and at that point the ruse would be exposed. Also the longer we are in Iran, the more likely the government will launch a search for her especially because of who she is married to."

Michelle says, "So, what is Plan B?"

Mark sits. "I guess if we can't get to the airport we drop Ethan in Tehran and hightail it for the border of Iraq."

Ducky speaks up. "Doesn't sound like much of a Plan B."

Mark looks around the table. "If we are stopped at any point in Iran, I plan to try to grab a gun and start shooting. Hopefully, I will be killed at that point. What I will tell Saarah is that she should tell the police that she was kidnapped by this crazy person, and stick to the story, no matter what."

Everyone stands mute at the implication.

Mark shrugs. "Yeah, so Plan A it is."

Michelle looks at Mark. "Are you sure you want to do this?"

"I have to rescue her. I can't leave her in Iran."

Michelle knows it's a losing battle. "Ok, we'll do all we can from here. But if you get caught, there will be nothing we can do."

Mark nods. "Let's get a flight to Ukraine, I'd like to be in Iran by this weekend."

Michelle's phone rings, she answers the call as she walks out of the meeting not knowing that this message will rearrange her priorities and could change the war on terror for decades to come.

Chapter 30

Genoa, Italy - August 13th

Clare and Diane are sitting in one of the corners talking about the Morse code and how she could deliver it while the terrorists are video taping her. "It won't be easy, you'll have to blink slowly. The CIA will figure it out. They will review every detail of the video tape to try to figure out where we are."

Clare shakes her head. "But we don't know where we are."

Diane takes her hands in hers. "We know it took us about thirty minutes to arrive. That will give them a search radius. Also the number of terrorists will help. Plus the main terrorist, Nimr Yazdi I think he said his name was. We need to get his name out to the CIA. That is our best opportunity."

The boys were sitting in another corner softly talking with Agent Lee. Clare looks over at her young sons and tears begin to form in her eyes.

The two continue to work on the Morse code when suddenly the door is opened. Yazdi walks in and motions for Clare to follow him.

Clare stands clutching the paper with her *statement.* She

looks at her boys, then Diane and follows Yazdi out of the room. Immediately she has a hood placed over her head. She is led to another room and seated on a chair. As the hood is lifted from her head she is blinded by several high intensity lights. In front of her is a camera on a tripod. Behind her is a sheet draped over a wooden frame.

Nimr Yazdi steps into the light. He smiles. "Clare, you will read the statement word for word. No adlibs. No pauses. Word-for-word. Do you understand?"

Clare nods.

Nimr steps out of the light and tells Clare to start when she is ready.

Clare looks up into the camera and then begins.

"My name is Clare Sweeney, I am the daughter of President William Baker. My two sons, a State Department employee and my two body guards were abducted by al-Qaeda today. We are being treated well and everyone is safe."

At this point Clare starts to tear up thinking of their driver, who was shot and killed in the attack.

"Stop. What is wrong Clare?"

Clare looks into the lights seeing just the outline of Yazdi standing off to her right. "I was just thinking of our driver. He was killed."

Yazdi steps into the light. "Yes, that was unfortunate. But your car had to be stopped and disabled. Take a moment to compose yourself, then continue."

Clare wipes her nose with her sleeve. "Ok." Then she continues. "We demand that the United States government pay one billion dollars as reparations for those true believers who have been killed in the war to establish a Caliphate. The money will be half in U.S. dollars, half in Euros. We will communicate how it will be delivered within two days. Additionally twelve of our brothers who have been illegally imprisoned at Guantanamo Bay, will be freed and sent to Afghanistan. We will send a list of those brothers also in two days time."

Clare pauses and looks up into the camera. "If these demands are not met, all of our prisoners will be executed. We do not wish to harm them, but they will die if our demands are not met."

Clare puts the paper into her lap and looks to her right.

"Excellent Clare. I will have another statement for you to read tomorrow."

Suddenly the hood is placed over her head and she is led back to the room. After she enters the room, the hood is removed.

The boys move to their mom and Clare pulls them to her. She starts to sob, really understanding the reality of their situation. Diane moves to her and puts her arms around her.

"We need to debrief while you remember as much as you can."

Clare nods. "Boys, would you please sit with Agent Lee while I talk with Aunt Diane.

The boys reluctantly move to the other side of the room.

Diane leads Clare to the opposite side and they sit on the floor. "Tell me everything you remember."

Clare pulls her knees to her chest and looks into her friends eyes. "They want one Billion dollars and the release of twelve terrorists at Gitmo."

Diane forces a smile. "Excellent, the government can deal with this. I suspect they will want to communicate a counter-offer. Probably less terrorists, maybe less money. But they will be playing for more time. The more time it takes, the more likely it is that they will be able to find us."

Clare nods, not really knowing how this side of hostage negotiation works. "He said they will send another video tape in two days, with the delivery information."

Diane considers this. "Ok, then we have two days to try to come up with a plan."

Clare looks at her boys. "He said they will kill us all if the demands are not met."

Diane looks away. "Probably not all of us. Probably one at a time starting with me, then the agents, then ..." Her voice drops off. "But I really believe the government and more specifically your father will move heaven and Earth to get you and the boys back safely. We just have to stay calm and be ready if some opportunity presents itself."

Clare looks into her friend's eyes. "I just can't believe we are here. Is this a dream?"

"It's real. Were you able to use the Morse code to send any of the key information?"

Clare smiles. "Yes, it was hard to read while at the same time blink a message. I was able to blink the thirty minute radius. I started to blink his name but then my eyes started tearing up and I had to stop. Then when I started again, I started blinking his name but I ran out of time and finished the statement."

Diane nods. "You did great. That will give the government some idea. They will know you at least are alive. I suspect they will ask for a proof of life of all of us. At that point, we can perhaps send more information."

At this point, the door opens again and Nimr Yazdi enters. "Clare, I would like you and your boys to follow me. You'll have to put on the hoods of course."

Clare looks at Diane, and then stands. The boys stand also and follow their mother out of the room.

Chapter 31

Dallas, Texas - August 13th

Walter Cartwright drove from New Mexico to Dallas stopping only once to grab a burger, fries and a chocolate shake. Once at Dallas / Fort Worth International Airport he parks his car in the long term lot and leaves the keys in the glove compartment. He then took the airport bus to the terminal and immediately walked into the nearest men's room carrying a small suitcase. He enters the handicap stall and takes out a change of clothes, a make up kit and mirror. He glues on a mustache and goatee. He then changes into a pair of shorts, a Hawaiian shirt and tennis shoes. The last piece of the disguise was a custom wig that matches the mustache and goatee. Once everything is in place, Walter looks into the mirror. Richard looks back at him. *Richard* smiles and stuffs his old self in the trash and walks out of the men's room confident his deception will work.

Sitting in one of the chairs facing the men's room is an Asian man reading a newspaper. He had followed Walter from Dallas and now had eyes on him again. But Walter was cleverer than they suspected. He had not only changed his clothes, but his appearance also. The Asian man smiles to himself. These

Americans feel they are so smart, but my people have been practicing deception for more than a thousand years.

After Walter passes through the TSA checkpoint, he walks towards the train line that will take him to his terminal. The Asian man moves in step behind him. As the train approaches, Walter enters with the Asian man just behind.

Walter puts his suitcase down and grabs onto the metal pole to maintain his balance during the short ride. As the train pulls out, Walter glances behind him. What he sees turns his blood cold. An Asian man is standing facing slightly away, but only three feet away. Could this be one of Bill's assassins? Walter quickly looks left, then right and makes a decision. As the train slows, he grabs his suitcase and moves quickly to another door squeezing between a mother and two children. He starts to exit, and then glances back at the man. He can't see him. Instead of exiting the train, Walter steps back and lets the doors close. Immediately the train moves to the C terminal. Walter tries to look out of his train to spot the Asian man, but he can't. He looks around his car but it only contains several businessmen and a flight attendant. He relaxes a bit.

The train comes to the C terminal and Walter exits. He glances around him now feeling silly that he overreacted. He glances at his watch and sees that he has almost an hour before his plane to Mexico City departs. God he needs a drink. Just then he spots a restaurant/bar just across from his departure gate. Richard slides onto a stool at the bar and orders double Bloody Mary. He is sipping his drink and eating some peanuts when a man sits next to him. Richard looks in the mirror opposite him and sees the Asian man. He almost falls off his stool. He puts his drink down with a shaking hand. Walter slides off his stool and walks quickly towards the exit. Just as he is about to leave he hears a man shout; "Hey buddy, you forgot your suitcase." Walter stops and looks around, the Asian man is holding the suitcase out for him. Walter walks slowly back and grabs the handle. He mumbles "Thanks" and moves away. Walking across to his gate he hears the call for all first class passengers. He wants to get on that plane and away from any potential assassin. He pulls out his ticket and is quickly processed. He enters the 474 and finds his 3A seat. He puts his suitcase up in the overhead and settles in for the three hour flight.

An attractive flight attendant comes over to him and smiles. "Good morning Mr. White, can I get you something."

Richard smiles looking at her expansive cleavage. "Yes, a double Bloody Mary would be excellent." The flight attendant smiles and moves to the galley to get the drink. Walter begins to calm down. "It was just your paranoia kicking in" he says under this breath. The flight attendant brings his drink and he takes a long swallow. The rest of the passengers board while Walter scrutinizes each person, no Asians that he suspects and he now fully relaxes.

The plane starts its roll out as Walter watches his former life racing past him. The plane lifts off and turns south towards Mexico City. Walter finishes his drink and asks for another. After the announcements that he totally ignores, Walter reclines his seat a bit and drifts off while watching the screen in front of him showing the planes altitude, speed and location on a map as they speed over Mexico and his new life.

Suddenly Walter wakes with a start. His eyes focus on the screen in front of him, they are half way to Mexico City, but then he begins to feel funny. Not drunk, just funny. He shakes his head and tries to focus. Suddenly he feels a slight twinge at the small of his back, like a spider bite. He tries to move his hand back, but he can't seem to move his left arm. He then tries to move his right but they are dead weight like when he would sleep on one or the other and he just can't make them move. He starts to call out, but he can't catch a breath. Then his muscles begin to spasm so hard he feels like his back will snap. In the back of his mind he remembers the Asian man handing him his briefcase. He was wearing gloves. Of course, poisoning. The handle had Cholinesterase Inhibitor on it and it did its job. Within minutes Walter is dead.

Chapter 32

Washington DC - August 15th

The President is nervously pacing in the Oval Office. He has called Michelle Samaha, asking her to come to the White House for a briefing.

"Sir, are you sure you want to bring Assistant Director Samaha into this?" Says Chief of Staff Randy Smith.

"Yes, Randy. We have gone over this, if we need to launch a rescue mission, she is the one I want to plan it."

"But Mr. President, again I just don't trust her. I am afraid her Muslim faith might get in the way when she has to make a key decision."

"Nonsense. Michelle would do the right thing. She is an American first. Her religion will have no bearing on her decision making."

They hear a soft knock and the President's secretary sticks her head into the Oval Office. "Mr. President, Assistant Director Michelle Samaha is here."

"Please send her in."

Michelle walks into the hallowed office and is humbled to be within its walls. She has been to the White House dozens of times since her CIA promotion to Assistant Director of Middle

Eastern Affairs, but each time it is a thrill. "Good afternoon Mr. President, Mr. Smith."

The President motions to the couch and they all sit. "I have some very troubling news and would like your take on it."

Michelle sits forward wondering what news the President was about to deliver.

"I was informed about eight hours ago that my daughter and two grandsons were kidnapped by terrorists in Italy."

Michelle first reaction is shock. "Oh no! Was anyone hurt? Has there been any contact?"

The President sits back. "Yes, just twenty minutes ago we received a video tape delivered to the American embassy in Rome. It contains video of Clare reading a prepared statement."

Michelle sits back also. "Thank God she is ok, what about the boys?"

"We don't know yet. The statement says all of the personnel are fine, but we know that isn't true. Six hours ago we received a report that their car was stopped on a highway from Pisa to Lake Como. The driver was shot and killed. They used tear gas to get them out of the SUV and they fled in two white vans. That is all we know for sure, until now."

The President stands and moves to a laptop on his desk. Both Michelle and Randy stand and watch the screen. "This is a copy of the video tape that was delivered."

As they watch, they see Clare sitting with a simple cloth backdrop behind her. She is reading a script. At first she is shaky, and then gathers strength as she continues. Finally, the tape ends.

"Play it again please." Says Michelle.

The President restarts the video.

Michelle smiles. "She is blinking in Morse code."

Michelle takes a pen from her folder and writes each letter. "T, H, I, R, T, Y, R, A... D I think, I, U, S. They are within a thirty mile or minute radius of the kidnapping site."

The President puts his hand on the Presidential desk and breathes out a sigh of relief. "Ok, anything else?"

Michelle had stopped the video, as she restarts it she says, "Y, A, S... That is it before the video stopped."

The President looks at her questioningly. "YAS? What could that mean?"

Michelle looks up into the hopeful eyes of the President. "I am sorry Sir, I have no idea."

The three of them ponder that clue. "Well at least they are alive, they want a ransom and we have a starting point to their whereabouts."

"Yes sir. We'll have our people analyze the video some more and have a Morse code expert check it out."

The President looks at Michelle. "We are going to discuss their ransom demands, but we'll try to stall them with a few counter proposals. That might give us a couple of days, but probably not much more."

Michelle nods. "I understand, Mr. President."

Chapter 33

Moscow, Russia - August 16th

Mark walks slowly into the Moscow airport carrying a briefcase and a small suitcase. Its early morning and most Muscovites are still in bed. Mark took the first flight to arrive before the customs agents are really fully awake. He knew that getting out of Ukraine was no problem, getting into Russia was the issue. Being a Canadian businessman will help, but the Russians are suspicious of anyone from the west.

He has business documentation created by the CIA to show that he is working with a CIA front company in Russia. He'll have a representative of the company there to vouch for him and take him to a safe house once he is on Russian soil. Mark knows that getting into Russia is critical for him to get into Iran. Russia has been a trading partner with Iran for decades, selling critical military and consumer goods over the past ten years during the embargos imposed by the United States and other Western countries.

The customs line for foreigners is fairly short. Mark stands casually glancing about and seeing many armed guards plus several FSB agents. The FSB (Federalnaya Sluzhba Bezopasnosti) is the successor to the Russian KGB. The Russian secret police are well trained, brutal and have almost unlimited power to seize any Russian citizen or foreigner.

Mark reaches the head of the line and is motioned forward to a customs agent. Mark slides his Canadian passport and his visa across and smiles. The agent looks at the passport and frowns.

"Ah, Mr. Brooks, are you a hockey fan?" he says in broken English.

Mark smiles, "Of course, I am Canadian."

The agent smiles thinly. "Then you are familiar with the 2015 IIHF World Championship?"

Mark searches his almost photographic memory, then pulls up the information he read several years ago.

"Ah yes, unfortunately for Russia, the Canadian national team beat Russia 6-1 in the gold medal match. But the most unfortunate result was that the Americans beat the host Czechs for third."

The Russia nods, "Yes but at least we got the Silver ahead of the Americans."

Mark smiles. "Of course, both Canadian and Russia children are born with skates on their feet. American children are born with silver spoons in their mouths, eh?"

The agent laughs. "Very good."

With that, the Russia customs agent stamps Mark's passport admitting him. Taking the passport, Mark turns and exits under the gaze of several FSB agents. Mark knows that he will be followed and will have to slip the tails to be able to return to the Moscow airport tomorrow for his flight to Iran.

As he walks out of the airport, he is met by Boris Petrov.

"Mr. Brooks, I am Boris Petrov the Vice President of KKR Wireless." Mark knows this is his Russian contact, and shakes his hand and smiles.

"Mr. Petrov, thank you for meeting me."

"My car is over by the curb and I'll be able to take you to our company's headquarters with meetings with our leadership. We are excited to talk with you about your company's technology and bringing it to Russia."

Mark nods, knowing they are probably being monitored. They slide into the Russian's Mercedes Benz and they head to the outskirts of Moscow.

They ride in silence for several minutes, and then Boris turns to Mark.

"The car is swept every morning for listening devices. We can speak candidly here."

Mark nods. "I am excited to address your board and bring this new technology to Russia."

The Russian knows that Mark is being careful and agrees to go along with the deception. "Of course, I am sure you will be welcomed enthusiastically."

After another twenty minutes they pull to the front of a three story brick building. The sign on the front of the building announces KKR Wireless in Russian. The men exit the car and enter the building. Mark notices several men sitting at the reception desk, but he is sure they are hired guns.

Mark signs in and is then led to a conference room on the third floor. The room is windowless and has just a desk and three chairs.

A small man in his late 40s is sitting at the desk finishing up a phone call. He has premature white hair, with a short cropped beard. He is well dressed with a red pocket square matching his red and black tie.

Mark knows he is the CIA's man in Moscow, undercover for the past seventeen years. Sergey Ivanov has been working for the CIA since Vladimir Putin came to power. Sergey's father and mother were purged when Putin came to power. They ran an international business and did a fair amount of trade with the United States, selling traditional Russian homemade gifts. The Russian government, after Putin took power, felt that the Ivanov's had too close a relationship with Americans and their business was taken and they were sent to Siberian labor camp. Sergey was a student at Moscow University and was shocked and dismayed at how his parents were treated. He vowed then to do what he could to bring Putin down. Sergey started a small wireless company with the help of the CIA, and has been funneling information ever since.

"Mr. Aldin, very nice to meet you finally. I have heard many good things about you from our mutual friends."

Mark smiles. "I assume this room is secure."

Sergey nods. "Of course, otherwise the secret police would be breaking down the door."

Mark knows of his operation and his hatred for Putin, but his love for Russia as a country.

Sergey continues. "I wish to see Russia become more democratic, get rid of Putin and his comrades. That is why I work with the CIA. Not for money, not to damage Russia but to try to move the country forward. Can you imagine how wealthy and prosperous Russia could be if it was a full trading partner with Europe and the U.S., much like Canada is now? That is what I would like to see. Curb the Russian expansionism and stop trying to take land from sovereign countries like Ukraine."

Mark can feel his passion and commitment. "Thank you for your support, I have just one objective. That is to get into Iran, get my sister out and return to the U.S."

Sergey looks surprised. "Iran? How did your sister get into Iran?"

Mark looks down at his hands and then looks up. "She and my mother were abducted by the Muslim Brotherhood when I was a child, they were sold to an Iranian businessman. My mother has died, but my sister continued to be a prisoner who is married to a powerful Iranian Guard Colonel. I am going into Iran to rescue her."

Sergey and Boris Petrov both smile. "I hope we can help you as we believe that Iran is a fundamental threat to both the United States and Russia. Putin has been working with the Mullahs for money, but when Iran gets what it wants, they will turn their terrorism toward us in their quest for a Persian empire."

Mark knows that neither of these men know about the close call the world had with the Iranian Red Death virus, but Iran is still a major threat to the region. "At this point, I just want to get my sister out and work on the other issues later."

At this point Sergey stands and extends his hand. "Good luck my friend. I hope you can safely get in and out with your sister. If there is anything we can do to help, please let us know."

With that, Mark heads for a hotel to check in, get some rest then in a few hours head for the airport for his flight as a Russian to Iran.

Chapter 34

Albuquerque, New Mexico - August 16th

The men drove the large truck into an empty warehouse. Park Kyung-soo steps out of the shadows and smiles. Inside is a most powerful weapon, one that his government would love to study and duplicate. *Bill* has been working toward this day for over two years. Additionally, he just received a phone call that his agent in Dallas was able to infect Walter Cartwright with the poison that would kill him within hours. Did Walter really believe he could take their money and just walk away?

Choi Hwan climbs out of the driver seat and says in Korean. "We had a problem. The woman guard wanted to inspect the crate. I couldn't allow that so we took her with us. She is tied up in the back of the truck."

Kyung-soo considers the situation. He could kill her now and depose of her body later, or he could keep her prisoner here until after the operation, and then dispose her. Maybe keeping her alive would be of benefit to them later. After some consideration, he orders his men to lock her into the berth, but keep her bound.

Kyung-soo opens his laptop and types a message on an international message board saying, the item has been procured and will be operational within two days.   Almost instantaneously, the message is picked up by a North Korean intelligence officer.   He was waiting for this particular communication because his dear leader instructed him to wait by his computer until the message was received.   Then he was to immediately contact his superior.   The intelligence officer knew that his job and perhaps his life depended on getting this message out quickly. He picks up the phone and asks for his Commander.

In New Mexico, Kyung-soo instructs his men to get the HEL system off the truck and onto a specially modified tractor trailer. As he watches, Hwan joins him. "When will we strike at America?"

Kyung-soo smiles. "We have to test the system to make sure we understand all of its capabilities. Take the other two men out to the desert and kill them. We will do this part of the operation by ourselves."

Hwan salutes. "Yes sir. We will be ready."

Park nods, "Tonight we will test the system. Then we will move to our primary location and wait for our instructions. We have no idea when the Army base will notice the Sergeant missing and check on the HEL systems. Because of your error, we must move quickly."

Choi bows knowing that because of the Staff Sergeant's curiosity, the operation could be in jeopardy and that her curiosity will cost her life.

Chapter 35

Washington D.C. - August 16th

The President is sitting in the Oval Office with his Chief of Staff and Michelle Samaha.

"Is there anything we can do now to be more proactive? Can you put together a team to get to Italy when they contact us again?"

Michelle replies. "Yes, we are pulling together the key people and a SEAL team to fly to Camp Darby later tonight."

The President knows the United States has multiple bases in Italy. "Is that base the closest to the abduction site?"

Michelle looks up from her notes. "Yes sir, the base is located in Tirrenia, near Pisa. We will fly directly into the camp and wait for some local information or their next demand. The only issue is that Mark Aldin is out of touch on a personal mission. As soon as he if available, I'll make sure he joins us."

The President leans forward. "A personal mission?"

"Yes sir. We located his sister in Iran and he is planning to go in and rescue her."

The Chief of Staff explodes, "What? Who authorized this operation? What if he is captured?"

Michelle sits back. "I authorized it. He has been looking for his sister since she was abducted by the Muslim Brotherhood when he was ten years old. He was traumatized. This is something he has to do, Mark would go to Iran whether we help or not. Our help will give him a better chance of success."

Michelle looks at the President. He seems lost in thought. "Ok, obviously if he is caught we can't acknowledge he is one of ours. What is his cover?"

"He is flying into Tehran from Moscow as a Russian businessman. He will meet with his sister, and then take her out with him as his wife hurt in a car accident. They will be flying to Germany for cosmetic surgery."

The Chief of Staff Smith takes a sip of his Starbucks. "Damn, I sure hope the documentation is world class."

Michelle nods. "Our guys have it all covered. The passports and visas are excellent. Plus Kelly Campos has hacked the Iranian customs computers and will show Mark's sister coming in with him under a false name and passport. So when they leave, their system will show her coming into the country and now leaving. But Mark knows that if they are detained, he will go for a guard's gun and try to shoot his way out, or die trying."

The President frowns. "Damn risky. I admire his loyalty, but if this blows up the ramifications will be damaging to the country."

The Chief of Staff gets back to the more immediate issue. "What are we doing to find Clare and the boys?"

Michelle looks down at her notes. "We have asked the Italian police and counter-terrorism to keep this under wraps. I think we have maybe 48 hours before the press finds out. Until then, we are asking all our agents to check with their contacts for any information regarding the kidnapping."

The President rises. "How the Hell could this happen? We need to find them before al-Qaeda gets nervous or time runs out."

Chapter 36

Moscow, Russia - August 16th

Mark Aldin walks slowly through the Moscow International Airport better known as Sheremetyeno. His flight was scheduled to leave at 2:15 pm and arrive in Tehran, Iran at 10:25 pm. Mark picked a late flight to Tehran for several reasons. One is that they are usually less crowded and secondly, arriving in the evening would enable Mark to transit through the Iranian Customs when the agents are near the end of their shifts and hopefully tired.

After his meeting with his Russian contacts, Mark went to his hotel then slipped out after changing into a Russian suit, shirt and tie purchased for him by Sergey. He has a small suitcase plus a briefcase with Russian wireless documents. After walking three blocks Mark waves down a taxi.

"To Sheremetyeno airport" Mark says in Russian.

The driver nods and flips the meter, then pulls from the curb heading to the airport about five miles away.

Mark checks his breast pocket for his passport, and then prepares himself for the customs check. His Russian is fairly good, but if he got into a long protracted conversation he might be found out. He is arriving less than an hour from the flights departure, hoping that when the custom's agent sees his flight ticket he will hurry him along.

The cab reaches the airport and Mark pays the fare. Mikhail Abramov now walks slowly into the airport terminal that Mark had exited just four hours before. He was wearing a hat and glasses to alter his appearance. Mark wasn't sure how sophisticated the Russian video capture capabilities were, but he didn't want to make it too easy. All he needed to do is fool the Russian customs for several hours and then Mikhail Abramov will disappear into Iran.

It's just after lunch and the terminal is very busy. Mark sees the lines for passengers and picks one with a woman customs agent. The thing he didn't need is to run into the same agent he spoke with as a Canadian entering Russia.

While waiting in line he pulls out his passport and flight ticket. Mark glances around and sees several SVR RF (Intelligence Agency for Civilian Affairs) agents watching the lines. He stands patiently like most Russians are taught to do. Finally he reaches the front of the line. He is motioned forward.

"Good afternoon, where are you traveling to?" The woman asks Mark.

Mark smiles, and then says in Russian. "Tehran Iran for business."

The agent looks at his passport, flipping through the pages with his travels out of the Motherland. "You travel quite a bit." She looks up. "Mr. Abromov, what do you do?"

Mark smiles again. "I am in sales, we are trying to interest the Iranians in our Russian wireless technology."

The agent nods while fingering one particular page. "Your trip to Germany last year, the return stamp doesn't look correct."

Mark's heart skips a beat. "I don't know, I just present my passport. You stamp it."

She looks at his flight document and glances up at a clock on the wall. "Ok, you have just 30 minutes to your flight." With that she stamps the passport, and passes it back to Mark.

"Have a good flight".

Mark smiles and takes the documents and walks at a good pace to his gate. Just as he arrives, they call for passengers to board.

As Mark slips into his seat, he breathes a breath of relief. The first step accomplished, Mark now focuses on getting into and out of Iran with his sister. As the jet takes off, Mark thinks about his sister and how much her life will change in just the next several days.

Chapter 37

Genoa, Italy - August 16th

Clare is dozing after finishing the video tape. It's early morning she believes and everyone is trying to rest. She hopes the blinking Morse code was successful, but has doubts that she did it right. Clare pulls the boys closer to her. They don't stir but she knows they are sleeping fitfully. She is proud of Oliver and Filip, they have been brave and helpful.

Suddenly the door opens. One of the guards enters and motions for Clare to follow him. He is carrying an AK-47 and he turns towards the Secret Service Agents who rise with the intrusion. He tells them in Arabic to sit. After they are on the floor, he motions for Clare to the door. He pushes her out into the warehouse and then closes and locks the door. Clare is confused, she is not bound and doesn't have the hood on her head.

She looks about and sees the warehouse. It's quite large with the two white vans that transported them after the attack. In another area is the video taping equipment and the sheet backdrop. It is dark outside but with just a tinge of morning light.

The guard pushes her forward towards an office at the opposite end of the warehouse. As Clare approaches the office she becomes more apprehensive. The light is not on and Yazdi is not sitting in the office.

The guard opens the door and pushes Clare in. She moves to the opposite wall and turns. The guard is a large man, well over six feet with broad shoulders. He has a full black beard and dark angry eyes, but his most distinguishing feature is a long scar on the left side of his face. He smiles and puts the AK-47 down on a table. At the same time he pulls out a long knife.

Clare now knows why she was taken here. She is determined to fight even if it means her death. The man moves towards her and says something in Arabic. Clare doesn't move. He smiles. With a quick step forward he grabs Clare's blouse and pulls her forward. She can smell his foul breath as he uses the knife to cut the top button from her shirt. With his other hand she can feel it on her breast. She is trying not to cry but the situation seems hopeless.

The man puts the knife tip to her throat and pushes her down to her knees. He pulls up his robe exposing himself to her. Clare just stares at it. He yells something as she feels his hand on the back of her head. Clare decides to fight and moves her head forward with a blow to the man's genitals. He is taken by surprise and doubles over with pain. The guard slaps Clare across the face splitting her lip and knocking her to the ground. The man is now enraged. He grabs the front of her blouse and slams her against the wall. He is shouting in Arabic while he pushes her down onto the floor. Clare can feel his hands pulling her panties down while she struggles under his weight. He spreads her legs as Clare tries to free her hands to fight him off. Suddenly a large explosion deafens Clare. The man slumps forward and Clare can feel wetness dripping down her forehead.

Nimr Yazdi is standing over them with a gun in his hand. Clare is dazed but slowly understands what just happened. Yazdi pulls the guard off her and sees the damage done. Clare looks over at the dead guard, a bullet hole in the back of his head, and the front part of his forehead blown away.

"Get up." Yazdi says to Clare. Clare tries to pull her blouse over her breast, and then realizes her bra is down around her waist. She pulls it up and positions it over her breasts. Then she readjusts her blouse which is covered in blood. Clare rises.

"I apologize for his actions," motioning towards the dead guard. "Come with me."

One of the other guards is standing at the door cradling the dead guards AK-47. Clare follows Yazdi out into the warehouse. She is led to a small bathroom in one of the corners. "Clean up and come out when you are ready."

Clare enters the bathroom and turns on the water. She cups a handful of water and splashes it onto her face. She rubs her hands over her face, then through her hair. Clare looks down and sees the water is rose colored. She shutters with the knowledge that she was within minutes of being raped and perhaps killed. Raising her head she looks into the mirror. The blood is gone but the memory remains. "Oh God" she moans. Her blouse is ripped and has the stains of blood remaining, but is still functional.

Yazdi knocks on the door. "Time is up" as he opens the door. Clare is standing there, arms crossed across her chest hugging herself. Yazdi motions with his handgun for her to come out. Clare exits the bathroom and is led to the room where the others are being held. "You must understand men like Nadheer do not respect infidels and feel they can do with them as they wish. It was a mistake of judgment and of orders. For that he paid with his life. He is now with Allah, the most merciful."

With that, Yazdi opens the door to the room and pushes Clare into the room. The boys run into her arms as Clare breaks down.

Chapter 38

Albuquerque, NM - August 17th

Park Kyung-Soo is riding in the passenger seat of an eighteen wheeler. It is specially modified with the roof removed. A custom tarp is affixed to hide the cargo. Choi Hwan is driving with Sergeant Davies in the berth.

It's just after dusk as the truck drives North on US45 near the Taylor Ranch area. They have passed the Double Eagle II Airport a small regional airport just North of Albuquerque. Park smiles as they pull off the road precisely under the flight path to the Double Eagle II airport.

Kyung-Soo, also known as Bill over the past two years, is now within minutes of proving his value to his "Dear Leader". Both men get out of the truck and Hwan puts out reflectors for any passing vehicles, while Kyung-Soo climbs into the back of the trailer.

Choi Hwan has already pulled back the tarp while Kyung-Soo starts up the generator. It purrs to life bringing the HEL system to life. Over the past several days the Major has poured over the operational manual of the HEL system. It is a fairly simple system, almost automated. The system locks onto possible targets and once the operator authorizes the target, the HEL system ramps up and then fires.

Kyung-Soo knows that with a low flying, slow airplane the system will not miss. The Double Eagle II airport caters to private planes and at night there are always dozens of private pilots wanting to improve their night flying skills.

The HEL system whines as the laser powers up. Kyung-Soo looks at the screen showing multiple targets. He only wants to bring one plane down to prove the system. If he shot down multiple planes that would certainly alert the authorities and possibly the military.

There are five targets all within several miles of the airport, making their approaches. Colonel Park selects one target and maneuvers the joystick so that the cursor is over it. He pushes a red button on the joystick and the system is locked on. Within five seconds the HEL system rotates and fires. It's all over within several seconds as the private plane suddenly loses power as the engine disintegrates... Kyung-Soo looks up into the sky and sees the plane cart-wheeling in flames down to the ground. The explosion as it hits could be felt from a mile away. He smiles and he and his lieutenant both congratulate each other.

"Ok, cover it up quickly and let's get moving." Lt. Choi pulls the tarp over the trailer while Kyung-Soo shuts down the HEL system. Within three minutes they are pulling out onto

Highway 45 heading south, then onto I-40 West towards Los Angeles.

In the berth section, Sergeant Davies is tied up but heard the laser whine and heard the men's cheers.

Chapter 39

Tehran, Iran - August 17th

The Russian jet smoothly lands and taxies to the Tehran Imam Khomeini International Airport.   Mark readies himself for the customs check. If he can not get through the check point, then he will have to either grab a gun and try to shoot his way out of the building or kill himself. He can't be captured. He knows that.

Since Mark is in first class, he is one of the first off the plane. He walks down a hallway, then down an escalator to the Customs area. He reads the sign in Arabic, Russian, French and English indicating non-Iranians to queue up in a line to the left. There are two people ahead of Mark as he tries to look relaxed. Finally his turn comes and he pulls his Russian passport from his pocket.

The Customs Agent eyes the passport then lifts his gaze to Mark's face. In Russian he says, "Your business in Iran?"

Mark smiles.   "I am trying to sell Russian wireless equipment to your government."

The Agent studies him. "How long will you be in Iran?"

Mark replies, "I'll be in Iran for one week, leaving next Tuesday."

The Agent nods. "Where will you be staying while in Tehran?"

Mark knows they want to keep track of visitors even from Russia. "I'll be staying at the Pasargad Hotel on South Jamalzadeh."

The Customs Agent nods again. Mark knows it's a cheaper hotel, but clean. The Agent probably knows of it himself. There are several minutes while the Agent notes the hotel, the dates and fills out an entry form. He stamps Mark's passport and waves him through.

After a sixty minute wait, Mark collects his luggage and heads for the exit. As he leaves the terminal a man approaches him. "Comrade Abramov, good to meet you." Mark smiles and greets his Iranian contact. They shake hands. "My car is over here."

They walk together is silence, and then enter his car and they pull into traffic. "I have been following Saarah for the past several days. She seems to be following her normal schedule. We have a planned snatch for tomorrow morning. The sooner the better. The longer we wait, the more chance something unplanned might happen." Mark nods and sits quietly watching the city of Tehran pass by.

Finally Mark speaks. "The toughest part will be snatching her off the street without attracting too much attention." He pauses.

"I think we should grab her as she arrives for school and not wait for her to go in and then come out with her sickness excuse to leave. They might insist on sending someone with her or call a doctor to the school."

The Mossad Agent nods. "She parks a block away from her school, and then walks to the front of the school. I think the best time would be as she gets out of the car. Move the van parallel to her and bring her into the van before she is really visible. Then we'll drive a mile away to prepare her bandages and brief her on the plan to get you both out. Then it's just a matter of getting you both to the airport and then hopefully out of the country."

Mark considers the plan. "What about someone seeing her getting into the van? Do you have weapons?"

The Agent shakes his head. "Weapons are extremely hard to come by. The Iranian government controls all the weapons coming in. But, I do have two Iranian-made pistols. They are the polymer body 9mm pistol that fires 15 rounds. It's fairly accurate. The best I could do on short notice. Also I have one silencer. Not Israeli, but should work." He says with a smile.

Mark smiles too. "Well, hopefully we won't need them."

The weave through Tehran and finally get to the Pasargad Hotel. Mark knows that the secret police will check on him to make sure he checks in.

"Get some sleep if you can. Leave the hotel at 7 am through the back entrance and walk two blocks to the Eslami Metro. Take the metro a few stops to Metro Shadman. If you are not followed, then come up to the street and I'll be waiting for you on Jeyhon Street. I'll be able to see if you are being followed. If you are clear, I'll put my lights on and get into the car. If my lights stay off, just walk by and I'll pick you up at the hotel."

Mark nods. "Ok, sounds like a good plan. I am going to take one of the guns and the silencer. Hopefully I won't need it. I'll leave it in the hotel when I leave. See you tomorrow."

Mark exits the car and retrieves his luggage. As he walks into the hotel, he sees Iranian secret police officer sitting in the lobby. He registers and gets his hotel room key. Taking the elevator to the third floor, he enters room 312 exhausted but excited; within twelve hours he will see his sister after thirty years.

Chapter 40

Washington D.C. - August 18th

The President is sitting with his chief of staff, Randy Smith, and several aides in the Oval Office. The President's chief of staff is reviewing the schedule for the week, but the President is only partially listening. His mind is focused on his daughter and grandsons. Where are they? Are they safe? How could this have happened? He is angry and disappointed in himself. He should have insisted on more security during his daughter's trip to Italy. He is determined to bring the full force of the American government to bear against these terrorists and al-Qaeda.

"Mr. President, you are scheduled for a quick trip to LA this week. You are meeting with the presidents of three major military contractors including a tour of one of their facilities. That will take up the majority of the morning. Then a stop in Michigan to meet with the leaders of the automotive industry on Thursday, then back to Washington D.C. on Friday."

The President nods.

The door to the outer offices opens and the President's secretary pokes her head in. "Mr. President, Michelle Samaha would like to speak with you."

The President stands. "Yes, can I have the room please?"

The aides and Randy Smith leave the office as Michelle enters. Randy gives Michelle a grim look as he passes her.

"Michelle, please sit down."

The President sits opposite Michelle and takes a deep breath.

"Mr. President, we think we know where the terrorists are holding your daughter, grandkids and the rest of her party."

The President sits forward. "How do you know?"

Michelle pulls out her laptop. "We have been monitoring warehouses within thirty minutes of the abduction site. Our analyst has come up with ten sites that meet the criteria and have the potential to hide the hostages. We looked at each warehouse extensively. Six are owned by businesses that would not allow terrorists to usurp their holdings. Two others are so busy with trucks and people coming and going would eliminate them as to secretly holding six people. So we have two warehouses that are currently not being actively used. We have placed a drone over both buildings and have been watching them, they are within two blocks of each other. One building has had several trucks come and go but we have not been able to identify any of the occupants. But the most critical information is that we did an infrared scan of the building and saw a group of six heat signatures in one part of the warehouse and four others at various points in the building that we assume are the exits."

The President grasps his hands in a silent prayer. "Michelle, that is promising. How can we be sure?"

Michelle nods. "We would like to try to get confirmation of any people entering or leaving the building. But I think I should get a team there as soon as possible and ready to assault the building."

"I agree. Mark Aldin is still on his personal mission?"

"Yes sir. We hope he will be available sometime this week, but as you know missions don't always go according to plan. It could be this week or next."

The President stands. "Ok, put together a team. Let me know when you are in-country? Also talk to the State Department, let Cindy Decker know what is going on since one of her people are involved."

"Yes sir. We will have a team there tomorrow. I'll be there to coordinate. Ducky will lead the team."

"Ok, let's move as quickly as we can. I just have the feeling that we are running out of time."

Michelle leaves the Oval Office determined to find the President's family and successfully rescue them.

As Michelle arrives back at the Black site and quickly assembles her team of Ducky, Jonathan Bardsley and Kelly Campos.

"We have a GO on a rescue mission. Ducky, I want you to pull in a special operator team that we will fly to Italy and be ready within 48 hours to assault that warehouse."

Ducky nods, "I have already spoken with six former special operators and they are on-board. We will be ready within six hours to lift off."

Michelle turns to Jonathan and Kelly. "You guys continue to monitor the warehouse and let us know immediately if more terrorists enter the facility or if the captives are moved. Let's get to work and save the President's family and the other innocents."

Chapter 41

Tehran, Iran - August 18th

It is 11 pm. Mark is dressed in all black and taking the Iranian 9mm and the silencer, he walks down the back stairs to the rear of the hotel. He walks among the shadows several blocks to a bus station. After only five minutes, a bus approaches and Mark steps on board. He has studied the bus schedule and knows that this particular bus travels to within three blocks of the house that his mother and sister had lived for many years. He is taking a big chance, but he doesn't want to come all this way without avenging his mother and sister. Javad Tousi is the master of this house but his abuse of Mark's mother and particularly his sister warrants the death penalty. Mark travels with just four other passengers on this late night route. After twenty minutes, Mark sees his stop. He rises slowly and moves to the front bus door. He exits and stands still for a minute getting his bearings.

The streets of Tehran are mostly empty as Mark walks with purpose toward his target. The house is a large one but not the mansion Mark would expect of a man with so much power. The home sits on about one acre he would guess. The house is dark but Mark knows he would have multiple guards.   But Kelly

Campos came up with the house blueprints and the electronic alarm system. The alarm system is a new one that allows for wireless communications by the owner. But it also allows for Campos to hack the system.

Mark checks his watch and sees that it's 12:10 pm. Mark puts on his wireless ear bud and microphone. "Eagle One, Check."

Mark hears one click acknowledging the transmission. "Going in, cut the alarms."

Walking up to the seven foot fence, Mark glances left and right. Seeing no one, he hops the fence landing lightly on his feet in a crouch. The one wild card would be guard dogs. Kelly Campos checked the property for dog houses, but that wouldn't guarantee they didn't keep them in the main house. Mark pulls his 9mm and ratchets a round into the firing chamber and attaches the silencer. "Moving."

One click acknowledges.

Mark moves from tree to tree moving stealthy towards the dark house. Suddenly he hears two clicks. He knows this means a guard is approaching. Mark stops and crouches with his 9mm out in front of him. He can smell the cigarette smoke before he sees the outline of the guard. He is standing in front of a stone stairway. Mark would prefer to use his Strider knife to control the body as it falls, but in this case he can't get that close to the man. Plus he had to leave his Strider at home as it would have been discovered traveling from Russia to Iran. Without moving, Mark takes careful aim at the guards head. As the 9mm spits its round, the guard's head rocks back and he collapses to the ground.

Mark rises and quickly closes the thirty yards to the body. He pulls the man into the bushes and continues up the stairs. A double click alerts him to another threat. He stops at the top of the stairs and crouches behind a large potted planter. Suddenly he hears soft footsteps. He waits for the guard to pass, and then puts a silenced bullet into the back of his head. He pulls the body into an alcove and moves to a door leading into the study. After picking the lock, he enters into a silent house. Knowing exactly where he needs to go, he walks quickly across the study and into a hallway. Mark then moves into the Kitchen and pulls a sharp twelve inch knife from its holder. Moving down the hallway to his left, Mark sees a large stairway leading up to the second floor. "Moving to target." He whispers.

Walking silently up on the plush carpet, Mark sticks his 9mm into the small of his back, while at the same time switching the knife from his left to his right hand. Moving down four doors, Mark pauses and listens. He hears a noise inside, then nothing. He pushes the door open and sees that the businessman is in his bathroom. Mark slips in and moves to a dark corner of the massive room. Sitting on his haunches he watches as the bathroom light is turned off and the target shuffles back to his bed. As he pulls the covers over him, Mark rises and moves quietly to his bedside.

Mark moves the knife to the businessman's chest. In Farsi he says, "Move and you will die." Mark can hear the surprise in the intake of air.

"Take what you want." Javad Tousi whispers.

"Oh, I will. But first I want to tell you a story. It's about a mother and daughter that were abducted by the Muslim Brotherhood in Syria. They were sold like cattle to an Iranian businessman."

At this point Mark can hear a sharp intake of air as Tousi knows he is talking about him.

"This mother and daughter were kept in isolation for years. This man then abused and raped the girl. Impregnating her multiple times, forcing her to have abortions."

Javad Tousi is now weeping. "In those days, it was the custom. I did nothing wrong."

Mark moves the razor sharp blade to the man's neck. "You raped my sister."

"I will give you money, how much do you want?"

Mark softly laughs, "I don't want your money Javad Tousi. I want your life." With that Mark slides the knife across the neck of his target severing the carotid artery. Mark watches as his sister's tormentor bleeds out. Mark then sticks the knife into his heart and slowly leaves the bedroom. After exiting the house, Mark retraces his steps, hops the fence then takes a return bus back to his hotel.

At 5 am after a short, fitful nights sleep. He knows that today will be either a spectacular day or he will be dead. He smiles. Just to see his sister again is worth it.

After taking a cold shower, he dresses in a soviet suit and grabs his suitcase. He has decided to slip out of the hotel early to take a more winding route to meet with his Mossad contact. Mark is sure the Iranian government has just one agent watching him. Last night Mark wandered around the hotel looking for a way he could bypass the lobby. After about twenty minutes he found an elevator that the maids use to bring sheets and cleaning materials up to each floor. He hoped that by the time the Iranian agent discovered Mark was missing, he would be on a flight to Germany with his sister. Looking around his room he lifts the mattress and places a folder containing false information implicating several high level officers of the Iran Secret Police in a plot by the Russians to overthrow the Iranian Regime.

Slipping out of his room, Mark quietly moves down the hallway and into the maids' elevator. He hits the button for the basement and waits while the elevator slowly descends. As the doors open, Mark breaths a silent prayer that the laundry room was empty. He exits and moves quickly to the door leading to an alley behind the hotel.

Mark sees the rising sun just showing on the peaks of the distant mountains. He knows he has just several hours to pull off his plan. There are several key parts of that plan that have to happen in sequence in order for Mark and his sister to leave Iran.

After exiting the hotel, Mark calmly walks onto the sidewalk and proceeds away from the subway station. There isn't much traffic at 5:30 am, but there are quite a number of workers heading for their jobs. Mark keeps his head down and walks briskly several blocks then ducks into a café. He orders a cup of coffee and sits near a window to watch the crowds walking by. After half an hour he can't see any persons waiting around watching the café. He finishes his coffee and exits out a rear door. Walking for over an hour, going in and out of buildings and stores once they open. Finally satisfied that he is not being followed, he enters the subway and takes it several stops. As he exits the station, he walks slowly up Jeyhon Street. He spots the Mossad agent and advances towards him. The vans headlights come on and Mark angles towards him.

After entering the van, the agent pulls away into traffic and heads for the language school.

"Did you get the medical kit?"

"Yes, it will take me about twenty minutes to apply the bandage and wire her jaw. Even if they take the bandage off, unless it's a doctor who specializes in head, neck, throat medicine, they will not be able to determine the extent of the injury."

"Ok, I have her passport. We just need a photo that can be added."

Mark slips into the back of the van while the agent drives the forty minutes to the school.

The agent passes Mark an Iranian pistol. Mark sticks it under his seat, but within a quick reach.

"The school is coming up on the left. I asked your sister to park one block away. We will park on her side of the street and when she gets out of her car, we will drive up and snatch her. I found a parking area within two miles where we can sit and you can take the photo and apply it to the passport, I'll wire her jaw and apply the bandage. At that point, we'll head for the airport. Your flight will be less than an hour from the time we arrive. Close timing but will help with customs."

Mark nods. "After you drop us off, sanitize the van and then make sure it gets stolen. I think you should get out of the country too. Once they realize that Saarah has left Iran, there will be a shit storm to find out how it happened."

"Yeah, I will dump the van, then head to the Mehrabad International Airport for a flight to Lebanon. From there to Israel."

Mark knows how dangerous it is for a Mossad agent. One slip and he would endure months of torture and finally a very painful death.

They slowly advance down the designated street. The van pulls to the curb and Mark moves to the back to prepare for the snatch. After twenty minutes, the agent says, "There she is. Get ready."

Saarah Nasir Al-Din Aziz takes a big breath. She has been waiting for the past two days for her brother to take her to freedom. Today has to be the day. She has been on pins and needles and the waiting has been some of the worst pressure of her adult life. Her husband, Captain Sajad Aziz noticed her nervousness. He made a comment last night at dinner, asking her what was wrong. She tried to pass it off as an issue at school, but she wasn't sure he bought it.

After turning off the car engine, she glances at her rearview mirror and sees a van moving slowly down the street towards her. She leaves the keys in the car and exits the vehicle.

The van moves forward slowly, then accelerates and stops next to her. Mark opens the sliding side door and pulls his sister into the van. Saraah lets out a soft "OH", and then the van is moving again with the door being slammed.

Mark is kneeling next to the woman. He has not seen a photo of his sister and only vaguely remembers her.

"Mailis? Do you remember me?" Saarah says in Arabic.

Mark smiles. "Yes Saarah. But I must ask you several questions."

Saarah smiles. "Of course."

"When the men came into our house. What did I do?"

Saarah smiles again. "You were a typical ten year old male, you wanted to see what was happening. So you stole out of the back bedroom to watch the Muslim Brotherhood invade our home." Her voice now hard. "They hit our father. Then you came into the room with money in your hand to buy our freedom. You were so brave. But of course it didn't work, they took our money and they took our mother and me."

Mark leans forward and embraces his sister. They are both crying softly, holding each other.

"We have a lot to do. Our cover to get you out of the country is that you have been in an automobile accident and broke your jaw. Therefore you can not speak. You are the wife of a Russian executive here on business and because of the accident, we are both flying to Germany for surgery. You will have a Russian passport. If we are found out, you will claim that you were abducted off the street and forced to come to the airport. You have no idea who this person is who abducted you. Is that clear?"

Saarah nods.

"This is very important. If you say anything about knowing me or what was going to happen, you will die. It doesn't matter who your husband is."

Saarah looks up into Mark's eyes. "Of course, but I would prefer to die today than return to my husband."

Mark smiles. "Well, we'll try to make sure you are out of Iran within the next hour."

While the van drives carefully towards the airport, Mark is kneeling in the back taking several photos of his sister using a small Fuji Film Square SQ10 camera. It is similar to the older Polaroid that rejects an "instant" photo, but it's digital and produces a much better photograph. He has film in the camera for ten photos but after six he is satisfied. He trims the photo to fit onto the Russian passport and once it's ready, he carefully examines the finished product. Mark carefully replaces the plastic cover over the photo and glues it.

He turns to his sister. "This is the best we can do with the time and materials we have. Hopefully the customs officer will not look too closely."

Saarah smiles. "Malis, I don't really care. Well, I do; but being able to see you, to talk with you, to hold you is worth this risk. I am just sorry that you are involved and might suffer for me."

Mark takes his sister's hand. "We will be successful, I know it. Now we'll have to wire your jaw shut and put the bandages on.

The van comes to a halt and the agent moves to the back of the van to prepare Saraah for her bandages. After approximately half an hour the agent moves away and Mark looks his sister over. The wiring of her mouth is well done. The bandages over her jaw and head show enough of her face for identification, but to an untrained eye look like someone who has been in an accident. The agent then takes some yellow, bale and purple glazing liquid and spreads it sparingly on her arms, rubbing it in and spreading it. It looks very much like a bruise. Then he does the same on her face and neck. When he is finished, Mark is amazed. It looks as if Saraah was in a horrific accident.

"Ok, we are ready. Are you ready?" Mark asks his sister.

With some difficulty, Saraah nods.

Mark looks to the agent. "Let's go."

The van lurches forward for the fifteen minute drive to the airport. Mark holds onto Saraah's hands. "Thank you for trusting me. Just to have this short time with you has been worth it for me. I love you."

Mark then spends the time in the van telling his sister about his life in America. About their father. His time as a Navy SEAL and his search for her and his mother in Syria. Then about tracking down the leader of the Muslim Brotherhood who abducted them and killing him. Then about his ex-wife, his children. He starts to tear up when talking about Paul and how he was killed in a terrorist attack, and his estrangement now with his ex-wife and daughter. Finally he smiles.

"Also, last night I went to the house of Javad Tousi. I killed him after I told him about what he did to our mother and to you. He will never bother you again."

Saraah eyes flow with tears. She nods and bows her head.

"But through it all, one of my main objectives is to find you and bring you home. Today we will do that."

Chapter 42

Los Angeles, CA - August 18th

Park Kyung-Soo directs the truck to a Walmart shopping center just south of LAX. The Walmart center on Inglewood Avenue in Hawthorne is the perfect location. It is located approximately one mile from the LAX and just South and East of the flight path. This will allow the HEL system to track a target coming from West to East over the Pacific Ocean landing at on the West-East runway.

Air Force One usually lands at March Air Force Base bringing Presidents for meetings in Southern California but because of the tight schedule, the President needed to land nearer to Los Angeles. Travel time from March AFB to Los Angeles is approximately eighty miles and would take two hours in the LA traffic. So Air Force One landing at LAX instead will be the perfect target.

Choi Hwan rolls back the tarp while Kyung-Soo starts the HEL system. They will not raise the system to target the President's plane until it is sighted coming in for landing.

Commercial airplanes come into LAX from the east and land to the west. But special flights like Air Force One come in from west to east and would not be confused with commercial airlines. Plus with Air Force One coming in, all commercial flights would be delayed or re-routed.

Kyung-Soo sits at the terminal looking at the monitor showing all of the airline traffic in the area. The President's plane will be easy to pick out. It will be the only 747 jumbo jet that will swing in from the west plus will have several fighter jets flying guard.

Suddenly, there is pounding on the rear door. Kyung-Soo looks at Hwan. "Find out who it is and get rid of them." Hwan checks his 9mm handgun and puts it into the small of his back. He pulls a tarp across to hide the HEL system.

Hwan unlocks the back door and sees a security guard standing looking up. Hwan jumps down and relocks the rear door.

"Can I help you?" Hwan says.

"Yeah, you can't park here. We have a commercial truck parking area on the other side of the lot."

Hwan eyes the man. "Ok, I have to call my office and figure out some issue with our order."

The guard screws up his face and his eyebrows come together. "What? What are you carrying?"

Hwan slips his hand to his hip and says, "We are carrying frozen chickens."

The guard looks over to the truck. "Where is the refrigeration unit? Isn't it usually on top?"

Hwan shakes his head, "It's an internal unit. Inside the truck."

The guard looks skeptical.

Making up his mind, Hwan says, "Ok, come inside and I'll show you." He unlocks the door and helps the guard in. As the guard steps in he notes that the temperature is not cold. As he starts to turn to ask the question, Hwan Choi puts a bullet in his head.

Chapter 43

Genoa, Italy - August 19th

The captives in the locked room hear the gunshot. Agents Bale and Lee immediately race to the locked door. Diane Fusco grabs onto Oliver and Filip and holds them close.

After a few minutes, suddenly the door swings open and Clare is thrown onto the floor. Her blouse is ripped and she is sobbing. Nimr Yazdi stands quietly for several seconds, and then receives a phone call on his burner phone. He steps back into the warehouse and locks the door.

"Yes." He says in Arabic.

He listens for one minute then hangs up. Nimr turns to two of the men guarding the door. "That was our American contact who has warned me that the Navy SEALs are coming and they know where we are. We have to leave immediately. Bind their hands and put the hoods on. Then get them into one of the vans. After we are ready, both vans will leave at the same time. Drive the van north up to the France border, and then abandon it. Get to Yemen when you can. I will contact you when I am ready.

Rik Thistle

The men tie up the six captives and lead them to one of the vans. After getting all of them in, Nimr hops into the drivers seat and one of the terrorist gets in the back. The other two terrorist get into the other van which contains the body of the guard shot by Yazdi.

The warehouse door opens and the vans speed out going in opposite directions. Nimr heading to the Italian coast, the other van heading north to the French border.

Chapter 44

Genoa, Italy - August 19th

Michelle, Ducky and six special operators have landed and are heading toward the warehouse. They are ten minutes out when Michelle's SAT phone beeps.

"Yes, what have you got?"

On the other end, Jonathan Bardsley clears his throat. "They just left. It appears the hostages were moved into one of the vans and then two vans exited, leaving in opposite directions."

"Are you following them both?"

"Can't do it. Only one drone, and it is almost out of fuel. We have another drone on the way but it won't be there for another twenty minutes. We are following a van heading north. The other van turned south."

"Damn. Ok, follow the first van and bring in the other drone to take over. We'll hit the warehouse anyway to collect as much information as we can. Get another drone overhead and try to find the second van."

Michelle turns in their SUV towards Ducky. "Missed them. They just bailed in two vans. Our drone can only follow one of them."

Ducky sneers. "Someone tipped them off. It can't be coincidence that they just decide to leave their safe house just as we are closing in."

Michelle takes a deep breath. "Well, let's hit the warehouse. Gather as much INTEL as we can find and let's chase the first van. I'll deal with the leak later."

As they arrive at the warehouse, the special operators surround the building. Ducky and two SEALs breech the building with their HK MP5N 9mm submachine guns ready. The empty building is quickly cleared.

"Hey Boss. Got something here." Ducky calls from an office off the main building. Michelle quickly strides over and stands looking at the spot Ducky is pointing to. "Blood on the floor and blood splatter."

Michelle looks at the site and frowns. "Get a sample and we'll get it to Langley for identification."

As they walk out of the office, another of the SEALs calls out to come take a look.

Michelle and Ducky walk over to where the terrorists obviously video taped the initial statement by Clare.

"Here is another blood pool. Lot's of blood. The body obviously laid here for some time period."

Michelle looks at the blood wondering if Clare or one of the boys were killed. Was it one of the Agents?

"Ok, gather another sample and let's get them to the U.S. Embassy so they can analyze the samples and do a search through the FDDU (Federal DNA Database Unit) to see if there is a match with any of the captives."

After handing off the samples, the group heads north chasing the van being followed by the drone. Michelle has a sinking feeling that they might have lost the trail. She pulls out her SAT phone ready to make a call to the President to tell him that they just missed the terrorists.

Chapter 45

Tehran, Iran - August 19th

The van drives into the airport traffic and creeps along at a snails pace. People dropping off loved ones, clogs the terminal parking area. The Mossad agent carefully maneuvers the van to the curb fairly near the terminal entrance. He parks and hops out and moves to the rear door. After pulling out a collapsible wheel chair from the back, he sets it up. With that, Mark helps his sister out of the van and into the wheel chair.

Mark shakes the agent's hand and expresses his thanks for all he has done. "Get out quickly." He says.

Then turns and wheels his sister and one bag into the airline terminal.

It is busy as usual with Iranians flying to various vacation spots around Iran and to Europe. Mark carefully makes his way to the ticketing for Lufthansa. In Russian then halting German, Mark speaks to the Lufthansa agent and presents his tickets. "My wife was injured in an automobile accident here and we need to get her to Munich for surgery."

The agent looks down at Saarah and sees the bruises and her bandaged head.

"I am very sorry. Let me see if we can get one of our agents to expedite the process."

Mark smiles and thanks her.

Within minutes a Lufthansa agent walks with Mark directing him to the customs area. As they approach the customs queue line, the Lufthansa agent uses his official badge to approach a customs supervisor. Mark watches them talking. He would prefer to just go through the normal process. But the Lufthansa agent has taken the initiative to try to expedite their passage. Unfortunately it could make the process more complicated. After a few minutes, the agent walks back and tells Mark that he and his wife will be able to pass through a special customs area. Mark thanks the agent and reluctantly they proceed to an area adjacent to the main passport control area.

The supervisor is waiting clearly not happy having to give this couple special treatment. Mark presents their Russian passports and waits.

The supervisor looks the fake passports over and then looks up. "Why did you come to Iran?" He says in Persian. Mark screws up his face and pauses several seconds. "Do you speak French or German or English?" Mark says in broken Farsi.

The supervisor nods. "I speak French."

Then in French, he repeats the question.

Mark smiles and replies in French. "My wife and I are here on business. I am looking for business opportunities here for Russian companies in Iran. Yesterday my wife was involved in an automobile accident. I am taking her to Munich for surgery to repair her jaw, the surgeons in Moscow are not quite as good."

The supervisor looks down at Saarah and nods.

Mark gives the supervisor the medical report. While he reads the report, Mark reaches down and puts his hand on Saarah's shoulder.

There are two Iranian guards with AK-47 submachine guns standing nearby. Mark turns to the supervisor. "I see your guards have our guns."

The supervisor looks up and smiles. "Yes, they are excellent weapons, very reliable." Then the man turns to Saarah. "Is your name?"

Mark says, "My wife was in a horrific accident and her jaw is wired shut. She can't speak without a lot of pain."

The supervisor moves closer to her examining her bandages. "Please ask her to try."

Mark kneels next to Saarah and speaks softly in Russian repeating the question.

Saarah looks up at the supervisor. "Mon nom est Saarah Ivanov" she says in French, grimacing.

The supervisor looks at her photo on her passport again, and then nods. He walks back to an unused terminal and types in their names.   After several minutes he returns and hands the passports back to Mark.

"Please come this way. I will walk you to your gate."

Mark wheeling Saarah says, "That is not necessary, I know the way."   But the supervisor persists.   Along the way, Mark glances at a television hung in one of the gate areas.   On the screen is a photo of Saarah.   With a TV announcer saying something about her being abducted.   Mark takes a deep breath and picks up the pace towards his gate.

They arrive and Mark sees that the passengers are queued up waiting to board. The agent moves forward and speaks to the Lufthansa gate agent. The agent smiles and motions for Mark to come forward.   As he wheels Saarah forward he hears some shouting from behind.   Mark glances back and sees two police officers checking identification papers in the gate next to him. He helps Saarah up and taking her arm, leads her into the walkway. Giving the Lufthansa tickets to the gate agent, Mark walks slowly down towards the airplane.

They take their business class seats but Mark gets ready to take the policeman's gun if necessary and highjack the plane. As passengers start to board, Mark looks at each one. Finally after twenty minutes, the outer door is closed. Mark looks at Saarah and smiles.

The Lufthansa flight backs out, and then moves to the taxiway. After another half an hour, the plane lifts off bound for Germany and freedom.

Chapter 46

On board Air Force One - August 19th

The President of the United States is sitting at his desk aboard Air Force One as it cruises at 35,000 feet at a speed of 575 MPH. He knows he has to maintain his normal Presidential schedule, but wishes he could be in the White House command post receiving the latest INTEL on his daughter's abduction. Instead he is heading toward California to meet with industrial leaders in Los Angeles.

"What is the latest?" the President says to the command post general.

"Mr. President, the team hit the warehouse but unfortunately they had packed up and left. There were two vans. The captives were in one, the other we believe was a decoy. We have a drone following one of the vans, the team is trying to pick up the trail of the other."

The President sits forward. "Damn it, how could they know we were coming? This doesn't make sense. I don't believe in coincidences. There must have been a leak!"

"We are checking on any communications picked up by the NSA. But right now we are focusing our efforts on finding the second van."

"Ok, let me know as soon as you have any additional information."

"One other thing, Mr. President. They found two pools of blood in the warehouse. Unknown origin. They are testing the samples now."

"Jesus. I pray they are not Clare or the kids."

"Yes sir."

There is a few seconds of silence. "Thank you General."

As the President hangs up the phone, he puts his head down. Being the most powerful man in the world doesn't help much at this point. His chief of staff, Randy Smith is on his phone talking with the advance people in LA.

"Mr. President, we have the meeting with the industry leaders set for 11 am. We will be landing shortly at LAX. From there it will be just a fifteen minute drive to BAE Systems. You will meet twenty presidents of the top aerospace and electronics companies in Southern California. After that meeting which should last two hours, then we'll head north up to Seattle and a meeting with Boeing."

The President nods absentmindedly. His mind not on the upcoming meeting, but on the safety of his daughter and grandchildren in Italy.

"Mr. President and the members of the press. We are starting our descent to Los Angeles." The message is broadcast over the airplanes communications system.

As everyone on board buckles up, they can feel the steep descent and the swing over the Pacific Ocean, then a wide sweeping turn to line up with the LAX runway.

Suddenly Air Force One lurches as the plane shutters and begins to pitch to the left. Some of the items on the Presidential desk slide off and crash to the carpeted floor. The President grips the arms of the chair to maintain his balance.

Randy Smith tumbles to the floor and then climbs onto a couch, holding on.

The aircraft pitches right, while the engines whine trying to gain altitude. Suddenly there is another shutter and then silence.

The President looks at his Chief of Staff. "What the Hell?"

The President buckles into his chair which is bolted to the floor. Air Force One is dropping fast.

The Air Force One pilots are struggling. Captain Blair Rodney has over thirty-one years of flight experience, twenty-five years of flying Air Force jets in various combat conditions, and now over six years flying Air Force One. Highly decorated, he is one cool customer, but he has not flown a 747 dead stick with the President of the United States onboard. First one engine of the modified 747-200 stopped. He corrected for that, but then the second engine quit. That can't be a coincidence. They are under attack.

"Mayday, Mayday. This is SAM28000 on approach to LAX. Both engine failure. Requesting immediate clearance."

"SAM28000, clearance approved SIX Romeo Twenty Four Left"

"Roger, Twenty Four Left"

Captain Rodney turns to his co-Pilot, "get ready to drop the landing gear but not until I tell you, I don't want too much drag."

The Boeing 747-200 has a glide ratio of 15:1 with a dead stick landing. The Captain Rodney knows that. The 747-200 glide would be 93 miles from a cruising altitude of 33,000 feet. The only issue is that he is at 7,000 feet approaching LAX and will only have minutes to set the plane down. He quickly calculates that he will be able to dead stick the aircraft onto the runway, but it will be close.

As the plane continues to fall at a controlled rate the pilot sees a flash and the windshield of the cockpit explodes sending glass and metal into the two pilots. Captain Rodney looks over at his Co-Captain and sees that most of this head gone. Fighting for control, the Captain dips the yoke slightly to gain some speed and lift as he drops towards LAX.

"Mayday, Mayday! We have been hit by a laser or something. Co-pilot is dead. Have emergency vehicles on standby."

The LAX tower responds. "Roger"

The Captain feels blood running down his face while he tries to keep the crippled aircraft on line for a controlled landing at the runway.

"SAM28000 lining up for landing on 6R24L."

"Roger, good luck SAM28000"

Air Force One continues to glide with the runway coming up fast. The pilot tries to keep the 747-200 online while dropping the landing gear. With only part of the cockpit windshield intact, the pilot can see the runway looming. The wind is howling into the cockpit. The plane hits the ground hard and bounces, then starts its rollout. The Captain applies the brakes as the end of the runway is fast approaching. The brakes are smoking, and then several tires explode due to the heat. Suddenly the aircraft landing gear collapses on the left side and the plane slides to that side. Flames explode from the left engine. After several seconds, suddenly there is silence as Air Force One comes to a stop.

Rescue vehicles rush to surround the aircraft. Fire retardant and foam are sprayed over both engines and the landing gear.

As smoke starts to fill Air Force One, the press and white house staff slide down the emergency slides.   The   Secret Service rush into the Presidential office intent on moving the President to the rear slide and get him off the plane.   As the President emerges from the rear office he sees smoke filling the plane.   "What about the pilots?"

"Mr. President, our job is to get you out safely."

The President shakes his head.   "Get them out first, they landed this plane.   Let's check on them."

The group moves through the several sections of Air Force One that was evacuated by the press and aides.   One of the Secret Service agents enters the cockpit.   He emerges with the Captain pulling the body of the Co-pilot.

The President swears softly, and then helps to cover his head with his suit coat.   One of the agents holds the body and slides down to the ground.   Then the Chief of Staff jumps on the slide, then the President, followed by the senior Secret Service agent and finally Captain Rodney.

Smoke is spiraling up into the air over the LAX airport. Dozens of emergency vehicles are on the tarmac, a hundred first responders are fighting to put out the engine fire, while the Air Force One occupants are moved into a secure area within the terminal.

#   #   #

The terrorists pull the tarp over the truck roof. Seeing the smoke from Air Force One during approach was initially satisfying, but then the plane continued on approach. Kyung-Soo expected to see the airplane explode but it seemed to only hit one of the engines. He quickly retargets the HEL system and shoots again, this time at the other engine. He can't tell if he hit the plane so he again retargets and fires directly at the plane's canopy. After the third shot the plane starts a steep descent and Kyung-Soo is satisfied that he has destroyed Air Force One. He and Hwan pull the tarp over the top and hop out.

"We should see smoke when the plane crashes."

As they pull the doors closed, the truck suddenly starts up. Both men don't realize what is happening until the truck begins to quickly pull away. Kyung-Soo pulls his revolver and starts to run toward the truck cab. He realizes now that the Army bitch they planned to rape and murder had gotten out of her constraints.

"Stop her." He yells to Hwan.

Both men run the length of the truck. Kyung-Soo fires two shots into the back of the cab. The truck is accelerating but Kyung-Soo is catching up. He jumps up onto the cab and grabs

226

onto the door handle. Just then, Master Sergeant Davies kicks the door open and the terrorist hangs on for his life. While hanging onto the door he raises the revolver to shoot Davies.

Just as Kyung-Soo fires, the Master Sergeant ducks and loses control of the semi. The semi truck crashes through a fence and hits several cars parked on a street adjacent to the Walmart. The impact throws the terrorist from the door and onto the street.

The Master Sergeant knows she has to get the semi moving and away from these terrorists or she is dead. She puts the truck in gear and pushes two cars out of the way and heads for the 405 freeway. As she directs the semi forward she sees both terrorists on the ground. She hopes they are dead, but then sees one pull the other up and start to limp away.

She wants to stop and call the authorities, but is afraid the terrorists might have backup. She wants to drive the HEL system to the closest military base. Susie knows that the LA Air Force Base is just a few miles south, so she heads that direction knowing she must first get this Top Secret system to a safe location, and then tell what she knows about the terrorists and their attack on the President.

Chapter 47

Genoa, Italy - August 19th

The white van moves slowly through the narrow streets of Genoa towards the Port of Genoa. Inside are six hostages, all bound and gagged with hoods over their heads. Nimr Yazdi is sitting in the passenger seat holding the official looking paperwork allowing them into the port, then into one of the twenty private terminals. This was part of the plan all along, just accelerated by a couple of days due to the tip about the SEALs. Of course the guards have been bribed to admit the van and look the other way on any cargo they are carrying.

Nimr hands the paperwork to the driver as they pull up to the guard shack. The guard notes the van, and then takes the paper. He has been alerted to their arrival and has been paid. He glances at the driver then the passenger, but knowing he doesn't want to see too much he turns to his partner and shouts "Admit". The barrier is lowered and the van moves forward. Nimr knows that this phase of the plan is the most dangerous.

The van moves through several streets of the port then pulls into the back of one of the private warehouses used to store goods ready to be shipped out of the Port of Genoa to locations around the world. It is dusk and the street lights are just starting to come on. Nimr gets out of the van and approaches a man with a flowing beard.

"Is the container ready?"

"Yes, we have worked on it all day. The food, water and communications equipment is inside and we are ready to go."

Nimr nods. "Back the van up to this container."

The van is turned and the rear door is opened. The guard emerges holding his AK-47. He takes his post to oversee the transfer of the abductees. Another guard pulls each of the Americans out of the van and puts them inside the container. After they are inside, Nimr closes the door.

"What time will the crane put the container on the ship?" Asks Nimr.

The burly man consults the ship schedule. "Within an hour, the crane will pick up the container and place it on the Al Safat container ship. We have paid the Captain to make sure the container is on the deck, not on the stack."

Nimr looks over at the ship. He has not been on a ship before and is a bit uneasy about being at sea for several days. But the trip from Genoa to Algeria will be 497 Nautical Miles. At 10 knots, that should take just two days. The route will be a straight shot past Corse and Sardegna to Algeria. Once there, Nimr plans to deposit the hostages into a safe house and then communicate with Hamza to implement the next phase of the plan. But right now, his main concern is to get the container onto the ship and dispose of the van.

The hostages are sitting at the back of the container on blankets. They still have their hands bound and the gags and hoods on. Nimr looks at them and decides that they are ready.

"Ok, we'll enter the container. Let's go. Sameer, take the van and drive it to a poor area and leave it on the street with the keys in the ignition."

Sameer nods and moves to the container door. As Nimr and the two guards enter the container, they turn on the flashlights. Sameer closes the door and affixes a lock. He then places a white half moon on the door.

Inside Nimr moves with one of the flashlights and sits on a blanket. "Once we have been lifted and are on the deck of the ship and underway, we can remove the hoods and gags from our guests." He says with a smile.

The two guards settle down keeping their weapons on safety, waiting for the lift.

After forty minutes, suddenly they feel the crane grabbing the container and lifting it into the air. The container is lifted up and transported over to the Al Safat ship. It is a Liberian vessel that is 306M long and 40M wide. It carries 75,000 gross tonnage. It is not one of the larger ships, but it is one that al-Qaeda trusts.

Its Captain is a true believer and has been trusted to transport people and material to and from Libya and Algeria.

The container is placed on the deck. Nimr breathes a silent pray of thanks to Allah, and then rises to pull the hoods off of the six captives.

"I will remove your gags, but if you yell or make any noise I will put them back on. Do you understand?"

The six all nod.

Nimr turns to one of the guards. "Remove the gags. Once we are underway, we will unbind your hands and give you food and water."

After another thirty minutes, they feel the ship beginning to move. A tugboat is pushing the Al Safat out into the bay. After almost an hour, the container ship turns on its engines and the ship gets underway for the two day voyage to Algeria.

Chapter 48

Munich, Germany - August 19th

Mark and Saarah walk off the Lufthansa aircraft and onto German soil. As they head towards the German customs area, several German uniformed officers approach them.

"Mark Aldin?"

Mark nods and says, "Yes, I am Mark Aldin."

"Would you please follow me?"

The couple walks with the two officers and enter into an office off to the side of the customs area. As they enter, Mark sees Michelle Samaha and smiles. The two German officers exit for privacy.

"We were worried about you." Says Michelle.

A fourth man in the room is a dentist and is removing the temporary wire bracing on the Saarah's teeth while she is sitting in one of the chairs. After a few minutes, he puts his tools in his medical bag and hands Saarah a bottle of water.

"Thank you for coming on such short notice." Michelle says to the dentist.

As he is leaving the room, Mark turns to Saarah and says. "Saarah, I'd like you to meet Michelle Samaha. My boss."

Saarah smiles and with some difficulty says "Very nice to meet you." In English.

"Here are both your U.S. passports. Saarah your new last name is Aldin. We will fly you directly to Colorado Springs, Colorado to a CIA safe house for a debrief, where you will live until we can determine your final destination."

Saarah looks at her brother. "Mailis, can I live with you for a while until I get acclimated to life in America?"

Mark looks at Michelle. "I am sure we can work something out. But initially, you'll have to trust the CIA to take care of you. If your husband discovers that you have fled to America, he could try to snatch you back or have you killed."

Saarah smiles. "I would never go back and I would prefer to die than return to Iran."

Michelle steps forward. "Well, we will make sure that doesn't happen. But first we have to get you to America and we have a private CIA plane to take you there. Unfortunately Mark will have to stay here. We have a major issue that we've been dealing with over the past week."

Mark raises his eyebrows.

Mark wraps his sister in his arms. In Arabic he says, "Saarah, I am so happy to have you in my life again. We will have years and years to reconnect. As soon as I can, I will come to Colorado. Right now I have to help Michelle with this... issue."

Saarah smiles. "Of course. I understand." Then she switches to English. "I will fully cooperate with the CIA and wait for you to return. I have waited thirty years to see you again Mailis. I have waited thirty years to tell you my story."

Mark kisses the top of her head and gives her a hug. "I will see you in a week or so."

With that Michelle leads Saarah out of the room where two CIA agents are waiting to take her to a secluded part of the Munich airport and a flight to America.

Michelle returns to the room to find Mark smiling.

"I am amazed the plan worked." Says Mark. "We were lucky and the timing was just perfect."

Michelle motions for Mark to follow her. They walk out of the room and through a door out to an area outside the terminal. It's an area where airport employees can go to grab a quick cigarette. Michelle sits down as her facial expression changes. "The President's daughter and two grandchildren were abducted by al-Qaeda several days ago."

Mark's face shows his shock. "How did this happen? Didn't they have security?"

Michelle nods. "It was a coordinated attack. Multiple vehicles, six to eight terrorists. They took the President's daughter, two grandchildren, a daughter's college roommate who works in Italy for the State Department and the two secret service agents."

Mark shakes his head. "Either the agents screwed up big time by being too predictable or the terrorists knew where they were going. Have you had any contact?"

"Yes, the daughter – Clare Sweeney, sent a video message to the White House. We think she blinked a message in Morse code. Our INTEL believes they are in Genoa. We are currently searching for a white van. We believe they are holding them for a ransom."

Mark sits, thinking about his own son killed by a terrorist. He can't imagine how much pain the President is dealing with having his daughter and two grandchildren in harms way. "What is the plan?"

Michelle pulls a map from her briefcase. "They were abducted here." Pointing to an area between Florence and Milan. "They were taken south to Genoa to a warehouse. We raided the warehouse less than twelve hours later, but they were gone. Plus there were two pools of blood. The DNA is being checked now."

"Damn. They are either very lucky or were tipped off." Notes Mark.

"We agree. We are back checking now to see who knew their schedule, plus who would have known about the raid."

"'"Ok, so what do we know now?"

"We think they are still in Genoa. Just before you and your sister arrived I got a message that the van was found in a poor area in Genoa. Obviously dumped to try to throw us off. We think it was al-Qaeda."

"You sure it's al-Qaeda? What do you think they want?"

"It is al-Qaeda, maybe in response to our bombing of the al-Qaeda leadership, stopping the virus, killing Nimr Yazdi. What do they want? Money, GITMO prisoners and maybe revenge?"

Suddenly Michelle's face shows shock. "Oh no, how could we miss it?"

Mark looks confused. "Missed what?"

Michelle pulls out a piece of paper. "The Morse code blinked by Clare Sweeney was translated to..." She refers to her notes. "T-H-I-R-T-Y-R-A-I-D, then Y-A-S. There were other blinks but we think she was either confused or didn't remember the Morse code for those letters. We believe she was saying thirty radius either in minutes or miles. That led us to Genoa. So that was accurate. The second one of YAS confused us. But what if she meant YAZ?"

Mark's face goes white. He stands. "You think she was saying Yazdi?"

"Could be. Do you think he could have survived the attack?"

Mark shakes his head. "I shot him in the head, but maybe I missed. I was shot in the shoulder just as I pulled the trigger. I was not able to check that Yazdi was dead."

Michelle looks up from her notes. "It would make sense if he survived. Al-Qaeda generally and Hamza bin Ladin specifically might have been driven to let Yazdi run this operation."

Mark can't believe this, but it would make sense. "OK, we have to assume that Yazdi is somehow involved."

Michelle stands. "Well, we have to get to Genoa and set up an organization there. But we'll probably have to wait for their new communication. In the meantime, we are pulling in every snitch and asset we have in the area to try to gather some leads."

Mark agrees with a nod.

"I have a plane ready to take us to Italy. We should be there tomorrow morning. Hopefully we'll get some good news when we land."

Chapter 49

Los Angeles, CA - August 19th

Los Angeles, CA - August 19th

The Secret Service quickly escorts the President and his Chief of Staff to a private terminal. Guns are drawn as the President is in a circle of protection. Air Force One is being hosed down with flame retardant as it sits leaning on one of its wings. The smell of burning tires hangs over the runway.

"Damn, what the Hell happened?" The President snaps.

"Sir, we are interviewing the pilot. We believe at this point it could have been a multiple bird strike taking out both engines and then hitting the cockpit windshield killing the co-pilot."

The President sits down. "I flock of birds could do all that damage? Hell of a coincidence."

The door to the conference room opens and one of the other Secret Service agents brings in the Captain. His head is bandaged and he has the blood of the Co-Pilot all over his shirt. The President stands and shakes hands with Captain Rodney.

"Thank you Captain for bringing the plane down safely. I am very sorry about your Co-Pilot."

Captain Rodney nods. "Mr. President, I believe this was a terrorist attack. It was definitely not a bird strike. It was some kind of high power laser. We lost the left engine first, then the right engine. When we started to glide, I saw a flash and the cockpit windshield exploded. That is what killed McNeal."

The President turns to his Chief of Staff. "Get me General Hayes, he needs to know what happened."

The Press Secretary comes into the conference room. "Mr. President, thank God you are ok. We need to get a statement to the press. They are currently filing all kinds of wild reports from bird strikes to terrorism."

The President smiles. "Good. Let them guess until we know for sure. But it definitely wasn't a bird strike."

The Chief of Staff's secure SAT phone rings. "Mr. President, General Hayes is on the line."

The President takes the phone. "General, Air Force One was attacked by what the pilot thinks was a high energy laser. Could one of our HEL systems been used in this attack?"

The Chief of Staff can hear the General try to explain how that would be impossible.

The President explodes. "Well, God Damn it, my plane was brought down by some kind of laser and I want to know who did it! This is an act of war!"

The General replies, "Mr. President, I will get to the bottom of this and get right back to you."

"Damn right you will. I want some answers within an hour General!" With that, the President tosses the SAT phone to Randy Smith. "Did everyone get out?"

The Chief of Staff nods. "Yes sir. There are some minor cuts and bruises, but overall we were all very lucky. With so many press on board, it will be impossible to keep a lid on this. I would recommend a public statement. Plus it will quell any stories that you were killed in the attack."

The President looks down at his hands. They are shaking slightly and he is feeling nauseated. One of the flight attendants enters the room with several bottles of water and some packaged cookies. "I am sorry Mr. President, this is all I could find."

The President looks up and smiles. "Thank you, just what I need."

As the flight attendant leaves, the President turns to his Chief of Staff. "Could this be a coordinated attack. Abduct my family and try to kill me?"

The Chief of Staff shakes his head. "I doubt it."

"Ok Randy, set up the TV interview. Let all of the press know. I'll make some notes and go live in 30 minutes."

"Yes sir." With that, he turns and leaves the room to gather the press together and set up an address to the nation.

Chapter 50

Cyrrhenian Sea - August 20th

The freighter is making good progress and is forty miles off the coast of Sardegna, an island 300 Km off the coast of Italy. The weather has been good and the Captain has not seen any other vessels over the past 24 hours.

Within the container marked with a half moon, the passengers and the captives are making the best of an uncomfortable journey. With the pitching ocean, the closed environment and the building heat, conditions are becoming dangerous. The door to the container is not locked, just secured.

"How much water is left?" Nimr asks his top aide.

"We have eight jugs which would total several gallons. It's not enough in this heat."

Nimr looks over at the captives. "Ok, we will unlock the door and I will go to the Captain to get more water and relieve the heat in the container."

The two guards flick off their safeties and move in front of the hostages. However, after a full day on the ocean with the heat and lack of water, the six captives are dehydrated and in no shape to mount an attack and try to escape.

Nimr lifts the lever to release the container door. He pushes against it and rush of ocean air and spray blows in. He pockets his 9mm pistol and slips out leaving the door slightly open. The change in the temperature is dramatic. Even though the container had several dozen holes drilled into the sides and top, it seems that was not enough.

"I will be back shortly." With that, Nimr steps onto the deck of the freighter and closes his eyes against the bright Mediterranean sun. As he moves from the container, he sees the steps up to the bridge. Climbing slowly, he scans the main deck and sees the fifty containers that accompanies their temporary home. On the second deck Nimr knows there is the hospital room, life rafts and various staterooms. He could have stayed in relative comfort in one of those, but felt he had to stay with his captives. After climbing up to another deck, Nimr finally reaches the Bridge.

Nimr pauses to catch his breath and look over the ship from this high spot. At the stern are two seamen who do not seem to be armed, otherwise he doesn't see another sailor.

Nimr takes a deep breath and walks slowly towards the bridge. As he enters, he sees four men. One is manning the wheel, steering the large ship along a course set by the navigator. Sitting at a desk is another sailor with the Captain standing beside him. They are in conversation and don't notice Nimr standing behind him. Nimr knows that he is aware of the illegal cargo on the deck, having been paid handsomely for taking the container.

"Excuse me Captain." Nimr says as he steps fully into the room. The Captain turns with a start not expecting anyone to enter his bridge.

In English, the Captain says, "Yes, what can I do for you?" The rest of the crew stare wide-eyed at the visitor.

Nimr smiles. "Perhaps we could talk in private?"

The Captain nods and turns to his second in command. "Please maintain the current heading." With that the Captain and Nimr step into the corridor.

Nimr eyes the Captain. He is older in his mid-50s, slim and seems very composed. "Excuse the interruption Captain but our conditions in the container were becoming intolerable. We are almost out of water and the heat inside is quite intense."

The Captain nods. "I will have more water brought to you. As for the heat, there is little I can do. You can open the container door at night but we do have guards walking the deck at regular intervals. The main issue is that you have now exposed yourself to my crew. This could cause issues when we offload."

Nimr knows all this but nevertheless listens quietly. "I will compensate you more to pay the crew to keep their mouths shut."

The Captain smiles. "Of course, that will be acceptable."

With that Nimr turns and starts to the ladder. "When will we be docking?"

The Captain turns around, "We should dock tomorrow afternoon. Perhaps by 4 pm."

Nimr nods. "Please make sure our container is the first to be offloaded. We will have a truck waiting to be loaded."

The Captain nods also and without a word, turns back to his bridge.

Nimr climbs down and returns to the container. One of his guards is just inside the door watching his approach. The heavy metal door is swung open and then closed as Nimr enters.

"They will bring us more water and at night we can open the door."

Clare looks at her boys who are sleeping, drenched in sweat. "How long will we have to be in this container?"

Nimr sits down on a crate. "Tomorrow afternoon we should reach our destination. Tonight we will open the door to let in some cooler air. Once we arrive, we should be able to disembark and get into more acceptable accommodations."

Agent Lee speaks up. "Where are we going? What do you want?"

Nimr smiles, "We are going into the stronghold of al-Qaeda, and I want to bring the United States and this President to their knees."

Chapter 51

Genoa, Italy - August 20th

Michelle and Mark enter the nondescript building and are buzzed into the "War Room" after being seen on the multiple CTV cameras that keep the facility secure. As the pair enter the room, they see over a dozen analysts pouring over reports, photos and data.

"Hey boss" says Ducky Duckworth. "You too Mark, how was your vacation in Iran?" He says with a grin.

Mark smiles back, knowing Ducky was trying to downplay the danger he faced in Teheran. "Easy Peasy."

Michelle laughs. "Yeah, rescued his sister under the noses of the Republican Guards, killed his mother's evil husband and planted false information that will disrupt the Iranian secret police."

Mark grabs a cup of coffee and smiles. "Yeah, all in a days work."

Michelle walks over to Kelly Campos. "How was the flight over?"

Kelly Campos, a 20 year old former MIT computer science major, had never been on a plane before. "It was a great way to travel. A private jet, get amazing food and travel the world. What's not to like?"

Michelle then pulls together the team. "Ok, what do we have on the President's family."

Campos pulls up several photos of the Genoa harbor. Ducky continues the debrief. "We know the family was taken to Genoa and kept in a warehouse, where the video was shot. We raided the warehouse, but just missed them. There were several blood stains there and we took samples. We just received the results from the FBI. They were not of any of the hostages."

Michelle takes a long breath. "Thank God."

Ducky continues. "The hostages were transported in a white van. One was found sixty miles away, but we believe that was a red herring. A second white van was found in Genoa. We believe this was the one used to transport the President's family."

Mark interrupts, "A great way to get them out of the country would be using a container ship."

Campos smiles. "Exactly. We believe they were taken to the Genoa harbor and put in a container and put on a ship. The trick is finding the ship. What I did is look at all the ships in the harbor that day and which left Genoa that night or the next day."

Kelly sits back and grabs a handful of M&Ms and pops them into his mouth while he thinks. "There were eight freighters that fit that model. Two were traveling to the Far East to China and Japan. We ruled them all out because of the length of the trip and their destination. Three others are traveling to European cities; Liverpool, Madrid and Hamburg. Maybe candidates, but probably not."

Everyone is now leaning forward waiting for Campos' final analysis. "Finally we have three freighters. One is the Ocean Music shipping under the Moldova Flag. Left port this morning for Egypt. The second is East Dinamik under the Turkish flag. It is heading to Darnah, Libya. It left last night and moving at 12 Knots. Finally we have the Al Safat under the Liberian flag. It is scheduled for Algeria. But of the three, I think the East Dinamik is the one to watch. The drone should be on-station early this morning. "

Michelle stands up. "Is there anyway they could have been put onto any other ships?"

Campos shakes his head, his long hair moving back and forth. "Could be. But I'll monitor each of them. It's one of the three if they were transferred to a ship. The issue is that at first light tomorrow when the drone arrives, they will be just two hours from the port of Darnah in Libya."

Mark shifts from one foot to another. "I think Ducky and I should fly to Libya and HELO near Darnah to get there before the ship docks. If the President's family and the Secret Service Agents are in one of the containers, then we need to be there to track them to their safe house."

Michelle nods. "Ok, but we have no assets there on the ground to help you."

"We understand. We can go in as locals but we'll have several tricks up our sleeves. We'll carry a Beretta M9, a M4 with a ACOG scope plus of course our Strider knife. We'll also have our TEA Multi-Com ear buds for communication." Mark looks over at Ducky.

"That should do it. Let's get geared up."

With that, the two men leave the meeting and Michelle puts her hand on Kelly's shoulder. "Keep them safe."

"Will do."

Kelly Campos pops some M&Ms into his mouth and leans back waiting for the drone to get over the ship and be able to take photos of the containers. He just hopes they picked the right ship.

Chapter 52

Los Angeles, CA - August 20th

Master Sergeant Susie Davies pulls the 18 wheeler into the secure area of the Los Angeles Air Force Base in El Segundo. She knows that if she can get HEL system on the base, it will be safe. As she pulls up to the guard station, both guards un-sling their M4 Carbines.

"Halt!" Shouts the Sergeant.

Susie brings the large truck to a slow stop. She knows they are concerned about a truck bomb. She raises her hands and unlocks the door. The Sergeant moves around with his M4 pointed at the door. Susie kicks the door open while her hands are raised. She is in her Army uniform.

"I am Master Sergeant Susie Davies and I have a classified weapon in the truck. We have to get it onto the base as soon as possible. Plus I know who tried to assassinate the President."

Both Air Force security officers order her out of the truck. Susie lays on the ground with her hands behind her back. One of the officers zip ties her hands while the other checks the back of the truck.

"Holy Crap!" Says the Sergeant.   He immediately radios their base headquarters. "Sir, we have a truck here with a large weapon system in the back. A woman claiming to be a Master Sergeant says she drove it here to keep is secure. Also, she said she knows who assassinated the President."

The communications officer is dumb founded. "What?" Then he recovers his composure. "Ok, I'll send a team to clear the truck. Bring the woman to the interrogation room."

"Yes sir!"

Susie is lifted onto her feet and marched to the bases interrogation room. As she is seated behind table, but the zip ties remain.

One of the guards leaves the room just as a Major enters. "My name is Major Jackson. Tell me how you came to be in possession of a military weapon?"

Susie takes a breath, and then begins to tell her story. How she was kidnapped, how the two people posing as Navy officers were able to turn on the HEL weapon and how they targeted Air Force One. Then when she was left alone while they were shooting the HEL system, she got out of her binding and hot wired the truck and drove it out of the Walmart shopping center and down to the LA Air Force Base.

The Major sits silently for several seconds. "What about the President?"

Susie sits forward, "Oh yeah. They were shooting the HEL system at Air Force One. I don't know if they hit it, but they cheered with the third shot."

The Major turns to his aide. "Find out if Air Force One has landed at LAX?"

The aide leaves the room and the Major turns back to the Master Sergeant. "So who were these men?"

"They were Asian, I would guess Koreans. They had U.S. Naval officers uniforms and falsified documents to pick up a demo HEL system. It had to have been an inside job. Someone, perhaps by my commander, falsified the order."

The interrogation room door is opened. Susie and the Major both see the aide white faced with eyes like saucers. "Air Force One was shot down. But I think everyone on board survived."

The Major stands. "Get me General Orr, immediately."

The aide rushes out of the office and the Major orders the guard to release the Master Sergeant arms from the zip ties. "Thank you." She says. "Could I have a glass of water?" They then move together towards his base office. "I want you to explain exactly what you know to General Orr."

"Yes sir."

Chapter 53

Los Angeles, CA - August 20th

"My fellow Americans. Today a foreign nation attempted to shoot down Air Force One with some of my staff, the press corps and two brave Air Force pilots on board. The plane took three direct hits which disabled the plane, but with the skill and bravery of the Air Force One pilots, they were able to glide the 747 to a successful crash landing at LAX. Unfortunately the co-pilot died. Everyone else was able to get out of the plane with only some minor injuries."

The President pauses to take a breath and sets his face in a stern manner. Looking directly into the camera, "We will discover who was behind this attempt and if it is a nation-state, that country will suffer the full might of the United States of America. Thank you for your continuing support. God bless America."

The camera lights dim and the President stands. "Randy, get the Joint Chiefs on a conference call. I want the military to go to DEFCON II. Call the FBI and let's figure out how terrorists could have gotten their hands on a HEL system."

"Yes Mr. President. Also I just received a call from a Major at the LA Air Force Base saying that a Master Sergeant just entered their base with the stolen HEL system and she thinks she knows who is behind the attack."

The President looks surprised. "Get her over here, I want to talk with her."

The Chief of Staff leaves the room to carry out the President's order.

"Get the Co-pilot's next of kin information. I want to call them to personally let them know of his heroism."

The Press Secretary enters the room. "Mr. President, the press wants more information beyond your nationwide address. What should I tell them?"

The President leans back against the desk. "Their reports on the crash, plus my address should give them plenty of material for the next twenty-four hours. Tell them there will be no additional information until tomorrow. That will give us some time to gather data and craft a response."

The Press Secretary nods and leaves the office. As he exits, the Chief of Staff returns. "Mr. President, I received a message from Michelle Samaha."

The President stands. "What is the latest?"

"She said that they believe the family is still alive and have been moved to a container ship. The blood samples were negative to your family or the Agents."

"Oh thank God. What are the next steps?"

"Michelle said Mark Aldin and Ducky Duckworth are going to HELO into Libya where they believe the freighter is headed. Once the family is identified, Mark and Ducky will follow them to the safe house. After that we'll mount an operation to free them."

The President nods. "Ok, keep me appraised."

At that point the door opens and a young woman in a military uniform is led in. "Mr. President, this is Master Sergeant Davies." The President salutes.

"Thank you Master Sergeant. Tell me what you know about the assassination attempt."

"Yes sir." She told her story with as much detail as possible. The President listening intently, only interrupted occasionally. When she was finally silent, the President asks her to sit down.

"Can you remember anything more about the two men?"

The Master Sergeant closes her eyes. After a few seconds her eyes flew open. "Oh, when I was tied up in the back of the cab, one of the men said something like chin-aeharnun jidojaga gippehal geos-ibnida." She says haltingly.

Rik Thistle

The President turns to the Chief of Staff, "get a Korean translator on the phone." Randy Smith nods. He places a call and within a minute he has a CIA linguist on the line.

"Master Sergeant, would you please repeat the phrase?"

The Master Sergeant nods. "chin-aeharnun jidojaga gippehal geos-ibnida or something like that."

On the other end of the phone, there is a pause. Then a woman's voice says. "The dear leader will be pleased."

The President looks at his Chief of Staff. "Kim Jong-un is behind this. He is going to pay."

Chapter 54

Cyrrhenian Sea - August 20th

The Al Safat container ship is making good time and the Captain knows they will reach the target port within the next several hours. The paperwork he completed in Genoa shows his destination as Algeria, but he has been instructed by his passengers to dock at Tobruk, Libya. The Captain knows this will be unusual, but he can claim an engine issue and spend a day in port fixing the "problem". The amount of money given him more than makes up for a two day delay in his schedule.

Last night, the half moon container had its door open throughout the night cooling the passengers inside. The Captain does not want to know who is inside, the less he knows the better. Take the money and keep your mouth shut. That has served him well over the past twenty years.

In the container, Nimr is setting up his camera system. He wants to get a communication out to the White House to reassure them that the family is fine, but also to give them al-Qaeda's demands for their safe release. A large al-Qaeda flag has been hung on the back wall of the container. While the video camera is being set up, Nimr moves to sit in front of Clare Sweeney.

"You will read this in front of the camera. No deviations. I would also like your children to be sitting next to you to prove that you and your children are being treated well. We will start filming in ten minutes."

Clare looks the message over. "There is no way the U.S. government will pay you one Billion dollars and release twelve terrorists from GITMO."

Nimr stands. "Well that would be very unfortunate for you and your children. If the demands are not met, we will kill your friend first, then the two Secret Service Agents, then each of your children, and finally you. All will die on camera for the world to see."

After a ten minute break, Clare sits cross legged in front of the al-Qaeda flag. Oliver and Filip are on either side. They have been told to not say anything. Looking into the camera, Clare begins; "We have been treated well and all of us are in good health. To secure our release, al-Qaeda demands that the United States pay one Billion dollars with half in unmarked U.S. dollars and half in unmarked Euros."

Clare looks up from the page she is reading and takes a deep breath. "In addition, al-Qaeda demands that twelve of their brothers who have been unjustly imprisoned at GITMO be released immediately and sent to Somalia. If these demands are not met, one of the hostages will be killed each twelve hours on camera starting tomorrow at sunset."

The camera lights turn off along with the camera.

"Very good. We will transmit this as soon as we dock and will monitor the results." Says Nimr. He takes the thumb drive and downloads the video onto his laptop. After reviewing it several times, he is satisfied.

The ship will dock in several hours, and then the U.S. Government and the American President will understand that the game has changed.

Chapter 55

Los Angeles, California - August 20th

Colonel Park Kyung-Soo and Lieutenant Choi Hwan are on the run. They know that the United States government is looking for them. Kyung-Soo is limping badly. When the stupid bitch drove the truck through the fence, he was thrown down to the pavement and just missed being run over.

Lt. Choi is helping his commander along the street. He is looking for a car to steal and get out of the area. Staying locally is death. Suddenly he sees a woman outside a grocery store loading food into her SUV.

"Wait here."

Choi moves quickly across the parking lot and pulls his gun as he approaches the woman. He hits the woman across the back of the head and pushes her into the back of the SUV. He quickly closes the rear door and grabs her purse lying on the ground. Going through the purse he pulls out her wallet and keys.

Hopping into the front seat he starts the car and backs away heading for Kyung-Soo who is laying on the grass medium. Suddenly a man is pounding on the driver side window having seen Choi hitting the woman. Choi tries to accelerate but knows he has to stop for Major Park. He jams on his breaks and the man is thrown forward. Choi picks up his revolver and exits the car. The man stands and puts his hands up. Choi fires twice hitting the man in the chest and stomach. While the man goes down, Choi is back in the SUV driving towards his hurt friend.

After getting Park into the SUV, Choi speeds out of the parking lot. In his rearview mirror Choi can see a group of people around the man. Several of them on their cellular phones.

"We need to get to the safe house. I'll call our U.S. contact and tell him to meet us there." As Park pulls his cellular phone. "He will get us out of the country."

As Choi maneuvers through the choked streets of Los Angeles, he knows he is probably already being tracked. Weaving between streets, the SUV moves down a side street then comes to a halt. "We are just two blocks from the safe house. Can you walk?"

"Yes, just help getting me out of the car."

The two men leave the SUV and start down the alley. Overhead they hear the rotors of a helicopter circling. Choi looks up and shades his eyes. What he can see is a police helicopter hovering nearby. He knows they have probably been spotted. "Quickly, we need to get to the safe house."

As the men make their way through several backyards, Choi sees the safe house ahead. They stop beside a house trying to keep the house between them and the helicopter. Instead of running to the safe house, Choi uses his elbow to break the window of a side door. Reaching inside he unlocks the door and the men enter into a kitchen area.

Choi sits Park down at a table and starts a search of the house. As he enters the family room a large black man stands and yells. "What the hell, get out of my house!" Choi pulls his revolver from behind his back and shoots the man in the chest.

Suddenly behind him he hears a door being kicked in. "Federal Agents, hands up!"

Lt. Choi starts towards the front door just as it explodes inward. He raises his weapon but is immediately hit with two well placed shots.

Chapter 56

Genoa, Italy - August 20th

Kelly Campos has been up for more than twenty-four hours tracking the three freighters. At first light he has programmed a satellite to take high resolution photographs of each of the ships. Kelly has been reviewing each photograph and just noticed something strange.

He pulls up the photograph of the Al Safat freighter taken six hours ago. Kelly adjusts the zoom to focus on one particular container. He notices a half moon on the door, and then he sees what looks like holes in the container. "What the Hell?"

Looking through the other dozen photos of the ship, only one shows this container. "Damn."

He picks up his phone and calls Michelle Samaha.

"Boss, I got something very interesting in a photo of one of the ships. There are holes in one of the containers."

Michelle immediately leaves her office and comes down to Kelly Campos' SKIF.

As she enters, Kelly puts the photograph up on a large screen monitor. "I noticed that it looks like this container has holes all around the top and sides. I can't figure out why they would do this unless..."

Michelle picks up the conversation. "Unless they have human cargo in the container. Where is the ship now?"

Campos looks at the live feed. "Ah, that is interesting. In the last six hours they have adjusted their course." He pulls up a sheet of paper with the Genoa shipping logs. "The Al Safat was supposed to be heading for Algeria. But it is now just coming into the Tobruk, Libya harbor. Over night it made the correction and will be docking in several hours."

"Damn, I'll get a hold of Mark and Ducky and let them know. The ship isn't the East Dinamik but the Al Safat. We are lucky that the Al Safat choose Libya to put the hostages on shore. Mark and Ducky may be able to HELO nearby and get to the coast before the container is unloaded. Can you watch that specific container and track it?"

"I'll try. If there are clouds, that might obscure the satellite. But otherwise I can track it." He picks up a handful of M&Ms and pops them into his mouth.

Chapter 57

Los Angeles, California - August 20th

Park Kyung-Soo opens his eyes but can't see. This confuses him. He can hear some noises in the distance but they were indistinct to his ears. He tries to move his arms but they are immobile as are his legs. His breathing starts to come in short gasps. He wonders what is going on.

Suddenly he hears a soft female voice. "He is awake."

He can feel some movement on his left, then a male voice.

"What is your name?"

"Park Kyung-Soo"

"What is your rank?"

Kyung-Soo is unsure he has his voice. He clears his throat. "Colonel."

"Are you an agent of the Democratic People's Republic of Korea?"

Park wants to resist but for some reason his mind won't cooperate. "Yes."

"Was it your intention to bring down Air Force One and kill the President of the United States?"

Park suddenly realizes that he is being drugged. They are using a truth serum he thinks. But regardless, he seems not to be able to lie.

"Yes."

"Who is are your partners in this crime?"

"Lieutenant Choi Hwan and Walter Cartwright."

There is a pause as the interrogator notes the name. "Who is Walter Cartwright?"

"He is an American, a sub-contractor who got us the paperwork. He worked at the base. He is dead."

There is a pause in the questioning. Park is enjoying the silence while his body floats in space. He thinks about his daughter in Pyongyang. Why is she not in school?

"Are there other people involved?"

Park thinks back. There is someone but he doesn't know his name. "Not that I know."

"Are there any other assassination plots that you know of?"

"All of you will die."

"Who are you talking about?"

"The American people."

"What will happen to the American people?"

Park smiles internally. "You will suffer. Your country will suffer. Every American will suffer..."

He hears the voice telling someone to let him sleep and that they will try again in a couple of hours. Park smiles to himself. He was able to keep one secret despite the use of drugs on him. The dear leader will be pleased with him.

Chapter 58

Tobruk, Libya - August 20th

The occupants of the container feel the crane lift them into the air and begin to move them to the dock. It is a relief on one hand that the seasickness that overtook all of them would end. The issue now is that they are on land again and the clock will be ticking down on their lives.

The container is put directly on a truck and locked down. Everyone could hear the workmen shouting instructions in Arabic.

"No talking or I'll shoot the youngest." Says Nimr moving his gun in the general direction of Filip. Filip crosses his arms and stares defiantly at Nimr.

The group sits quietly while the straps are secured and the truck is started. As the truck moves out, a CIA satellite twenty-two miles up is watching. Kelly Campos received authorization to re-direct the satellite to watch the Al Safat container ship. He has been watching the ship dock, the half moon container was the only container offloaded. That was the final confirmation he needed.

Nimr knows that the journey to the safe house will take several hours. He passes out some of the food and the last of the water in the container. He had transmitted the video file to the American President last night using the ships Wi-Fi. Nimr realizes that the American government would not pay a Billion dollars even for the President's child and grandchildren. But when he executes the two Secret Service Agents, they will understand his commitment.

The ride is somewhat rough with the truck taking the highway to Tobruk, a moderately sized city of 120,000 people in Northeastern Libya.

The passengers are dozing as the truck slows and then stops. "Stay seated." Says Nimr. After several minutes the container is stifling hot. Suddenly the door of the container is opened. Nimr and the two guards point their guns at the opening. In walks Nimr's key aide smiling.

"Omar!" Nimr says standing. "The plan worked well. Thank you for your help."

Omar embraces Nimr. "Hamza sends his greetings."

Diane knows Arabic and catches the name Hamza. She looks at Clare and she gives her friend a slight nod.

Omar looks toward the group of seven huddled in the back of the container. "I have two SUVs to transport the prisoners. The safe house is fully stocked and secured. Everything is in place."

Nimr claps his hand on the shoulder of his aide. "Let's get going. The longer we are here, the more exposed we are."

Turning back to the Americans, "Get up and follow the guards. No talking."

Each of the zip tied hostages is led out into the bright daylight. The Sweeney family is placed in one SUV, the other three in the remaining SUV.

The convoy pulls out and drives several miles with small buildings and homes passing by.

Both Diane and Clare are looking around during the trip to try to get an indication of where they are. Diane has been trying to figure out how far a ship can travel in three days from Genoa, Italy. She believes based on the terrain that they are in Northern Africa. Probably Libya or maybe Algeria. Suddenly she sees a sign that points to the Tobruk Airport only 4 km away. It is in Arabic which she knows well. So they are in Tobruk. She mentally pulls up a map of the area. That would mean they are only two or three hours by car to the Egyptian border. If they could escape, that would be where they should head.

The convoy then turns into a walled compound with a large two story home and two outbuildings. The SUVs come to a stop kicking up a lot of dust.

The hostages are quickly hustled into the house and down into the basement. Guards are then deployed around the perimeter.

Once in the basement, the six are freed from their zip ties. Now the waiting begins to see the reaction of the President of the United States.

Chapter 59

Los Angeles, CA - August 21st

The President sits back after hearing the audio tape of the interviews with the two North Korean captives. His staff and the military Generals watch the President's face turn from anger to rage. "That fat little bastard tried to kill me, my staff and perhaps hundreds of people on the ground. That is a declaration of war." Everyone was quiet, letting the President vent. "We should have taken him out years ago." He says quietly. "God-dammed Bush and Obama, letting this asshole continue to get away with killing millions of his own people, building a nuclear arsenal, then trying to assassinate an American President?" The President sits back with his hands steepled over his chest. "It will end now. General I want you to put together two plans; one to individually assassinate Kim Jong-Un and two for a first strike attack to totally disable the North Korean military establishment. The probability of success and how quickly could they be implemented."

The General nods, and then says "Yes Mr. President."

The President looks around the room. "Nobody and I mean nobody in this room is to discuss this topic with anyone else. Am I clear?"

Everyone says, "Yes Sir."

"OK, clear the room except for Randy."

As everyone shuffles out, the President stands. "I want to get back to the White House as soon as possible. Also do you have any additional information on Clare and the boys?"

The Chief of Staff shakes his head. "I haven't had a chance to contact Michelle Samaha since the crash."

The President nods. "Sorry, I know everyone is pretty shaken up, but I want to talk with her now."

"I have a secure phone set up in a conference room, we could call Michelle and get an update."

"Ok, set it up. I need to know what is going on there."

A few minutes later the President enters the conference room and the international secure call is placed. After just one ring, Michelle Samaha answers.

"Mr. President. We are happy to hear that you were not injured in the assassination attempt. Is it related to al-Qaeda?"

The President responds, "I don't think so, we believe it was directed by North Korea."

Michelle whistles. "Wow, I am surprised they have the sophistication to pull off something like this."

"Well, we have proof they did. Maybe they had help, but at this point we are holding North Korean and their leader totally responsible. So, what is the latest information on Clare and the boys?"

Michelle pauses, "Well, Mr. President we believe the hostages were transferred to a shipping container in Genoa and the ship sailed to Tobruk, Libya. We will have Mark Aldin and Ducky Duckworth on the ground in Tobruk shortly tracking the container."

"How do you know they are in the container?" Asks the President.

"Our analyst spotted air holes drilled into a container plus the ship was scheduled to travel to Algeria, but twelve hours ago the ship altered its course and docked in Tobruk. The target container was the only one unloaded. Since the ship was not scheduled to go to Tobruk, so why was one container unloaded?"

"Excellent detective work, Michelle."

"Thank you Sir. But at this point we only have unverified evidence that Clare, the boys, Diane and Secret Service agents are in the container. But we believe they were. We should have more definitive answers in two or three hours."

"Also, we received a video message from al-Qaeda."

The President's brows rise. "Let's see it."

The CIA black site head nods to her analyst. Suddenly the

screen is filled with an image of Clare Sweeney and her two children.

The President sits down with tears in his eyes. This is the first time he has seen his grandchildren since they were abducted. He sees Clare looking into the camera. She begins with a deep breath.

"Al-Qaeda wanted you to see that your daughter and grandsons are being treated well and no harm has come to them. In order for this to continue, they have three demands; first, the U.S. government will release twelve brothers who were unjustly imprisoned at Guantanamo Bay, Cuba. Those names are listed at the end of this email. If they are not all released within the next forty-eight hours, one of the hostages will be shot on camera. Then another every twelve hours until we end with your daughter." With this, Clare's voice catches as she looks over from her note at her two children. Then after a couple of seconds, she continues. "Additionally, the U.S. government will drop one Billion dollars to a predetermined latitude and longitude that will be transmitted to you when you have communicated that half U.S. unmarked dollars and half in unmarked Euros are ready. Third, if any rescue attempt be made. All of the hostages will be executed. You have forty-eight hours."

With that the video stops. The President had been leaning forward, now he sits back. "Who are the twelve terrorists?"

Michelle reads off the list of names.

The President looks at Randy Smith. He shrugs his shoulders. "Ok, figure out who these people are and the level of danger they pose. Contact the Treasury Department to come up with a plan."

"Mr. President, we are working on trying to trace the transmission of the video file. If we can do that we'll have a good idea of the general area of the hostages. "Says Michelle Samaha. "But we believe all of the hostages are in the Tobruk. Another thing we noticed is that the camera seemed to be tilting slightly back and forth. We believe this is because the video was shot on a ship. This confirms our belief that they are in a container on a freighter."

"Ok, thanks Michelle. Keep me updated."

With that the President hangs up the phone and sits back. "I want to get my daughter and grandchildren back safely and kill all those bastards." He says to himself.

Chapter 60

Tobruk, Libya - August 21st

The three SUVs roll into the town just outside Tobruk, just at sunset, their tires sending up blooms of dust as they pull into a large compound. Surrounded by a ten foot wall, the two story house was unremarkable except for the size of the compound. Located in an upper class section of the city where military officials, business owners and professionals have build houses. An al-Qaeda operative bought the house in 2014. Since then, several men and families have been housed there, usually for a brief time, before moving on.

As the SUVs come to a stop, several armed men close the gates of the compound and open the doors. Nimr hops out and embraces his number two man; Muhammad Abbar.

"My friend, how was your trip?"

Muhammad smiles, "Uneventful. No issues at all. I was able to take a flight from Rome to Tunis, then a bus to Tobruk. I am sure I was not followed."

"Excellent. I have transmitted the demands to the President and we will know in forty-eight hours if they are serious. If they do not make progress towards our demands, then I shall begin killing the hostages. I am confident our brothers will be released and al-Qaeda will have one Billion dollars to fund our work."

Muhammad smiles. "I will supervise the perimeter security. We also have a dozen people in and around the city who are looking for anything out of the ordinary and will contact me."

Nimr nods. "We must be weary of the U.S. military trying to free the hostages. I underestimated them once; I will not do that again. Make sure the SUVs are out of the compound as soon as possible. I don't want a spy satellite seeing them here."

"I will tell the drivers to leave immediately after the hostages are in the house."

Nimr nods to one of the guards in the SUV and each hostage is lowered to the ground. Each has a hood put over their head and their hands are zip tied. After the six are unloaded, they are lead single file into the house.

After they are led to the basement, the hoods and the zip ties are removed. As the heavy wooden door is closed and locked, the secret service agents begin a search of the basement. Clare pulls her boys to her and makes sure each are doing ok.

"Oliver and Filip, how are you guys doing?"

The boys sitting next to their mom nod. "Mommy when can we go home?" Says Filip.

"I don't know honey. But I do know that Poppy is looking for us and he will be able to rescue us. We just need to be strong. Ok?"

Both boys nod and Clare hugs both of them.

The door opens and everyone looks up. Nimr enters along with two guards. One has his AK-47 at the ready, the other is carrying a tray of bread, butter and some fruit. He puts the food onto a table in a corner and retreats back to the door.

Nimr looks around the room. There are no windows and a dirt floor. Six small rugs are thrown into the room. "Get some sleep, tomorrow we will do hopefully the last video. Of course if your father does not meet our demands, I will be forced to kill one of you every twelve hours. I pray to Allah that I will not have to do that, but I will."

With that, Nimr turns and leaves the basement. The door is closed and locked.

"Mommy, are we going to die? Asked Oliver.

"No honey, he is just trying to scare us. Don't worry." Clare says looking at Diane.

Agent Bale comes over to Diane and Clare. "I think we should try to dig a tunnel under the wall. Most Middle Eastern houses do not have a foundation. I think we could dig under this wall and perhaps be able to get out. The issue will be the dirt we excavate. Where can we put it?"

Everyone sits for several minutes thinking. Suddenly, Clare says, "What about each time we are taken to the bathroom, we empty our pockets along the way or in the bathroom?"

Diane nods. "The problem is that if they see the dirt in the bathroom they will know what we are doing. With a dirt floor here, it will be fairly easily to spread the new dirt around."

Everyone agrees. It will take a while, but it seems to be doable.

"The other issue is a digging tool." Says Agent Bale. "We can use our hands, but also maybe our bowls."

"Ok, I'll start the process." Moving to the opposite wall. The Agent says, "I think this wall faces the back of the house." With that, Agent Bale gets on his knees and begins to dig with his bowl at the base of the wall. The dirt is hard, but after about ten minutes he is starting to make real progress. With each bowl of dirt, everyone takes turns spreading the dirt throughout the room. He pulls his rug over and covers the hole when the door is unlocked and two guards enter.

"You each will be able to go to the bathroom, one at a time."

Clare rises. "Ok, I'll go first but I want to take my boys with me." The terrorist looks at this partner. "Ok but only one boy at a time, and each boy must wear the hood." Clare nods in agreement. Agent Bale is sitting against the far wall on his rug. He is hiding the hole his has dug.

One of the terrorist looks around checking on each hostage. Satisfied he backs out and closes the door while Clare and one of the boys are led upstairs to the bathroom.

Chapter 61

Washington D.C. - August 21st

The President has returned from Los Angeles to Washington DC amid the chaos of the assassination attempt. The mainstream press is going crazy. As the President departs Marine One with the first lady, the press shouts questions. A grim faced President gives a short wave and ignores the questions while continuing to walk into the White House.

As the President enters the Oval Office, he turns to his Secretary of Defense. "I want a Security Council meeting as soon as possible."

"Yes, sir. What are the topics?"

The President turns suddenly. "God Damn it. I want to know about my daughter and grandkids and I want to know what our options are to take out Kim Jung-Un."

The Secretary of Defense is caught off guard. "Take out Kim Jung-Un?"

The President glares. "Damn right. That fucker tried to kill me and my staff. He is a crazed dog; we have to put him down. We let this lunatic and his father develop nuclear weapons over the past twenty years. Not one President was willing to stand up to his guy. That stops now. I want several options to stop him. Is that understood?"

"Yes sir." The Secretary of Defense turns and strides from the room.

The President turns and faces his CIA Director and Chief of Staff. "What's the latest on Clare and the boys?"

The CIA Director refers to his notes. "We believe with 96% accuracy that they were put in a shipping container and loaded onto a ship at Genoa, Italy. We were able to identify the container and track it to Tobruk, Libya. At that point, the container was loaded onto a truck, and then hostages were taken to a compound on the outskirts of the city."

The President nods and leans against the Resolute Desk. "What is the plan?"

The CIA Director says, "Michelle Samaha has two operatives on the ground tracking the container. They have eyes on the house right now. But there are only two of them. We didn't feel comfortable sending in a large group. The two there are Mark Aldin and Ducky Duckworth?"

"Yes sir."

"Ok, they sent us their demands. Of course we won't free those terrorists in GITMO or give them a Billion dollars, but we need to play for as much time as possible." The President says. "How much time do we have?"

The CIA Director frowns. "Probably twenty-four hours, maybe less until they start killing the hostages. They will want to see some progress."

The President turns to Randy Smith. "Get the Secretary of the Treasury in here."

"Yes sir." The Chief of Staff turns and pulls his cellular phone and makes several calls.

"What I want to see is if we have half a billion of counterfeit dollars that we could send them, see if the Brits have half a billion in counterfeit Euros or Pounds."

The CIA chief looks surprised. "Counterfeit?"

"Sure, I doubt the al-Qaeda people on the ground in Afghanistan or wherever they want us to drop the payment will be able to easily determine if the money is real or not. At least it will buy us some time."

The CIA Director nods. "I like it. But we'll have to raid the compound shortly after the money is delivered in case they have someone who could spot a counterfeit bill. The other issue is finding that much fake money."

The President sits on the couch. "Let's just start on this track. We only have twenty-four hours to let them know we are cooperating."

An hour later the Secretary of Treasury, Cosette Alexa comes into the Oval Office. "Good morning Mr. President." She stands patiently as the President rises to greet her.

"Good morning Coco. Good to see you again. You are doing a great job over at Treasury. The economy is humming and you are a big part of that."

"Thank you sir. Your economic initiatives have created the environment for the American economy to accelerate. What can I do for you?"

The President invites the Secretary to sit on the couch. "Coco, I have known you for over twenty years. We both have run companies and you know me. I am going to ask you to do something that you may not agree to, but this is very important both to the U.S. Government and also to me personally."

The Secretary of Treasury leans forward. "Of course Mr. President. What do you want me to do?"

"What I am going to tell you is highly classified, you are not to share this with anyone else, understood?"

"Of course Mr. President."

The President sits back and takes a sip of coffee. "One week ago my daughter and two of my grandsons along with a State Department person and two Secret Service personnel were kidnapped in Italy by al-Qaeda."

Coco sits back, shock on her face.

"They have asked for two items to facilitate their release. One would involve your department. They are asking for one

Billion dollars, half in U.S. dollars and half in Euros."

"Holy Moly" says the Secretary.

"I have no intention to give them half a Billion dollars, but I would like to send them some counterfeit dollars. How many counterfeit dollars do we have?"

The Secretary of Treasury considers the question. "Well, not sure we have half a Billion counterfeit dollars, but we could print some. How much time do we have?"

"Excellent. We probably have twenty-four hours but we'll have to fly the money to Afghanistan for the drop. What about Euros?"

Coco thinks for a few seconds. "Twenty-four hours? I could place some calls to our EU buddies and see what they might have."

"Ok, get on it and get back to Randy as soon as you have a handle on this issue. Lives are on the line and we need to move quickly."

The Secretary stands. "Yes sir, I'll get back to Randy by the end of the day."

They shake hands and she exits the Oval Office. Then the President turns back to his Chief of Staff. "Find out about the Gitmo situation and let's figure out how to make it look like we are moving those twelve."

"Yes sir."

"Finally I want to meet with the National Security Council this afternoon to figure out how to take Kim Jong-Un out."

Chapter 62

Tobruk, Libya - August 21st

Mark Aldin and Ducky Duckworth are dressed in their Arab clothes to blend into the environment. Both are wearing a loose cotton shirt over dark trousers, they have a dark cloak over their shoulders and are wearing a flat brimless cap. Under their Arab clothes they have two weapons; a Strider knife and an H&K 9mm pistol.

They are separately moving slowly through a market that is within a block of the target compound. Mark stops at a fruit stand that has an unobstructed view of the house. While he is buying a bag of dates, he watches the front gate.

Ducky is on the other side of the street just sitting down at an espresso café. He orders a frothy macchiato and opens a Libyan paper. Mark strolls over and joins him. In Arabic he says, "Hello old friend how is your day?"

Ducky smiles and offers Mark a seat. "Fine my friend. Please have a seat."

Mark orders a coffee and offers Ducky some of the dates he just bought. Both men sit covertly watching the compound. In the Libyan culture somewhat shaped by the Italian occupation of its colonial past, it is customary for business to be conducted over coffee in a café for hours. Mark and Ducky know they can sit for several hours without drawing any notice. Sipping coffee they both watch the compound and all the people walking around the market. Several people seem to be watching them, but then they move on. Mark is satisfied that he can pass as an Arab. He is less confident Ducky can. Both have the language skills, but Ducky's light brown hair might be problematic if his keffiyeh, the head covering, that is common in Libya was removed.

Last night the drone made a pass over the house and was able to pick up only five heat signatures. If the six hostages are in a shielded room or if the house has a basement, then the drone would not pick them up on the thermal camera. Mark knows that but it would have been good to confirm that they are there.

Mark finishes his coffee and puts down several Libyan Dinars. "We should get back." He says in Arabic. Both men rise and walk by the compound looking for any other way in. There isn't.

After they are several blocks away, Mark says quietly. "I think we'll need six other operators, gear to breech the wall and small charge to blow the door."

Ducky nods. "What about the exit plan?"

"Well, we are less than three hours by car to the Egyptian border. If we hit at night, we might catch the Libyan police by surprise and by the time they figure out what happened, hopefully we will be in Egypt."

"We could have six operators from Fort Campbell HELO in within forty-eight hours. If the President can delay, then we can have everyone here and run through several scenarios before the raid."

Mark nods. "Ok, set it in motion. I have the feeling we are running out of time."

Chapter 63

Washington D.C. - August 21st

The National Security Council has gathered in the situation room in the basement of the West Wing at the invitation of the President. It is one of the most secure facilities in the world. Sitting around an oblong table is the Vice President, the Secretary of State, the Secretary of Defense, the Chairman of the Joint Chiefs, the Director of National Intelligence, the Attorney General, the Director of the CIA, the White House Chief of Staff and Michelle Samaha. Everyone knows Michelle or has heard of her. They are all wondering why she is in the meeting but if the President invited her, they stay silent.

Suddenly the door opens and the President of the United States rushes in. Everyone sitting moves to their feet and stand. "Please have a seat. I have called you all here for one reason. As you all know, an assassination attempt on me and many of my top staff was made by North Korea. Cam, would you give us a summary of your investigation?"

Cameron Anderson is the Director of the CIA and one of the most respected spooks in the service. "We have captured one of the North Korean perpetrators and he was questioned using

Congressional approved practices." He says looking toward the Attorney General. "During the questioning, he admitted their roles stealing a HEL system and the attempted assassination. They fired the HEL system three times. The first shot disabled the right engine. The second shot shutdown the left engine. Air Force One then went into a glide trying to reach LAX. The final shot hit the cockpit windshield and partially destroyed it, killing the co-pilot. Fortunately the pilot was able to bring the 747 down in a controlled crash and all of the passengers including POTUS was able to walk away."

Everyone is on the edge of their seats. Some had heard a few details, but now they were getting a complete briefing.

Continuing, the Director of the CIA says. "Several hours later the local police and the Secret Service captured one North Korean national and killed the other. We flew in a CIA interrogator. She was able to get the man admit that they stole the HEL system with the intention of assassination of the President of the United States. He admitted they were agents of the North Korean government. We are convinced that Kim Jong-Un ordered the attempt."

Cindy Decker, the Secretary of State spoke up. "Why would they try to kill the President? What advantage would that give North Korea?"

Andy Cobb, the Director of National Intelligence responds. "Our sanctions have had a significant affect on the Hermit Kingdom, also China has been doing its part to limit the amount of oil they sell North Korea. We do not believe that China was involved in the planning or even knew in advance about the assassination attempt. I believe it is strictly designed to take our eyes off their nuclear capabilities. I received a new report yesterday that our analysts believe that North Korea has 30 plus nuclear missiles all are capable to hit North America."

There is a murmur among the attendees.

The President leans back. "So if they assassinate me, they feel the U.S. government would be in disarray for weeks or months, then what?"

Director Cobb stands. "We believe they are at their breaking point. Their population is starving. Their military is disgruntled. China is reining them in. I think Kim Jong-Un has made the decision to strike first. China would love to see a nuclear exchange. They could sit back and watch the carnage."

With that comment, most of the National Security Council members start talking all at once. Some yelling and others talking quietly one on one. Finally the President has enough.

"People, people. Please quiet down. A nation state has tried to assassinate a sitting U.S. President. This can not be allowed to stand. I have asked the CIA to give me several options to end this stalemate once and for all. Cam, would you give us your options?"

Cam Anderson stands. "Mr. President, there are two options. First is to send in special operators to set up an assassination. There are multiple problems with this option. Getting the people in country is doable. SEALS could land on the coast, and then using one of our North Korean contacts to take them to Pyongyang. There are many check points that they would have to pass through. It would be tough. The SEALs could land in Namp'o about 35 miles from Pyongyang, and make their way to the Capital at night. The main issue is that Kim Jung-Un does not announce where he will be when he might be most vulnerable. We don't have any agents that high in their organization."

The Director takes a sip of water. "The second option is a preemptive strike of Kim Jung-Un and their nuclear weapons."

There is stunned silence.

The President speaks first. "What is your opinion on the likelihood of success?"

"The first option is estimated at 20-25% chance of success. Getting the Special Operators out of North Korea would be extremely tough after an assassination or an attempt of Kim. Plus there is no guarantee that his successor would be any better.

The second option is believed to be 80-90% chance of success. We know where all of their nuclear sites are and where Kim might be."

The Attorney General Susanna Brockway stands. "Mr. President, the assassination of Kim Jung-Un might not be legal. Executive Order 12333 prohibits the act of state-sponsored assassination."

Andy Cobb stands. "HR 19 titled the Terrorist Elimination Act of 2001 allows for the military to kill terrorists. I believe all of us understand that Kim Jung-Un is a terrorist and leads a terrorist nation."

The President stands and both Brockway and Cobb sit. "The issue with North Korea has been festering for the past twenty years. Multiple Presidents have passed on this responsibility; both Republicans and Democrats. That ends now. Kim Jung-Un ordered my assassination." The President's voice rising. "Except for the skill and experience by the Air Force One pilot, I and many of my staff would be dead!" The President slams his fist to the table. "This will not stand."

Turning to General Seibert. "General I want to go to DEFCOM 2. I want a plan on my desk tomorrow for the elimination of the North Korean nuclear theat."

Suddenly the room erupts into verbal chaos. About half of the members disagree with the President's order, the other half agreeing with the President.

The President stands and with the Vice President and his Chief of Staff, they leave the room entering the elevator to take them to the West Wing.

"Mr. President, are you sure you want to risk a war with China over this action?"

"The Chinese will watch and won't intervene. The real damage will be to South Korea if we don't take out their artillery and conventional missiles at the same time. The nuclear sites will be reasonably easy. We will have to alert the South Korean government just before we strike."

The Chief of Staff looks over at the Vice President, and then says. "Mr. President, to declare war on North Korea we will need approval by Congress."

"Nonsense, The United States, South Korea are still technically at war with North Korea. We are responding to an Act of War by the North Koreans. As soon as we alert Congress, it will be on the front page of the New York Times the next day! I want this top secret. No leaks. I want Kim Jung-Un dead."

Chapter 64

Tobruk, Libya - August 21st

Nimr is on a SAT phone talking with one of his top Lieutenants located in Germany about his plan. "We have to set up a direct communications link with the target (meaning the President of the United States of America). I want you to listen to his tone, measure what he says and try to determine if he is being honest or trying to trick us."

Khalid al-Habi is excited to play a key part in the plan to humiliate and humble the U.S. "Yes, my leader. I will be happy to be the intermediary."

Nimr continues. "Your education in the United States and command of the English language will allow us to determine their honesty."

"What are the terms?"

"We are demanding that twelve of our brothers are released, I will send you their names shortly. You should know two or three of them personally. Secondly; we are demanding one Billion in either dollars or Euros to be dropped to a Latitude and Longitude that we will give to them just one hour before the scheduled delivery. We will send the location to you via the dark web by tomorrow."

"Yes leader. I will await your information, and then contact the White House."

Nimr sits quietly for several seconds. "You will be in great danger. I am sure that the Americans will try to trace your call back to you. If they do trace the call back to you, they will send their military. You can not be captured. I expect you to kill yourself if they find you."

Khalid al-Habi replies immediately. "Yes leader, if I am discovered I will kill myself gladly for the cause."

"Go with Allah. Contact me with any updates."

Nimr hangs up and smiles. The President of the United States will now be contacted and set the clock countdown to a blackmail payoff to al-Qaeda or the killing of one of the hostages.

Khalid al-Habi uses his personal computer to route a message through the Dark Web using a TOR plug-in to maintain an anonymity network and having his message rerouted and masked through a dozen servers located throughout the world. Khalid knew everything there was to know about the Dark Web. He graduated with honors from the University of California, Berkeley with a degree in Computer Science.

He dials up the computer routing information given by the White House to communicate with the President. He knows the

FBI, CIA, NSA will all be monitoring the call, but he is confident that if he keeps the call short they will not be able to trace it to him.

The phone rings then is immediately picked up.

"This is Special Agent Jones, who are you?"

"This is one of the al-Qaeda warriors who are holding the President's daughter, two grandchildren, a State Department employee and two Secret Service agents. You received our video and now we expect our twelve brothers to be released publically tomorrow. Second we will call you tomorrow at this time and give you a time for the drop of one Billion dollars or Euros or a combination today at 1600 hours Afghan time. One hour prior to that time frame we will send you the Longitude and Latitude for the drop."

The Special Agent on the other end says, "Please stand by for the President's Chief of Staff. He will have to communicate your demands to the President."

"We will not be trifled with! I want to speak with the President now or the consequences will be death to his family. You have our demands, if they are not met then one hostage will be killed on live video and streamed to the world."

The President, the Chief of Staff, the Secretary of State, the CIA chief, the NSA director are in the room, Michelle is on another line listening to the exchange. The President turns to the NSA director. "Damn, will you be able to trace the call?"

"We will try, but I am sure he is using multiple servers, try to keep him on the line as long as you can."

The President hit his call button, "This is President Baker. We are pulling together the money but getting a Billion dollars is not easy. It might take us another day or two to get all of it on pallets for shipment. As for the twelve prisoners at GITMO, we are processing them now and are planning to have them on a plane by tomorrow. However, I want proof of life of all the people you are holding before your prisoners are released."

There is a long pause. "The Billion dollars or Euros must be dropped in Afghanistan by tomorrow night at 1900 Afghan time. We will send you proof of life tomorrow morning." With that, the line goes dead.

The President heavily sits in his chair. "Ok, the clock is counting down. I heard from Treasury and they have approximately $250 million in counterfeit dollars. The Brits have about $100 million in counterfeit Euros. The bills are wrapped up and on a plane to Afghanistan as we speak. Ok, 1900 Afghan time, what time is that?"

The CIA Chief looks at his notes. "Kabul is approximately 9 ½ hours ahead of Washington DC. So 1900 hours would be around 7 pm their time, 10 am our time tomorrow."

The President looks at Michelle. "When will the SEALs be on the ground in Tobruk?"

Michelle replies over her phone. "Not until four hours after the drop. We can't get them there any quicker."

The CIA Director weighs in. "Once the drop happens, it will take them an hour to just load the pallets and transport them away from the drop zone. We will be able to track their trucks back to their hideouts. Then what we do is based on when we can rescue the hostages."

Michelle chimes in. "We do have Mark Alden and Ducky Duckworth on site. I could speak with them to see what ideas they might have?"

The President nods. "OK, alert the Air Force to drop the bills at the site at the correct time. We'll also make a show of transferring the twelve prisoners. Make sure the press picks up the news. That should delay them enough for the SEALs to get on the ground and we can conduct a raid on the site."

"Yes sir." Says the Joint Chief of Staff.

"Michelle, inform Mark and Ducky of the timeline and to try to keep the target under surveillance if they can. Report any changes."

"Yes Mr. President." Michelle replies.

"Ok, that is all for tonight. Keep this strictly need to know."

All members of the assembled staff nod and head off to implement their assigned roles in the coming show for the al-Qaeda terrorists.

Chapter 65

Black Site Italy - August 21st

Michelle Samaha returns to her office and summons her top staff and tells them the plan to fool the terrorists and rescue the hostages.

"The only issues are time and manpower." Says Jonathan Bardsley. "We have to convince the terrorists that we are acting on their requests to delay them from killing any of the hostages, then getting the SEALs on the ground and mounting an attack. Not sure we have either enough time or manpower to make this happen."

Kelly Campos speaks up, and everyone turns towards him. "I received the NSA data and transcripts of the phone call. I was able to trace the call to a six square mile area in Southern Germany. It's a town called Passau. It's about 100 miles from Munich and on the border of the Czech Republic and Austria. With a few more hours of computer time to crunch some analytics I should be able to narrow it down to blocks or maybe even houses."

Michelle stands. "Ok, keep up the good work. I'll contact Mark and Ducky and see what they know at this point and let's all get back together in three hours, ok?"

Everyone else stands and files out of the office. "Jonathan, wait a moment."

"Sure boss."

"Contact the Czech Special Forces and ask if they would be willing to conduct a mission in Germany. I need to know we have a reliable partner in the event the Germans are unwilling to do it."

Jonathan nods. "But why wouldn't the Germans want to take out a terrorist?"

Michelle sits suddenly the lack of sleep hits her. "Since they took in a million or so Syrian refugees, they are very sensitive about operations like this, targeting Middle Eastern peoples in their country. We may have to use the Czechs. They are one of our most trusted allies. Let them know we might have an operation in eight or nine hours, that we would have several senior special operators alongside them to lead the raid of a known terrorist. That is all they need to know at this point."

"Ok, I'll get right on it."

Michelle grabs some black coffee and heads back to her office. She picks up her secure SAT phone and dials the number for Mark and Ducky.

One the second buzz, Mark answers. "Yeah."

"Mark, this is Michelle. We are moving about $250 Billion fake dollars and Euros to Afghanistan and will make a drop about nine or ten hours from now. Secondly, twelve al-Qaeda prisons from GITMO are going to be transferred tomorrow morning. Several trusted news contacts will be alerted and will report on the transfer to make sure the news gets out."

Mark lets out a long breath. "Ok, it will take the al-Qaeda guys on the ground several hours to just transport that much money to somewhere they think is safe. I would bet they will have a dozen trucks waiting, then divide the loot up into maybe three or four parts, then have all of the trucks drive away at the same time to try to confuse any drones or satellites watching."

"Yes, I concur with your assessment."

"When are the SEALs due to HELO in?"

"That's the bad news. We've had terrible weather over Little Creek, Virginia and SEAL team 2 was delayed taking off. They won't be arriving until 2200 hours."

Mark swears. "Damn, that's three hours after the drop. It's possible by then they could learn the money is fake and start killing the hostages."

"Yeah, we have to come up with an alternative plan. Kelly is zeroing in on the German contact who has been the go between. We should be able to have more definitive information in a few hours."

Ducky is on the call too and chimes in. "What if we create a diversion, maybe an hour after the drop? Something that would create some chaos and delay their plan."

Michelle thinks about it for a few seconds. "What did you have in mind?"

"Well, there is a mosque just a block from the target. If we set a fire there, that would create all kinds of activity which we could use as cover to move around and get in close for an assault."

"I like it. The more chaos the better. Develop a plan and let's talk again in two hours. Good luck."

Just before Michelle hangs up she says, "Mark, we intercepted a communication from Hamza bin Ladin to someone he calls the Black Widow. Would you have any idea who that might be?"

Mark frowns into the phone. "Not at this point. But it might be Nimr Yazdi. Can you run the Black Widow name through the CIA database and see if that handle was used before by him or any of the al-Qaeda leadership? "

Michelle replies, "Sure, I'll let you know if we find anything."

Mark hangs up and turns to Ducky. "I think we have a big problem."

Chapter 66

Tobruk, Libya - August 21st

Clare is hugging both her boys knowing the clock is ticking down to their potential death. The Secret Service agents have been digging continually for the past six hours. The hole they have dug is about two feet across and four feet down. The going is slow using just their food bowls and they have made good progress, but they know they are running out of time.

"How is it going?" Asks Diane.

"We think the foundation of the building is probably four to six feet deep. We should be able to get under the foundation sometime tonight, and then maybe tunnel out by tomorrow night."

Clare looks up. "That will probably be too late."

Both agents look at each other, and then redouble their efforts. Suddenly Agent Lee lets out a muted shout. "We are under the foundation!"

Diane moves over and peers over the agents' shoulders. "Can I help?"

"Move that pile of dirt and spread it around. Dinner will be coming within an hour and we don't want the terrorists to see fresh dirt."

Diane grabs her bowl and scoops up a large pile of dirt and spreads it around the corners of the room.

After an hour, the Agents sit down and cover the hole with one of the rugs. They are sweating and trying to control their breathing when the outer door opens. One of the terrorist enters with an AK-47 at the ready. Nimr walks behind him holding a tray with bread, cheese and a pot of tea.

"Here is some food. We communicated with your father and they are complying with our demands. If they do not meet the timeframe, then we will be forced to kill one of you during a streamed video. If they meet our demands, then all of you will be released unharmed. We pray to Allah that will be so."

Nimr looks around the room. Only one light is on creating shadows throughout the room concealing the prayer rug and the hole underneath.

Clare watches his eyes as he looks around. She decides she should try to distract him. "Do you want me to do another video? Or have my sons talk directly to their Grandfather?"

Nimr turns towards her and smiles. "That is not necessary yet Clare. If your father does not meet our demands, there will be an opportunity for you to speak, but unfortunately with a dead body before you. Eat and drink and it should all be over by tomorrow morning."

With that Nimr and the guard leave the room. The hostages hear the door being locked.

"Eat something and drink the tea. We have to try to get the tunnel dug within the next twelve hours." Says Clare.

Everyone eats some of the bread and they all share the tea.

Agents Lee and Bale eat quickly and then resume their digging. Agent Bale stops and turns to Clare. "In order for us to dig out under the building, we'll have to significantly widen the hole, otherwise we can't get down there to dig upwards."

Clare stands and comes over near the hole. "What about Oliver going down there and digging and handing the dirt up for us to distribute. Then we can keep the hole that size. If it gets any wider, the rug won't cover it."

The Agents look at each other. "Ok, we can give it a go. They won't check on us for another few hours so we can see how far up he can dig. The only issue is a cave in. It might trap him before we could pull him out."

Clare looks at Oliver. "Want to give it a try?"

Oliver nods. "Ok, give me the bowl and I'll dig as much as I can."

Filip comes over to the hole. "I can dig too!"

Clare smiles. "Of course, we'll all take a turn."

With that Oliver drops into the hole and begins to dig under the foundation. Digging bowl by bowl down and out it is hard work and takes longer than they thought. After half an hour, Filip takes over for his older brother and continues their escape tunnel.

Agent Bale motions Clare over to the opposite side of the room and lowers his voice. "The issue will be that the hole will not be large enough for an adult to crawl through. It would have to be about twice the size to allow us to wiggle under and up. What might have to happen is that the boys go with you and Diane. Agent Lee and I can stay behind to try to disarm the guard and shoot our way out."

Diane thinks about the situation. "We'll just have to widen the hole. We are not leaving anyone behind."

The Agent nods grim faced. "Ok, but if they have to kill one of us, I want it to be me. Then after they do the video, all of you need to get out regardless of the time. Get a vehicle as soon as you can so you can hide and force the driver to take you to the Egyptian border. Agent Lee will take care of you and your boys."

Clare smiles. "I just hope that the Calvary comes soon."

Chapter 67

Washington D.C. - August 21st

The President is sitting in the Oval office contemplating the information just given him by the Director of National Intelligence. It is devastating data, it confirms their worst fears.

"Are we 100% sure?" The President asks.

"Yes sir, we have checked, double checked and triple checked each source. Kim Jong-Un ordered your assassination; put the people in place to carry it out and then tried to erase his tracks."

"Damn, I can't believe the gall of that little fucker. Plus he has nuclear weapons that threaten the United States and most of Asia."

The DNI shifts from one foot to another and looks down at his notes. "Additionally, the NSA detected that they are moving multiple nuclear tipped missiles on mobile platforms into firing position."

"Do you think he is planning a pre-emptive strike?"

"Hard to say at this point, but he knows that his assassination plot was not successful and he is probably concerned that it will lead back to him and about our response."

The President stands and starts to pace about the Oval office hands clasped behind his back. The DNI stands silently watching the Command-In-Chief weighing his options. After several minutes, President William Baker makes up his mind. Andy Cobb looks into the eyes of the President.

"Andy, this threat to world peace can not be allowed to continue. If I do nothing and he launches one or more of those missiles, I could not live with myself if Seattle, Portland, San Francisco or Los Angeles were destroyed."

The DNI stays silent knowing the President is talking through his arguments.

"Taking out this madman should be one of the top national security priorities. A surgical strike seems out of the question. Low chance of success, plus it will probably be a suicide mission. We can't do nothing, so the only option is a first strike."

Andy Cobb knew this was where the President was heading, but hearing it sends a shiver down his spine. Destroying another country would set off a wave to consequences not only to the United States but to South Korea, Japan and the world. Millions would die, not only in North Korea for sure, but also potentially in the U.S. If Kim could get off a few of his nuclear tipped missiles before the first assault could destroy them, then several U.S. cities could be incinerated.

Randy Smith, the Chief of Staff, has been sitting quietly on one of the couches watching the exchange. "Randy, pull together the Joint Chiefs to the PEOC (President's Emergency Operations Center) in two hours. I want a full briefing on our plan to take out Kim and all of his military capability."

Smith stands. "Yes sir." And quickly leaves the room.

Andy Cobb comes to stand next to the President. He has known him for over twenty years and knows the pressures that he is under. "Mr. President, I would urge caution. This is a world changing decision."

The President is looking out the side door at the Rose Garden. "I know, but someone has to stop this monster. You know what would happen if he had twenty or thirty intercontinental nuclear missiles? He could hold the U.S. hostage, he could take out all of the major U.S. cities for God's sake. Our country, our culture, our people could be wiped out. I can't allow that. I am not going to be the President that kicked the can down the road like Obama and Bush."

The DNI nods and places his hand on the President's shoulder. "I understand Mr. President. If we do this, let's make sure we do it right."

Chapter 68

Tobruk, Libya - August 21st

Mark and Ducky are sitting again at the café one block from the compound where the hostages are being held. They are watching the coming and going of several people through the morning. Unfortunately the SEAL HELO won't happen for another twelve hours and it might be too late. This evening the C140 plane will drop two pallets of money to al-Qaeda. At that point, the clock will be counting down until they realize that either the money is counterfeit or not the right amount, and that would trigger the death of one or more of the hostages.

Mark gets up. "I'm going on a little stroll. Keep an eye out on the main gate. I want to check out the back."   As he walks across the street Mark spots a young girl about ten carrying four bags of food towards the compound. He speeds up to intercept her and accidentally bumps into her. She drops two of the bags and Mark says in Arabic, "I am so sorry."   He bends down and picks up two of the bags. "I can help you take these where you are going." He says. The young girl is a bit confused. Libyan men do not help women or girls with anything. They are used to being waited on. Mark sees her confusion. "You look very much like my daughter who was killed last year. Excuse me."

The girl smiles. "Of course. I am taking the food to the house over there." Nodding toward the compound.

Mark smiles. "Ok, I will help you. I'll give you 500 pounds to let me help you. "

The girl is amazed at the offer. A 500 Syrian Pound is a lot of money. She smiles and Mark picks up two of the bags.

The two walk slowly towards the compound. Mark glances towards Ducky still sitting at the café. Ducky gets up and slowly begins to follow the pair.

As Mark and the girl reach the compound, she pounds on the door. After a few seconds, the door is unlatched and a man is standing there with an AK-47. He sees the girl, and then his eyes travel to Mark. "Who is this?"

Mark looks bored. "I am her uncle helping her with her job. Do you want us to just leave the bags here? They are heavy."

The girl looks straight forward.

"Just take the bags to the kitchen. Hurry up."

The girl and Mark trudge the thirty yards from the front gate to the house. There is another guard just inside the door also armed with an AK-47. Mark keeps his eyes down but also trying to take in as much detail as possible. The girl leads down a hallway, and then turns right into a large kitchen. In a room just off the kitchen Mark can hear two men talking. Suddenly Mark hears a familiar voice.

In Arabic, the man's voice says, "Within several hours we will know if we have been successful." They have a television on with the news stating that the United States government is releasing twelve terrorists to Somalia.

Mark knows that voice belongs to Nimr.

The guard tells them to hurry up and Mark and the girl put the bags on a table and the girl accepts a 100 pound Libyan note with a short bow. Mark follows her out of the kitchen, and then looks right. What he sees runs his blood cold. Down the hall is the President's daughter and one of her sons being led into another room.

Suddenly another man enters the hallway. It's Nimr limping towards the back of the house. Mark takes another quick look, then exits the house. After he and the girl leave the compound, Mark pulls out a 500 pound Libyan and hands it to the grateful girl.

"How often do you take food into the compound?"

"I have taken food there for the past three days."

Mark considers the information. "Do not take any more food there. Stay away. Do you understand?"

The girl nods. Mark gives her another 500 Libyan note. Then he walks away towards Ducky who was watching the exchange. As they meet, Mark says softly, "I saw the President's daughter and one of his grandkids in the house. They are definitely there. Also I saw Nimr Yazdi."

Ducky looks surprised. "He is there?"

Mark nods. As they walk, Mark tells his friend a story of his childhood. "When I was a kid in Syria we had a woodpile behind our house. Occasionally when it got cold enough there, my dad would ask me to bring in some wood for our fireplace. In the woodpile was a black widow spider. Nimr and I would use a stick to try to touch him or wiggle his web, just to see what he would do. Then one day I went out to get some wood and I reached in and he bit me. I could feel his fangs pierce my finger and the effects of his venom almost immediately. My dad took me to the hospital where I almost died. I recovered after a couple of weeks. But it was very painful. Nimr knows that story and that is why I think he picked that handle. Yazdi placed his web to capture the President's daughter and grandkids and now it's up to me to eliminate the Jihadi black widow. This time I won't miss."

Chapter 69

Washington D.C. - August 21st

The Joint Chiefs of the United States military are seated in the PEOC under the East Wing of the White House. In addition to the Joint Chiefs are the DNI, the Secretary of State and Michelle Samaha.

"Thank you all for coming so quickly to this emergency meeting. I have asked Michelle Samaha to attend also because I want to coordinate two operations."

The President looks around the room. "As you all know my daughter and my two grandchildren were kidnapped along with her secret service detail and a friend of hers who works for State." The President nods towards Cindy Decker, the Secretary of State. "As you all know, al-Qaeda is trying to blackmail me to release twelve terrorists and give them one billion dollars." The President looks around the table. "I will not be blackmailed! I have authorized an operation to rescue the hostages which will begin in about ten hours. Approximately $250 Billion counterfeit dollars will be dropped in Afghanistan within the next several hours. We believe it will take al-Qaeda at least two or three hours to realize that the amount isn't the one Billion they required. I doubt they will realize the bills are counterfeit for several weeks."

The President starts to walk around the room. "At the same time; as I know you are all aware, North Korea has reached the ability to build and deploy hundreds of nuclear tipped missiles. Currently the CIA believes that North Korea has ten to twenty nuclear missiles operational and targeted towards the U.S."

"I will not be blackmailed by al-Qaeda or Kim Jung-Un. We must act. If we do not eliminate this cancer now, we will see one or more of our cities in flames, millions of our citizens dead and dying and our country brought to its knees."

"Therefore, I am authorizing the military to launch a pre-emptive strike of the North Korea military complex, their nuclear development facilities, the 10-20 nuclear missile sites, and all of the artillery and missile batteries on the South Korean border. Finally, we will use bunker buster bombs to take out the Presidential Palace and every known location that Kim Jung-Un is known to sleep."

Suddenly the room erupts into chaos. Cindy Decker rises and with hands on the table. "Gentlemen, gentlemen!" The room quiets. "I can not support a pre-emptive strike without the opportunity to negotiate with the government of North Korea. An attack on another country requires a Congressional approval."

The President stands. "Ms. Secretary of State, the Department of State has been negotiating with The Democratic People's Republic of Korea for the past twenty years! During that time, they have starved millions of their own citizens and have developed nuclear weapons that could kill millions of our citizens. The time for talking is over. North Korea tried to assassinate me. That is an act of war. Therefore, I can act as the President of the United States without Congressional approval."

"Mr. President, I will have to resign if you move forward."

"Thank you for your service Cindy. I will expect your resignation on my desk tomorrow morning."

With that, the Secretary of State stands and leaves the meeting.

"If there is anyone else who can not carry out a Presidential order, please speak now."

There is stoic silence.

"Ok, I want to implement General Seibert's plan within two days. General Seibert would you please outline your plan?"

The Chief of the Joint Chiefs stands. "Mr. President, we have worked out a pre-emptive strike of all of the major military targets in North Korea. Nuclear weapons will not be used. We will use cruise missiles, stealth aircraft and B-52s with bunker buster bombs that will totally destroy the Presidential complex.

Other key operations will be to take out the artillery batteries targeting the south. We will also put the American troops in South Korea on alert and try to evacuate as many of the families to the South coast. Those in Seoul will be evacuated first to the Busan area on the Southeastern coast. We estimate that the initial operation will take twelve hours. At that time, the North Korean military will be 80% degraded."

The President leans forward in his chair. "General Seibert, what is your assessment of the Chinese reaction?"

The General takes a sip of water. "Mr. President, I believe that China will watch the carnage, assess our capabilities but will stand on the sidelines. They will lodge formal complaints with the United Nations, but most of the countries in the world will breathe a sigh of relief that Kim Jung-Un is out of power. Millions of North Koreans will die and perhaps millions of South Koreans. But I agree with you; that if we do not act, millions of Americans will eventually die at the hand of North Korea."

Andy Cobb stands. "Mr. President, I think it will be important for you to go on national television as the attack is underway. With social media, as soon as we drop the first bombs, the news will spread around the world like a wild fire. You will need to make your case to the American people why we had to act now. Also, you need to talk about reunionification of South Korea and North Korea. The issue will be China and in a minor role Russia. They will not agree to have a unified Korea on their borders. The other issue will be the humanitarian issues with millions and millions of North Koreans who are starving. You would have to rally the world to send food and medical supplies to pacify the population. There are lots of issues we will have to deal with, but with South Korea's help I am confident we can control the situation."

The President nods. "Thank you Andy." Speaking to Michelle Samaha on the conference call phone, "Michelle, I know you have an operation underway to rescue my daughter and my grandchildren and the rest of the hostages from al-Qaeda. That operation has to be completed before the North Korea operation starts. So that gives you two days."

Michelle replies. "Yes sir. The operation will begin tonight there in Libya. The SEALs are scheduled to HELO Tobruk and link up with Mark Aldin and Ducky Duckworth. Both of them have been onsite for the past several days. Also, I received a message from Mark just an hour ago saying that he saw your daughter and one of your grandsons in the facility and he saw Nimr Yazdi there also."

"Damn. At least we know where they are for sure. Ok, let's meet in the Situation Room later today when your operation starts."

"Yes sir. I'll bring my team over to help coordinate."

The President stands as do all of the other members of the team. "Let's move this along as quietly as possible. Everything on a need to know basis until the day of the attack. Ok?"

Everyone nods and files out of the room to begin the operation called *Enduring Unity.*

Chapter 70

Washington D.C. - August 21st

Cindy Decker is furious as her SUV pulls into the State Department parking structure. Her driver gets out and opens her door. As she steps out of the car, she is met by her second in command; Julia Barstow.

"God, I can't believe that asshole."

Julia is taken aback having never heard her boss speak that way. "What happened?"

The Secretary of State stops inside the State Department building. "The President is going to war against DPRK!" She whispers.

Barstow gapes at her boss. "What? How can he do that?"

Cindy Decker shakes her head. "He is going around Congress by declaring war without any negotiations, no talks with Kim Jung-Un and no input from State. I resigned today."

Julia is stunned. "Oh my God. You need to stay and fight!"

Decker and Barstow move to an elevator to take it to their offices. Once in the elevator, the Secretary of State pushes the button to stop the elevator.

"You will be named Secretary of State at least temporarily. You need to do everything you can to stop him. Or at least bring him down after the shooting ends."

Julia nods. "What happened with the President's daughter and grandchildren?"

"They are being held in Libya, we have the SEALs on the way to free them. The President is going to drop counterfeit bills to al-Qaeda and has a big show of releasing twelve terrorists to delay them until the SEALs can attack the compound and release the hostages."

Julia Barstow considers her next question. "When are the SEALs going to hit the compound?"

The Secretary of State starts the elevator, "I think it's within the next twelve hours or so. Hopefully they can free those hostages before the North Korea shit hits the fan."

The elevator doors open and both women exit. The Secretary of State's Chief of Staff is waiting with her public relations person. Cindy Decker heads straight to her office with most of her staff in tow dictating the process for her to leave State.

At the same time, Julia Barstow heads directly to her office. Once inside she closes and locks her door. She moves around her desk and unlocks a drawer and withdraws a secure cellular phone.

Julia sits down and takes a deep breath. Over the past four years she has transitioned from a committed State Department employee to a committed Jihadi. Her secret boyfriend has opened her eyes to the truth about America. He is a Saudi diplomat and Julia met him at a State Department party. She was swept off her feet by his sophistication, his rugged good looks and his unique sense of humor. They have been conducting a secret love affair for the past four years. They would meet at his apartment in Georgetown sometimes or at local hotels when their schedules permitted. As the Assistant Secretary of State, Julia knows she is being watched by enemies and friends alike.

She dials his secret cellular phone and waits while it rings several times. "Yes?" She hears his voice and it sends a thrill throughout her body.

"I know we agreed to communicate this way only if it's an emergency. I have some important information and I need to meet with you as soon as possible."

There is a long pause. "Ok, meet me at the West Potomac Park. I'll be sitting on a bench. I'll be there in an hour."

The connection is ended and Julia sits back. She knows she is committing treason by giving a foreign national top secret information, but she loves him and she believes that America is crumbling. Ahmed Bin Abdulaziz is a second cousin to the King of Saud, Mohammad Bin Salmal Al Saud. That is how he was awarded the assignment to the Saudi Arabia Embassy. He is committed to Wahhabism Islam and fully supports al-Qaeda. Wahhabism is an extreme interpretation of Sunni Islam supported by the Saudi government. The new ruler Mohammad Bin Salmal Al Saud has cracked down on the Wahhabism extremism, but it still is popular among the ruling class.

She is willing to convert to Islam and has been studying the Koran. She has kept Ahmed appraised of the hostage situation and he seemed very pleased that al-Qaeda was going to strike at the American President.

Julia puts the cellular phone in her purse and leaves her office, walking quickly to the elevators. "Julia, are you leaving the office?"

Julia stops and sees a person who works for her. "Yes, I am just too upset to stay in my office. I need some air. I'll be back in an hour."

With that, she turns and enters one of the elevators and descends to the ground floor. She then hails a taxi and heads to the West Potomac Park. During the short ride Julia thinks about what to tell Ahmed. She decides to tell him just about the al-Qaeda information and about North Korea. That action by the U.S. government against Kim Jung-Un will not affect Saudi Arabia directly, but he needs to know.

As the cab slows to a stop, Julia pays the driver with cash and exits. She looks up and down the park walkway. She must be early. Suddenly she sees him walking about 300 yards away from her. Julia picks up her pace and closes the distance by half just as he sits on a bench and opens a newspaper.

Julia slows and tries to collect herself. She moves behind him and catches a whiff of his cologne. It reminds her of their lovemaking and how happy she is with him. As she sits on the bench, he briefly glances over, then down the mall checking for others who might overhear them.

"Our friends are in trouble. The enemy has a group coming in the next twelve hours. You need to alert them as soon as you can."

Ahmed doesn't move, but she can tell that the news is surprising. "How sure are you about this information?"

"One hundred percent."

"Ok, thank you. I will contact you tomorrow. Do not contact me again today."

"Also, the U.S. will launch a pre-emptive strike against North Korea in three days." Her lover stiffens.

Julia rises and glances at Ahmed. As she passes him, "I love you" she whispers. Then walks back the way she came to return to the chaos at the State Department.

Chapter 71

Tobruk, Libya - August 21ˢᵗ

Their escape hole has been dug and the only thing to be done is to break through the twenty-four inches at the top, and then freedom. Oliver was the first to crawl under the foundation and dig at the other side, pulling dirt between his legs and out to the Agent Bale to lift it out and then either Clare or Agent Lee spreading it throughout their room. Diane was standing at the door with her ear against the metal listening for any sign of the terrorist approach.

After twenty minutes of digging, Oliver is dragged back under the foundation and up into the room. Agent Lee has been assigned to break through the dirt and see where they are. Hopefully they will break through in an isolated area and not next to one of the guards.

Agent Lee wiggles under the foundation and up to the other side. It is totally black in the hole. As she digs, she is on her back with the dirt falling onto her chest as she angles up. Suddenly a large piece of dirt collapses and she can see stars above. Kari Lee is excited, their escape is just several feet above her. She clears some dirt then braces herself. As she lifts herself

328

up she can see the high outer wall about twenty feet from her, but just five feet away is a pile of discarded wood. Agent Lee silently climbs out of the hole and pulls the wood pile next to their escape route. As she climbs back into the hole, she pulls several pieces of the wood over to cover her.

After wiggling back under the foundation, she is pulled back into the room. "We are through, just twenty feet from the back wall. Plus I found a pile of wood nearby and pulled some of it to cover our hole."

"Excellent. Now we just have to decide when to leave. It has to be tonight. At some point, they may notice all the extra dirt or do a search. Dinner is coming soon. We should eat, and then we'll make our escape." Everyone agrees and covers the hole and waits for their capturers.

Upstairs Nimr Yazdi receives a call on his SAT phone. He is surprised but it must be important. "Yes?" she says in Arabic. The voice at the other end is one he knows well. It is Hamza bin Ladin. "You have been discovered and the Americans are getting ready to attack your position. You must move the hostages now!"

Nimr is totally surprised. "How could they know where we are? We have been very careful."

"They know. Our contact at the State Department told us just two hours ago. You must leave."

Nimr shakes his head. "Ok. I will have to get the trucks back here. That will take an hour maybe two."

"Just do it and call me when you have relocated."

Nimr hangs up and immediately calls one of his lieutenants to bring the trucks back from the warehouse near the port, then walks downstairs.

As he opens the bolted door, Nimr sees the hostages sitting against the opposite wall. "Your father has agreed to deliver the one Billion dollars later tonight and he is releasing the twelve prisoners we asked for. However, your military has initiated a rescue mission that will fail. After dinner, you will be moved back to the warehouse. If the money or our comrades are not released, one of you will die."

Another of the terrorists enters the room with a plate of their normal fare; bread, cheese and fruit, along with six cups of tea.

"Eat quickly, we will leave in fifteen minutes." Nimr backs out of the room as the remaining terrorist watches them eat with his AK-47 at the ready.

The Americans eat silently not knowing if the guard knows any English. After eating quickly, they pile the plate and cups for the guard to remove them. He motions with the AK-47 to move back and they all do and sit on the floor. He then picks up the plate and cups and exits the room, locking the door.

Agents Bale and Lee begin to uncover the hole. "I will go first and make sure its clear." Says Kari Lee. "Then send the boys through, then Clare, and then Diane. Agent Bale will be last. If there is any danger, we will hoist the boys, Clare and Diane over the wall. If there is any shooting, run like hell. If the Special Operators are in the area, they will respond immediately."

Everyone nods knowing this could be it.

Chapter 72

Tobruk, Libya - August 21st

Mark and Ducky are dressed in their Arab garb but each have a AK-47, a suppressed Beretta APX Combat 9mm pistol and four 17 round magazines. Mark of course has his Strider knife.

Mark sees one of the guards hurrying out of the compound and driving down towards the port. He suspects that they somehow know about the operation and are preparing to leave.

"I think we should accelerate the rescue. Let's torch the Mosque now." It's just 9 pm and they were planning to wait until 1 am, but the key to a successful operation is flexibility.

Ducky is carrying two cans of gasoline that he has stolen from a car. Mark is guarding his six while they make their way. After arriving in the shadows, Ducky spreads the gas around the Mosque, then quietly breaks a window and dumps the rest of the second can inside, then throws the first half full can through the window. Mark lights a soaked rag and Ducky throws it inside. There is a swoosh and they can see the flames starting to spread.

Moving with stealth back to the compound, the pair wait for the chaos to ensue. Within a minute there are shouts of alarm and dozens, then hundreds of people rushing to the Mosque to put out the flames.

"Ok, lets go."

#   #   #

Inside the compound each of the hostages wiggle through the opening. Agent Lee first, then Oliver, then Filip, then Clare and then Diane. Finally Agent Bale makes it through. All six sit quietly listening for a guard.

Suddenly they hear shouting and see what looks like flames down the street. They realize this is the break they need. As they approach the wall, they hear "Halt" in Arabic. They turn and see one of the guards with his AK-47 leveled at them.

He is too far away to attack. With the AK-47 he could easily shoot them all before they get close. All of the hostages raise their hands.

It's over now, Nimr will probably take his revenge for their escape by killing one of them. Suddenly the guard staggers and falls.

The hostages all stare with disbelief.

"Ok, stop staring and get over the wall."

Six faces turn and see Mark Aldin laying on the wall with his suppressed Beretta in his hand and a big grin on his face.

"Come on, grab my hand."

The hostages scramble to the wall and are lifted one by one to the other side where they are greeted by Ducky. As Agents Lee and Bale make it over, they are given AK-47s.

"Ok, we have to get a vehicle and get out of here. The plan is to get to the Egyptian border."

As they make their way between homes nearby, they hear shouts of terrorists coming from the compound.

Running down an alley, they see a medical van. It has the markings of the green crescent and the emergency lights on top.

Mark moves to the drivers door and using his knife jimmies the door open. While Ducky, Agent Lee and Agent Bale form a protective cover, Mark works inside the van to get it started.

The engine roars to life and everyone piles into the back, with Ducky in the passenger side. Mark puts the truck in gear and they slowly creep out of the alley. Just down the street, the Mosque is fully enveloped with a hundred people trying to extinguish the fire with water buckets and hoses.

Mark turns the opposite way. He knows it will require him to drive past the compound, but he has no choice. Driving slowly, Mark sees people running towards the Mosque to help or just see what is happening. Out of the corner of his eye he sees three men exit the compound, one of which is Nimr Yazdi. Mark tries to keep his face passive, but he turns slightly to see his former friend and nemesis. Their eyes lock for just a second, and then Mark turns on the lights and sirens and speeds away.

Mark turns slightly to Ducky. "I think Nimr saw me." Ducky turns and glances back in his mirror. "I don't see a vehicle following, yet."

As they race out of Tobruk lights flashing, Nimr runs back into the compound to get into their van. "Call the local police, tell them to stop that medical van."

Mark pushes the accelerator to the floor increasing their speed to almost 70 MPH. He knows that Sallum, Egypt is 145 Km away which is 90 miles, so he just has to outpace Nimr to the border in the next hour or so.

"Get on the SAT phone and let Michelle know where we are and alert the Egyptian government to let us through."

"Roger" as Ducky pulls out their SAT phone.

Suddenly they hear some pounding on the section between them and the back of the van. Mark slides a communications panel and Agent Bale yells, "There are a couple of cars on our tail. They seem to be gaining."

Mark looks at his side mirror and sees two sets of lights gaining fast.

"Ok, as they get close open up with your AK-47s. See if we can back them off."

The heavier medical van only has so much speed and Mark knows the terrorist vans would probably top out at 90 MPH.

As the vans continue to close the distance, Agent Bale opens the rear door and laying on the floor spits out a dozen bullets at the vans. They slow slightly and begin to evade, but only have two lanes to use with desert on either side.

Suddenly several bullets ping off the medical van. Agent Bale shoots back trying to hit the front of one of the vans to try to damage their engine. After several exchanges the vans start to back off. Suddenly Agent Bale is shot. He is hit in the shoulder and is pulled back inside and the door is closed.

The vans behind continue to advance, but Agent Lee takes her turn to fire at the Jihadis. The vans back off as bullets fly at them. This continues for almost an hour.

Mark continues to press the medical van to its maximum speed. They come over a rise and they can see the lights of Sallum, Egypt. It is a small town, but the only border crossing for hundreds of miles.

"They are coming on fast." Yells Lee.

Diane Fusco lays down next to Lee and they both begin to fire a hundred rounds pinging off the vans. One of the vans starts to smoke and slows. Then they hear a wop-wop-wop of a helicopter closing in. Agent Lee spots a Libyan government helicopter closing in fast.

"Crap! Get inside and tell Mark to floor it. We have company."

Clare yells to Mark and Ducky letting them know that they have another issue to deal with.

The helicopter paces the medical van easily, and then slides in front with its spotlight on the front windshield. "Halt! If you do not stop, we will open fire!" the helicopter loudspeaker says in English.

Ducky turns in his seat. "Give me one of the AK-47s!" Agent Lee passes her AK-47 and a clip to him. Ducky slaps the magazine in and leans out the window. At the same time, several bullet rip through the windshield and into the back of the vehicle. Ducky levels the AK-47 and fires a dozen bullets into the helicopter fuselage. The helicopter wavers, and then starts to lose altitude. A flame shoots out of the back while the helicopter dips and then plummets to the ground in a huge fireball.

Ducky pulls back inside the vehicle and looks over at Mark. Ducky's face is white and he has a grimace in his face. Mark looks down and sees blood flowing from his right side. "Ducky, are you ok?"

Ducky gives his buddy a small grin. "A-Ok."

The medical van is racing down towards the small town of Sallum. Mark can see some flashing lights of police cars blocking the border crossing. "Damn, we may have to run through. Tell everyone to brace themselves."

Just as Ducky yells into the back, a volley of bullets slam into the back of the van. Mark looks in his side mirror and sees that the terrorist van has closed within 25 yards of them. They aren't going to make the crossing.

"Hold on!" Mark yells.

Suddenly he puts both feet on brake and the medical van screeches to a smoky stop. Within milliseconds the terrorist van crashes into the back bumper and veers off and flips. Mark starts to accelerate again, but then stops.

Mark looks over and sees Ducky slumped with a blood spurting from his shirt. Mark reaches over and tells Ducky to hold on. Ducky knows what Mark needs to do. "Go get him."

Mark exits the van with his Beretta in his hand. Mark knows his buddy has been hit, but he has to make sure Nimr is finally dead. As he trots over to the white van in a shooters crouch, suddenly the van explodes into a ball of flame and smoke. Mark shades his face as he creeps closer and sees a body burning in the vehicle. Suddenly he senses someone behind him. It is Nimr, standing unsteadily with his gun in his hand. He has his pistol leveled at him. Mark has his gun at his side.

"Well my friend. I guess this is where I finally get my revenge. You ruined my original plan, but now al-Qaeda will have one Billion dollars to use to fund our work in the West, plus twelve of our brothers to help in the effort."

Mark smiles. "You will not receive the money and those twelve will rot in GITMO. You lose again."

As Nimr tightens his finger on the trigger, a gun shot echoes through the local hills and Nimr looks surprised, and then drops. Mark looks over his shoulder and sees Clare holding the AK-47.

He walks over to Nimr and sees that he is trying to breathe, but blood is restricting his airway. Mark looks down at his boyhood friend. "Nimr, I am sorry it had to turn out this way but you killed my son and hundreds of others. It ends now."

Nimr creates a forced smile. "It will not end Mailis. The next stage will destroy your culture, your people and your country. In two generations, your people will be bowing before Allah."

With that, Nimr coughs once, then his breathing stops. Mark knows that now his emotional healing can begin.

Mark turns towards the medical van and sees a lot of activity inside. As he reaches the van, he sees Diane laying on the gurney. Blood is all over her blouse and Clare crying and holding her hand.

"What happened?" Mark says.

Agent Lee steps down and shakes her head. "One of the bullets ricocheted inside the van and hit Diane in the chest. I am afraid she is dead."

Mark turns to Clare. "I am so sorry, are the boys ok?"

Clare nods and hands Agent Lee the AK-47, then begins to sob from the loss of her friend.

"We need to get to the border as soon as we can before the Libyan government sends another helicopter." Mark says.

They can hear a second helicopter coming fast. "Let's get out of here!"

Mark helps Ducky get into the back of the van to receive medical treatment for his wound, while Agent Lee moves to the shotgun spot next to Mark as he floors the accelerator.

As the medical van approaches the border crossing, the police cars pull away and allow the van to pass unmolested.

A squad of Egyptian solders stand at the ready as a Major approaches Mark. "We received word from the U.S. Government to bring you to Alexandria where your Embassy will take charge of your security." He says in Arabic.

"Thank you Major. We have one person injured and one dead. We appreciate your help." Mark says back in Arabic.

Then the Major is taken aback seeing two women, two children and two men carrying a body exiting the medical van. He signals for the Egyptian military helicopter to start its rotors and for his men to help the Americans on their journey to freedom.

Chapter 73

Washington D.C. - August 21st

The President sits down with tears in his eyes. Michelle is standing in front of the Resolute desk after telling the President and the First Lady that their daughter and two grandsons are safe.

"Thank you, thank you Michelle."

The first lady comes over and hugs Michelle. "We are so grateful to you and your team."

Michelle smiles. "It was Mark and Ducky. They risked their lives to save those six. Ducky was wounded, but will recover. Unfortunately Diane Fusco was killed. They are the true heroes."

The President recovers. "I am so sorry, you said you think that Nimr Yazdi was killed?"

"Yes, he is dead. He was in one of the two vans chasing Mark. One van was disabled by gunfire and the other crashed and burned. After the crash, Mark ran to the van to see if Nimr was there, but he had been thrown from the van in the crash. While Mark was looking for him, Nimr pulled a gun and had Mark at a disadvantage. It was Clare who shot him."

The President raises his eyebrows. "Well, she was an excellent shot when I took her hunting in Colorado."

Michelle continues, "She saved Mark's life."

President Baker smiles. "She has a lot of grit. What about the boys?"

"They are fine, a little shaken. But ok."

"So when will the six be returned home?" Asks the President.

Michelle responds, "They are being flown to Italy now and will be checked out medically. Ducky will be flown to Germany for medical attention, Clare, the boys and the two secret service agents will be flown home using an Agency plane. Diane will be flown home after her mother and father are notified. Your daughter and grandsons should be back in Washington D.C. in a couple of days."

The President smiles for the first time in a couple of weeks. "Thank you Michelle and thanks to your team."

"Our pleasure Mr. President. I'd like to fly out to Italy to check with Mark and come home with him. Is that Ok with you?"

"Of course Michelle. Take whatever time you need. But remember that our operation against North Korea will commence in three days."

"Yes, Mr. President. I am very aware of that. We'll be back before the pre-emptive strike."

Michelle leaves the White House and drives directly to Dulles Airport and hops on a Gulfstream G650 compliments of the CIA to fly to Italy and to pick up Mark Aldin.

Chapter 74

Washington D.C. - August 22nd

The President is sitting in the Situation Room with the Joint Chiefs of Staff, the Director of National Intelligence, the head of the CIA and his Chief of Staff. These are the only people that are aware that the operation against North Korea is not a drill. The massive United States military is poised to strike at the rogue regime of Kim Jong-Un. Over the past two days the United States has quietly moved strategic forces into place for a quick attack.

Some new information just came in and has prompted the emergency meeting.

"Mr. President, our satellites show that North Korea is moving their mobile nuclear missiles and starting to fuel their ICBMs; their KN-14s and KN-10s missiles. Both missile types can reach the continental U.S. We believe they have 10-12 nuclear missiles at the ready."

The President shakes his head. "They must have been tipped off. I want a full investigation by the FBI. The only person in the Situation Room that is not here now is the Secretary of State. I want her questioned, who she talked with. I can't believe she would betray her country. But we have to cover all our bases."

"Yes sir." Says his Chief of Staff.

The President turns to General Siebert. "What are your recommendations General?"

The General looks up from his monitor. "I can't believe this is a coincidence. They know. We can't wait the three days to initiate the attack. We may lose track of their missiles. Kim Jong-Un will go into hiding. He will harden his defenses and he may initiate a pre-emptive strike on us and the south."

The President nods.

"I believe we should strike now or we will lose our surprise advantage." President William Kellan Baker looks resigned to his role. "Ok, initiate the strike."

The General picks up a secure phone and issues the order. All around the world U.S. military bases are notified of a DEFCON I. This is a notification of maximum readiness. The highest DEFCON level previous was DEFCON 2 during the Cuban Missile Crisis October 16 – 28, 1962 when President Kennedy confronted Russia who placed missiles just 90 miles from Florida. The normal DEFCON level is 5. Everyone will know America is at war.

"When will the first missiles hit?" Asks the President.

The Chairman of the Joint Chiefs looks at the large screen showing all of military assets in the form of small symbols on a global map. General Siebert takes a deep breath. "The first cruise missiles will impact their nuclear weapon sites in just over

346

thirty minutes depending on the position of the submarines. At the same time our stealth bombers will enter North Korea airspace and release their bunker buster bombs on the Presidential compound where we think Kim Jung-Un is staying. Then at that point, all hell will break loose. The South Koreans will take out the artillery batteries on the North side of the DMZ and will alert their citizens to seek shelter. There will be massive casualties in Seoul and many of the other Northern cities."

The President nods solemnly. "What about the families of American service people there?"

The Chairman looks down at his notes. "There are over 35,000 military personnel in the country and almost 100,000 family members. Over the past couple of days we have quietly moved most of the families to southern cities. Unless North Korea is able to launch a nuclear strike, they should be safe."

"When will the invasion start? How many troops will it take?"

The General again checks his notes. "We will have almost 220,000 joint South Korean and American troops that will flood into North Korea over the next week. We have an additional 40,000 troops ready in Japan to move in if needed. Our Special Forces are currently in country getting ready to observe the North's military reaction and capture the one person we believe can prevent massive bloodshed. That is Colonel-General Chong

Kang Hwan. Once Kim Jong-Un is eliminated, we will abduct Colonel-General Chong and convince him to stage a coup d'état. He is a moderate and has the authority once Kim is eliminated, to have the DPRK armed forces stand down."

The General takes a deep breath. "If he refuses, then it will be a four to six week battle and perhaps a million people will die. We have overwhelming fire power and their troops are malnourished, but until we can convince them that their Dear Leader is dead, they will fight."

The President sits with his eyes closed. "Damn, we should have taken out his father or little Kim years ago. How did it come to this? Ok, thank you General. Initiate the operation."

As the group watches the large screen, the General places the call that is relayed to each of the commanders in the Navy, Air Force, Army and Marines. The war with North Korea has begun.

An aide to General Seibert enters and hands him a note. The General turns to the President. "Mr. President, your daughter and two grandsons just landed at Dulles. They will be taken to the White House presently."

The President nods.

Suddenly the door to the Situation Room opens and four armed U.S. Army personnel, the Senate Majority Leader, the House Majority Leader and the Chief Justice of the Supreme Court enter the room.

"Mr. President, we must ask that you come with us, you are facing impeachment for high crimes and misdemeanors."

The President sits calmly. "Gentlemen, this is a breach of security to have you in this room."

The Senate Majority Leader, Jordan Claiborne says, "Mr. President, you have violated the Constitution by attacking another country without consent by the House and the Senate. Therefore, we are invoking the Article I Sections 8 paragraph 11 and Section 3 paragraphs 6 & 7 and Article II Section 4. We are impeaching you and the Vice President for high crimes and misdemeanors for planning to initiate a war with the Democratic People's Republic of Korea."

The President sits quietly considering the Senate Majority leaders words. "Those are very serious charges Mr. Claiborne, however the President of the United States has the ability to declare war under a threat to the United States and I submit that North Korea presents a clear and present danger to our homeland. Over the past twenty years former Presidents and Congress have failed to act to rid the world of the madmen in the DPRK. Now North Korea has nuclear weapons that can kill millions of Americans, South Koreans and Japanese. I was forced to act. I have sixty days to come to Congress for your approval, but right now I am fully engaged."

"Mr. President, we are also invoking Article II Section 1, paragraph 6 which allows the Congress to remove a President for the inability to discharge the Powers and Duties due to you being mentally ill."

The President is surprised. "Mentally ill? What proof do you have?"

The Speaker of the House, George Watkins steps forward. "Clearly your actions today demonstrate your lack of mental acuity and have caused our actions, Mr. President. Plus your secret payment of one Billion dollars and the release of twelve terrorists to al-Qaeda"

The President glances at the large screen showing the path of the cruise missiles just launched from the U.S.S. Michigan submarine. "How did you find out about our plan?"

The Speaker smiles. "The Assistant Secretary of State, Julia Barstow has been very helpful. She informed us of your actions yesterday."

The President nods. "The actions I took regarding al-Qaeda were to save six American lives, including my daughter and two grandsons." The President's anger rising. "Additionally, al-Qaeda was tipped off to our rescue operation, only five people knew about the plan. One of which was the Secretary of State who resigned when told about how we were going to rescue them.

I suspect that the Secretary told Ms. Barstow and she is involved in a treasonous act."

The Speaker and the Majority Leader of the Senate look surprised. "Mr. President, I would be very surprised if she is somehow involved. But we will investigate. However, we are here now to stop your actions with regards to DPRK."

The President stands. "Gentlemen, you are too late. As you can see from the screen, we have launched our cruise missiles from multiple nuclear-powered submarines just off the coast of North Korea. These are conventional warheads. We will take out all of their nuclear weapons in just over twenty minutes, and then we will launch a full scale military action to destroy the DPRK ability to counter-attack the U.S. or South Korea."

All of the men stand silently with their mouths open.

"We are officially at war with the Democratic People's Republic of Korea. Under the war powers act I have the ability and the duty to protect the nation."

Looking at the four Army Rangers, "Sergeant, as your Command-In-Chief would you please remove the Speaker, the Majority Leader and the Chief Justice from this secure room and keep them incognito until I can address the nation?"

"Yes sir." The Rangers march the three men out of the Situation Room.

As soon as the door is closed, General Seibert looks at the screen. "Mr. President the North Koreans have launched ICBMs!" The General quickly calls his NORAD (North American Aerospace Defense) commander. "Yes, ten ICBMs from DPRK, shoot them down."

The assembled men watch as the red squares signifying the North Korean missile tracks race toward the U.S. mainland. The NORAD communications center authorizes the launch of the United States strategic defense shield of missiles to try to shoot down the incoming ICBMs. The United States has forty-four ground-based mid-course defense interceptors in California and Alaska that have been designed specifically to shoot down ICBMs. After ten minutes, the staff sees the missile interceptors on the board as blue streaks racing to stop the North Korean ICBMs at stage 2 or 3. As each blue streak intercepts the red square, the color changes to green indicating a successful intercept. After another five minutes, the General smiles. "Mr. President it looks like we were able to intercept eight of the NPRK ICBMs and two of the ICBMs 2 or 3 stages failed in flight. As the President and his military staff watch, each of the red squares indicating a North Korea ICBM is intercepted or blink off the board. The President and the Generals congratulate each other.

Suddenly a red phone rings and General Seibert picks it up.

As he listens, his face turns to shock. "Mr. President, we are picking up multiple ICBM launches from Syria!"

The President turns and stares at the global map on the wall. "What the hell?"

The General picks up a phone and calls the U.S. Missile Defense Agency. "Have you picked up the launches from Syria?" He listens for several seconds then receives an affirmative. "Ok, launch the remaining missile interceptors. Mr. President, we believe the missiles are Russian R36 ICBMs. The CIA thinks the Iranians moved them into Southern Syria to give their government cover. They are probably operated by Russians or Iranians with some al-Qaeda involvement. We just don't know at this point. But the R36 missiles have multiple warheads and have evasive capabilities that may defeat our counter-measures."

The President looks grim. "When were you going to tell me that they had Russian ICBMs? What is their range?"

The General responds, "The CIA told us last year that they suspected that Russia was sending missile parts illegally to Iran, but that they couldn't confirm it. The R36 or better known as the SS-18, has a range of 16,000 Km. They easily can reach the U.S."

The President looks at Randy Smith. "Get the leadership to safety. We have approximately 30 -45 minutes if we can't shoot them down."

General Seibert says, "They launched three ICBM missiles. Our analysts believe one will hit Denver, the second will hit Kansas City.

The President looks puzzled. "I understand Washington D.C. but why Kansas City and Denver?"

The General looks at his second in command and nods. The three star Air Force general speaks up. "Mr. President, because there are only three ICBMs and they are spaced out, I believe the Iranians will detonate their nuclear packages at 100 to 150 miles above the Earth to cause an EMP."

The President knows all about an Electro-Magnetic Pulse. He was briefed on its affects and they can bring a nation to its knees for months or years without destroying the infrastructure. Detonating at that altitude will spread the EMP over a wide area allowing the pulse to spread out over the U.S. and affecting all of the country. Every electronic device within the pulse will be fried. The nation's telecommunications system will fail, the transportation system will fail, and the electricity grid will fail. After those three major systems are no longer working, chaos will ensue. Riots in the major cities. Food shortages within two weeks. No running water. Millions of Americans will die.

"What can we do?" Asks the President.

"We have several Aegis destroyers on the East coast but we have little chance to shoot the ICBMs down once they re-enter the atmosphere. We will try, but I am afraid we are venerable.

"Mr. President, you need to get into the bunker and make sure the Vice President is secure."

The President wants to stay where he can be involved in the action. But he knows that is the right decision at this point.

As President Baker is rushed out of the Situation Room and down to the secure bunker under the White House, he wonders if he will be the last American President.

Chapter 75

Over the Atlantic - August 22nd

Mark and Michelle are relaxing on the Agencies' Gulfstream 650 ER. It's the top of the line jet that cruises at Mach 0.85 and can travel over 13,000 miles.

They have caught up on the operation and are both happy that Ducky, the first daughter and her grandchildren are safe. Ducky, due to his injury was evacuated to Germany for treatment. But the prognosis was good.

Michelle takes a quick sip of her favorite scotch. "What I don't understand is how Nimr knew about the operation. He was getting the hostages out just as you moved in. He either saw you guys, or was tipped off."

Mark takes a sip of his scotch and shakes his head. "No way they saw us. I guarantee that."

Suddenly, Michelle's SAT phone rings. "Michelle." She says. She listens for several seconds, and then says "Damn. Ok, let me know when she is arrested."

Mark raises his eyebrows and waits for Michelle to finish her call. Michelle hangs up and faces Mark. "We were betrayed by the Assistant Director of State, Julia Barstow. She apparently had a secret relationship with a Saudi agent. She passed information to him, who then told an al-Qaeda operative. Nimr knew you were coming."

"Damn, I hope she swings for treason."

Michelle nods and sits back.

"I wonder if al-Qaeda knows at this point that the money is counterfeit?" Mark muses.

"And that their twelve terrorist brothers are still sitting in their GITMO cells?" Says Michelle.

Mark puts his drink down. "Doesn't really matter at this point. I am just happy that Nimr is dead thanks to Clare Sweeney. That was a great shot at night."

Michelle gets up and heads for the on-board kitchen. "Do you want a sandwich or something to eat?"

Mark gets up also and follows Michelle. "Sure what do we have?"

Michelle bends over the refrigerator and peers inside. "Looks like a cooked chicken, some veggies, several sandwiches and a couple of desserts."

Mark is standing behind Michelle as she leans over. She senses his presence behind her. She can feel his body heat and it makes her smile. Standing up, she turns and faces him with a twinkle in her eyes. "So what would you want?"

Mark is just several inches from Michelle and he can sense her interest. He reaches out and moves a lock of her hair from her forehead to behind her ear. They stand silently for several seconds, and then both move forward and kiss softly. She can feel his strong arms envelope her and pull her to him. The kiss is short but sweet. Both linger in each others' arms for several more seconds, then separate.

Mark smiles. "Well, that beats anything that is in the refrigerator."

Michelle is somewhat embarrassed but also relieved that their feelings for each other is now out in the open. "Well, we didn't check out the deserts."

Mark laughs. "I guess then I'll settle for a sandwich and some chips."

The spell is broken for the moment and Michelle smiles. "Coming right up."

At that moment, Michelle's SAT phone rings again. Michelle moves past Mark, brushing by thinking of the possibilities with him.

"Michelle." There is a long pause as she listens to the speaker. "Oh No! When were they released? Which cities are targeted? Ok, Ok.... Good luck. Thank you for the information."

Michelle hangs up white as a sheet.

"What's wrong?" Asks Mark.

"The President moved up the pre-emptive strike on North Korea and somehow they got tipped off. Five minutes ago they launched ten ICBM missiles at the U.S. Looks like we are at war and we'll get hit within the next thirty minutes."

Mark immediately thinks of his ex-wife and daughter. He grabs the SAT phone and dials the number he knows by heart. It rings four times, and then his ex-wife's voice comes on. "This is Jennifer and Mary, please leave us a message."

"Jen, this is Mark. This is not a joke. North Korea just launched nuclear tipped ICBMs at the U.S. and they will land in just thirty minutes. Get inside or down in a basement. Don't go outdoors for several days. Take water and food if you can. Sorry for all that has happened between us, tell Mary I love her. Good luck!"

Mark then calls his ex-wife's office number and gives the same message. She is probably with a patient and Mary is probably at school. He puts the phone down and sits. There is nothing else he can do.

Michelle calls her parents and leaves a similar message, then sits down next to Mark. She grabs his hand and gives it a gentle squeeze. "God, I can't believe Kim Jung-Un would launch his missiles. But I guess a rabid dog will fight when cornered.

What about the millions of Americans who could die. It will be horrible. I wish we could do something."

Mark pulls Michelle into his arms. "There isn't anything we can do at this point, but survive. Hopefully the U.S. military can stop the attack. But at this point, we have to figure out where we are going to land this plane."

Michelle sees Mark considering all their options, "We have to divert the plane. There could be a third world war. Where should we land?"

Michelle is trying to clear her head. She can't believe this has happened. "We want to be close enough to the U.S. to get there after a few weeks or months, but not in the way of the trade winds that will carry the radioactive fallout."

"Ok, what about Mexico? Or Puerto Rico? Or Belize? We have to tell the pilots and change course."

They both get up and inform the pilots. They are shocked, but professionally alter course for the Caribbean.

After returning to their seats, they try to wrap their heads around the new reality.

"Being on an Island like Puerto Rico would be beneficial in the event the U.S. is invaded. But there would be limited water, food and services if the U.S. is no more."

Mark considers the situation. "We will have to fend for ourselves at least for a month or two. Mexico will be largely unaffected, and it would be easy to get into the U.S. once things calm down or the government can establish control, but the issue would be the Mexican narco gangs and if they would take over in the chaos. Belize might be the best choice. They speak English, they have abundant resources and they are far enough south to not be contaminated. We'd have to keep the jet safe, but we have some weapons here and could set up a watch with each of us taking turns."

Michelle nods. "Ok, I agree Belize would be best. There is an American Embassy there too."

Mark gets up. "Do you think China or Russia will try to exploit the situation or just sit back and see what happens?"

Michelle shakes her head. "I don't know. Depending on how many missiles get through, the U.S. military will still be intact. We will also have the submarine force lurking in the Pacific and Atlantic. I don't know if they will have Command & Control, but the commanders have their orders and will not hesitate to unleash their nuclear missiles if China or Russia attack."

Mark nods. "I think both countries will wait and see what the damage is. NATO will support the U.S., but everyone will be on edge. If we can get to the U.S. Embassy, then hopefully we communicate with whoever is still there and in charge. Either way, it's not going to be pretty."

Michelle nods then smiles. "I am happy I am with you during this crisis."

"Me too. Nobody I'd rather have covering my six." Mark says with a smile.

Michelle gets up and Mark pulls her into his arms. They kiss softly at first, then with more intensity. Michelle can feel Mark responding to their embrace. After a minute, they break the kiss. Mark looks into her beautiful brown eyes flecked with green. "I hadn't noticed how beautiful your eyes are."

Michelle smiles. "Yours are pretty nice too."

Mark gives Michelle a soft short kiss, then goes to inform the pilots of their new destination.

The Gulfstream gently banks left heading southeast to their new temporary home.

#   #   #

The End

For a sneak peak at the third book in the Jihadi Series,

turn the page.

JIHADI
White Christmas

Al-Qaeda delivers a deadly present to the unbelivers

Continuing the Mark Aldin Series

A Suspense Thriller Novel

RIK THISTLE

Jihadi

White Christmas

Next in the Jihadi series due out Christmas 2018

By Rik Thistle

Turn the page for a preview of Jihadi White Christmas…

Chapter 1

Pyongyang North Korea
August 22nd

Kim Jong-Un is in shock. After his generals told him that the United States president's decision to attack the DPRK was imminent, the dear leader fled the Presidential palace knowing it would be one of the first targets of the American bombs. In the middle of the night Kim, his wife and three of his children rushed out of the presidential palace and into a bullet-proof SUV. Waiting in a separate SUVs are eight of Kim's personal guard. The Chairman and his generals pile into his bullet-proof limo.

Knowing that most of his military sites would be attacked, Kim makes the decision to head for a secret underground facility just forty-five miles from Pyongyang.

In the limo with Kim is his most trusted Generals. General Gim Chi-Sung is the head of the Korean People's Armed Forces. He is the key player for Kim. General Ri

Pyong-Chol, the person who can launch the DPRK conventional and nuclear arsenal and finally Jeong Jha-Ji who heads up the secret police. Kim knows that this will just speed up the plan he and Iran had hatched just weeks ago. Iran and North Korea had been working together over the past decade both helping the other to develop nuclear weapons. Both countries believed it was the only way they could survive the imperialist threat of the United States and Europe. The Iranian Revolutionary Guard general contacted General Ri about accelerating their attack on America, but now apparently the Americans have found out about their plan and decided to attack first.

"Dear leader, if we are going to launch our nuclear missiles we must to act now. If we wait, the Americans could launch first and take out our military facilities."

Kim Jong-Un is regaining some of his senses as the limo and three SUVs race out of the city. "Are we sure the Americans are planning an attack?"

General Ri nods. "We have been told by our Saudi contact who told us that his contact within the U.S. State Department confirmed that the President is committed to overthrowing North Korea and unifying Korea. Plus General

Aziz with the Revolutionary Guard confirmed the information."

Kim looks absentmindedly out of the tinted window at the dark North Korean countryside as it flies past. "What do our Chinese brothers say?"

"Our Chinese *brothers* have not replied to my call." Says Jeong Jha-Ji.

Jeong Jha-Ji is the head of the secret police and is one of the most feared men in North Korea, besides Kim Jong-Un of course. "My leader, we are running out of time. The Americans could be launching their missiles. Once they attack, all of our military facilities will be vulnerable. We need to activate the Red Guards; that will put 3.5 million workers on alert to stop the South Korea army that will invade."

Kim knows the General is right but he wants to be the one to give the order. His people believe he is a god, just like his father and grandfather before him. "I should go on television, talk directly to the people."

The Generals glance at each other; they know that only a very few people in North Korea have a television. Those who do are the elite and would be warned by their high level friends and family. General Ri looks at the other Generals, then says. "We do not have the cameras and systems to broadcast from facility 358." The General leans forward and lowers his voice so as to not be overheard by the driver. "We should also consider the aftermath if the Americans invade our country. We are heading to facility 358 near Anju and that will give you and your family an opportunity to leave North Korea and flee to China."

Kim Jong-Un turns his head slowly and stares at his General and hisses. "I will not leave my country! We will stop the Americans. They must not be allowed to invade. Every man, woman and child will fight to the death to push the Americans into the sea!"

The outburst quiets the Generals. After a few minutes of silence, General Ri responds, "But sir, we need to consider all possibilities. Your survival is critical to the government."

Kim sits back, calming down. "Yes of course." Kim closes his eyes considering the situation. "Alright, launch the ICBMs. When we get to facility 358 we can coordinate our forces and truly understand what the Americans are up to."

The Generals look at each other but say nothing. General Ri places a call from the limo to his second in command authorizing the launching of their twelve ballistic missiles. It will take several hours to fuel and target the missiles but the General is confident they can release the nuclear storm on the Americans before they can react. The issue is the aftermath; they know that the bunker called facility 358 has 1980s equipment given to them by the Russians and can barely keep up with information in real-time. The computers breakdown and spare parts are no longer available, no matter how hard they search. The Generals know they are hopelessly over-matched by the military of the United States of America, both in technology and their firepower. But disputing the Chairman could lead to a bullet in the brain as Kim Jong-Un has done to countless other military and political adversaries.

Suddenly the limo and the trailing SUVs pull into a barbed wire compound that shows three buildings guarded by several hundred special-forces troops. As the limo rolls to a halt inside a large garage, the North Korean leader steps out to be greeted by four of the top facility military leadership. As the three Generals step out of the limo, the military leaders are shocked. They snap salutes, nervous that both the Dear Leader and his top Generals have come to their facility.

The family and the Generals are led to an elevator that takes them three hundred feet down to the underground bunker that the leadership believes will safeguard them in the event the Americans attack.

As the Kim Jong-Un enters the command center all of the personal stand and clap. "Thank you. Everyone please take your seats and continue to monitor the events outside of our country. We are about to launch our first volley of ICBMs at the United States. What are the Americans doing?"

The Generals look at each other. Nobody wants to give the dear leader bad news.

Finally General Ri stands up. "We will successfully launch twelve ICBM missiles in just over an hour. Then after launch they should be hitting the American cities within thirty to forty minutes."

The Chairman smiles. After forty years of delay and deceit, the North Korean leader is about to deal the West a shocking blow. His grandfather, his father and now he faced the Americans and the West and negotiated concessions and time. Now he has developed what his father could only dream of; a nuclear arsenal. He knows it will probably result in the loss of his country, but that was going to happen anyway. He is confident that the Chinese will take care of him and his family.

"Contact our Iranian brothers and let them know we are initiating our part of the bargain. Now they need to do the same."

The Generals know about the triad of power with Iran and al-Qaeda Kim has cultivated over the past decade is now ready to act. This plan they believe will result in a world war and the overthrow of the western governments. Kim has read the papers about the racial discord in America, the college students rioting in the streets, police being shot in the major cities. America is coming apart by the seams. He intends to rip it apart and allow his partners to tear it down. It is a dangerous game that North Korea is playing, aligning themselves with the Iranians and in proxy with al-Qaeda, but the old saying that the enemy of my enemy is my friend, is true in this case. Kim Jong-Un smiles to himself.

After the fall of America and Europe, he will be the one to unify Korea under his control.

Chapter 2

Washington DC
August 22nd

The President had just arrived at the Situation Room when all hell broke loose.

President Baker's chief of staff rushes up to the President eyes wide with panic.

"It looks like Kim is going to launch his ICBMs."

The President looks to his Generals. "What?"

General Seibert turns and salutes the commander-in-chief, "Sir, somehow Kim must have been tipped off. We need to move our forces into position for a counter-attack. There is no way he could have detected our troop build up and the positioning of our air assets. Someone leaked our plan. We just detected the fueling of their ICBMs. They have also started positioning their troops along the DMZ."

"How the hell did he know? Can we hit his ICBMs before they are fueled?"

The General shakes his head. "No sir. We have just ten minutes until they are ready. Then it will be up to Kim to decide to launch. They may be just fueling to provoke a response from us or just to be ready. But personally I think he knows about our plans and has decided to launch first."

"Damn. Ok, continue with our plan. What about defensive systems if they do launch?"

General Seibert reaches over and picks up a folder and flips it open. "We have several dozen THAAD systems along the Alaska and Northwestern U.S. ready to shoot them down. We also have THAAD systems in Japan and South Korea in the event that bastard shoots any birds in their direction."

The President knows that the THAAD system is the U.S. designed Terminal High Altitude Area Defense system designed to shoot down short, medium and ICBM ballistic missiles in their terminal phase of descent and re-entry by intercepting it with a hit-to-kill approach. The system has been promising, but it has only been tested on single incoming ICBMs. The President looks at the large monitor and sees the might of the United States military positioned for an attack on North Korea, but now worries that all that might could be for nothing if the North Korean ICBMs get through and destroy American cities.

Suddenly an Air Force Major tasked with monitoring the North Korean ICBMs yells, "Launching!"

All eyes turn to a satellite real-time feed over North Korea. The software shows a red circle rising from the surface, and then another, then another. Twelve in all.

"God-damn. General how long until they hit us?"

The General shakes his head. "We will have to determine the trajectory of each missile. That should take our software just under a minute, but probably 30-40 minutes depending on their targets. We have put all our THAAD systems on alert."

All around the situation room, every person seemed to be moving with determined purpose.

"We are sending out an alert to all communications centers telling all citizens to take shelter" says the communications officer. "We just went to DEFCON 1."

"Seven ICBMs are targeting the U.S. mainland. One ICBM is heading for Hawaii. Two ICBMs are heading for South Korea. Two for Japan!" Yells the Major.

The President watches the monitor and sees two missiles racing south towards Seoul, South Korea. "Six minutes to impact."

Suddenly they see two blue circles intercepting a pair of red triangles and they turn to green squares. "Got them both! The THAAD system shot down both missiles!"

Over Japan, the two missiles heading east are reaching their zenith. As the missiles begin their decent towards Japan, the THAAD system fires multiple defensive missiles. The President and all of the military staff watch as the missile tracks race towards each other. This is a tough mission, like shooting a bullet at another bullet. One trace of a THAAD missile slides by the North Korean ICBM, but then another THAAD intercepts and the software confirms the kill. A joyous yell goes up from all of the military personnel in the room. The second ICBM now is racing down its trajectory towards Tokyo. A THAAD missile trace moves toward the ICBM and then misses. A second THAAD missile is right behind the first. Just seconds behind. Everyone, including the President, is holding their breath. As they all watch, the ICBM and the THAAD missile traces intersect, but then the ICBM continues on its decent.

"Crap! Their ICBM is going to hit Tokyo."

"What about the eight aimed at us?"

"Sir, within the next five minutes our THAAD systems will begin to shoot our defensive missiles. We are tracking the North Korean ICBMs up on the main screen. But three of the eight failed in launch."

All eyes in the room focus on the five red triangles moving slowly across a large map of the world, heading for the continental U.S. and Hawaii.

As the ICBMs begin their descent, blue circles begin to rise up to meet them. Several miss, but the sheer number of THAAD missiles is impressive.

One after another, after another of the North Korean ICBMs is intercepted and the screen shows green squares signifying a hit. After just ten minutes it's all over. All of the North Korean ICBMs have been neutralized.

"Mr. President, we should get your family into the PEOC (Presidential Emergency Operations Center) just in case the North Koreans have more ICBMs."

The President grimly nods. "Ok, but they just gave us the justification for an all out attack. Launch the attack. Conventional arms only. Give'm hell boys!"

The President had tried to negotiate with Kim Jong-Un.   It seemed to be going well until the Americans discovered a secret nuclear arsenal and ballistic missile program.   When confronted, the North Koreans broke off talks and prepared for war.

After kissing his wife, the first lady, his daughter and grandsons are led to safety under the White House in the secure bunker.   Clare's husband and the other two of her children were moved to Cheyenne Mountain where they will be safe from any additional nuclear attack on Denver. Several of the President's top aides and multiple military leaders are all watching a large screen showing the detonation of multiple missiles that take out the remaining missile sites that had not yet been hit. Also shown are the B-52s, Stealth bombers and Stealth fighters taking out the NKPR military installations.

Kim had launched twelve ICBMs. This surprised the American military, but they were prepared.   Once in the Situation Room, the President has been on the phone with the leaders of Britain, France, Germany, South Korea, India and other key leaders as well as Russia and China.   Those last two phone calls were not pleasant. But the President was clear. The North Koreans fired eight ICBM missiles directly at the United States. The U.S. responded as any other country would at being attacked. Additionally Tokyo has been nuked. Both China and Russia understand the use of power when provoked.

"Mr. Xi, we understand your concern about a unified Korea. Our military will try to negotiate a transition to peace, but Kim Jung-Un must step down and be tried for crimes against his people. If he is still alive, we would ask that China help with the cease fire after our troops have taken P'yongyang."

The President listens to the translation and the reply. He smiles.

"Yes Mr. General Secretary. We will keep you and your military appraised of our progress, but we expect no interference with our mission."

The President hangs up and lets out a long breath. "Well, at this point both the Russians and China are on the sidelines. Both I believe are relieved that Kim has been taken out, hopefully taken out. But from their standpoint a nuclear Korean peninsula was very dangerous and they both know that Kim was a rabid dog."

The generals are busy directing the war and moving military assets towards North Korea. Even though the THAAD systems shot down the nuclear missiles, other conventional missiles did get through and caused considerable damage and killed thousands of civilians in South Korea. But several hours after the start of the war, the Americans and South Koreans have destroyed most of the military assets of the North. Unfortunately one of the nuclear missiles did get through and hit Tokyo. The world is shocked that Japan has suffered another nuclear attack, seventy-three years almost to the day after the Americans dropped two nuclear bombs on Hiroshima and Nagasaki to end WWII. Several hundred thousand Japanese were killed or injured from the North Korea attack.

Communications has been spotty at best, but the NSA and the CIA have continued to stream the latest information and data to the White House.

"Mr. President, we have confirmed that one NKPR ICBM missile did get through and hit just north of Tokyo."

The President shakes his head. "Damn. What about South Korea?"

"No communications yet Sir. But it will be bad."

The President sits and considers this new information. "What about civilian casualties in Japan?"

The General is handed a piece of paper from his assistant. "From the nuclear attack directly? Too many died. Before the ICBM exploded, they had almost five hundred commercial airliners in the air. Unfortunately because of the short distance between North Korea and Japan, they had only fifteen minutes warning before the missile hit. Almost sixty airliners crashed. Some were coming in from overseas and couldn't get down, but several were just too far from airports that could accommodate them and they tried to put down on highways. At this point with communications very limited, we have no idea how many people may have survived."

The President rises and walks over to a table with water and packaged snacks. "So what is the situation on the ground?"

The General clears his throat.

"The South Koreans have pounded the North Korean missile batteries and the troops just north of the DMZ. Of course some of the North Korean's missiles have gotten through and have hit Seoul and other cities.

"Well, thank God we were able to shoot down Kim's nukes. I knew we couldn't trust him."

Suddenly an aide to the Joint Chiefs enters the PEOC. He hands the General a note.

After reading the note, the General turns to the group. "Mr. President, we have detected a launch of three ICBMs from Syria. We are attempting to bring them down, but we used most of our interceptor missiles to take down the North Korean initial launch. Our analysts believe they will get through."

The President stands up straighter. "Syria? What the Hell? "What are the targets?"

"Looking at the altitude and direction, our analysts believe they are targeting Western, Central and Eastern United States.

"Could this be Iran?"

The General shakes his head. "Could be Iran, could be Russia or could be al-Qaeda."

"What about THAAD sites in Europe?"

"We can only hit the ICBMs during their re-entry. The

missiles are coming in from an orbit that won't allow us to hit them until they get closer."

An Air Force staff sergeant turns from his terminal and yells. "The ICBMs are tracking to three targets in the U.S., that don't make sense."

"The Iranians probably moved Russian RT-12M2 missiles on portable launchers into Syria for deniability. They control the Southeastern quadrant with the Syrian government forces and working hand-in-hand with al-Qaeda and ISIL. "The three ICBMs were launched near Deir Az Zor, in Eastern Syria." Says the National Security Advisor.

The General moves over and looks at the monitor. "Damn. They are going to detonate the ICBMs over the U.S., not hit us. They are going to do a HEMP. A High Altitude Electromagnetic Pulse."

The President reacts immediately. "We have to warn the Congress, the Supreme Court, the White House staff and the American public!"

"Yes sir. We have put out a general warning on the Emergency Warning System by FEMA has already been initiated. I will place calls to all branches of the government, but unless they get to a hardened site within thirty minutes they will be exposed."

The President runs his hand through his hair. "I want that area destroyed. Every military force taken out. I don't care if they are Iranian, Russia or Syrian. Then we'll deal with Iran."

General Seibert nods. "Yes sir! We have several drones in the area and they are tracking the launchers and the troops that were responsible. We have multiple assets available Qatar. They have been launched to take them out."

The Secretary of Defense speaks up. "I just heard from Israel; they have put their military on alert and would be available to hit Iran if we determine that the ICBMs are Iranian. They of course are also concerned that Iran will shoot a few nukes their way. But if they do Israel will destroy Iran with their own nukes."

"Mr. President, you should move into the PEOC along with the rest of the Joint Chiefs of Staff."

The President nods and leaves the Situation Room knowing he can follow the troop movements in the PEOC but wanting to be in the middle of the action.

In the PEOC, the President and the rest of his staff continue to watch the American attack unfold in North Korea while three nuclear missiles are streaking towards the American homeland.

Chapter 3

Belize

August 22nd

The Air Force pilots maneuver the CIA jet towards the Belize City International Airport. The plane is cleared for landing and swoops onto the 9700 foot runway. After landing and roll out, the jet taxis to a private hanger that the pilot arranged for after the change in destinations.

Mark and Michelle disembark after talking with the Air Force officers. The jet has onboard a small arsenal of weapons including four M16A rifles, six Beretta M9 pistols, two XM2010 Enhanced Sniper rifles, two XM 25 Counter Defilade Target Engagement Systems and a box of grenades. They discuss the protection of the jet.

"We will refuel while we can and we've rented this private hanger for two weeks, we can extend as we need to." Says the pilot.

Mark nods, "Ok, great. One of you should stay with

the jet at all times. The other doing a parameter patrol varying the time. Each of you should be armed and use deadly force if required to protect the jet. We'll take over when we get back."

Michelle jumps in. "I'll contact the Belize military and see if they will assign a few of their men as an extra level of protection. We'll head to the U.S. embassy and try to get more information on what is happening back home, the extent of the damage and what our next steps are."

The two pilots nod affirmatively and one directs over a fuel truck to refill the tanks and begin his maintenance review.

Mark and Michelle walk into the terminal and look for a car rental site. As they walk down one hallway, Michelle sees a television in one of the bars showing a photo of Washington D.C. and several commentators speaking.

"Let's check this out." Motioning towards the television, they see that it's a BBC broadcast.

They move into the bar and ask the bartender to turn up the sound. After he does, they hear one of the commentators saying; "... the United States attack on North Korea has been for the most part very successful. Over eighty percent of the North Korea military capability has been destroyed as reported by Reuters. It is reported that North Korea fired a dozen missiles first at the United States, and then President Baker responded with overpowering force."

Another commentator breaks in. "It seems that the NKPR fired those missiles in response to the United States moving military assets towards North Korea. They were justified."

"Justified? The United States moves military assets around the world on a regular basis, it looks like Kim Jong-Un feared an American attack and reacted first." Say the other commentator.

The moderator takes over. "To bring everyone up to speed. The United States and North Korea went to war this morning. The information we have at this point shows that North Korea fired a dozen ICBM missiles, eight at the United States, two at South Korea and two at Japan. All of those missiles launched at the U.S. were shot down by the U.S. missile defense system, but one of the missiles reached their target in Japan. Just coming in, our latest information from the Canadian government says that the three missiles were detonated two hundred miles above continental U.S. with one over the state of Colorado, one over the state of Iowa and the third over Northern Virginia.

The moderator takes a deep breath and looks directly into the camera. "At that point, all communications from the United States has ceased. These were EMP blasts that would impact most electronic devices including cellular phones, car electrical systems, airplane systems, and the United States electrical grid and of course it's telecommunication systems."

One of the commentators starts to describe Electromagnetic Pulse devices and how they work and the damage they can do.

At this point Michelle and Mark leave the bar to find a vehicle.

"Damn, this could be really bad. I was briefed on EMP attacks and the aftermath, it's not good. First the public will stay calm for a few days waiting for the Federal government to turn on the lights. The food supply will be consumed within a week. Because the trucks that bring food to stores stop, there will be no resupply. Within a week there will be riots in the major cities; New York, Chicago, Los

Angeles, San Francisco, Atlanta and others will collapse into total chaos."

They take an escalator down one level and spot the car rental companies.

"The medical system will breakdown, disease and societal collapse will kill millions. The study I saw was that within a year unless the government can restore order and electrical power, the United States population will drop by 80-90 percent."

Mark can't believe what he is hearing, but he knows Michelle understands what she is talking about.

"We need to get to the embassy as soon as possible and try to establish a connection with the White House. Hopefully the President and his family are safe."

Chapter 4

Tehran Iran
August 23rd

The leadership of the Iranian Mullahs has gathered along with General Aziz the head of the Revolutionary Guards. After the decision was made to move the Russian ICBMs into Syria, General Aziz knew it was only a matter of time before either the Israelis or the Americans spotted them. The Mullahs didn't want to attack America unless there was no other choice. But now that their gambit of releasing the Red Death virus upon the world was stopped, the European Union, the Americans and even the Russians and Chinese were against them. All were calling for a regime change and an end to the Islamic ideology in Iran. They are pushing a government much like Turkey that has both Muslims and non-Muslims ruling the country.

The theocracy guided by the Islamic ideology has ruled Iran for the past forty years. The supreme leader and the clerics will not have their power usurped by the West. After receiving the $1.2 Billion dollar payment from the United States for the nuclear deal in 2015, the military was upgraded and now they believe they are capable to destroying Israel.

Of course the agreement was suppose to stop the Iranian nuclear program, but Iran had built a totally secret underground facility that continued the development of both a nuclear warhead and ballistic missiles to deliver them to anywhere in the world. But the most important part of the agreement was the lifting of the sanctions. Those sanctions were strangling the Iranian economy. They were not able to sell oil and therefore could not buy much needed food, medicine and other basics to keep the Iranian population pacified. The nuclear agreement happened just in time. There were millions of Iranians that were getting ready to revolt. But with the sanctions lifted, it was like taking the top off a tea kettle just before it blew. Now the Iranians are reaping almost $1 Billion dollars per month from oil exports. More than enough to fund their economy and export terror to the West.

General Aziz stands before the supreme leader and the Mullahs and informs them of their progress. "As you know, we moved three Russian RT-12M2 missiles with 5 KT nuclear warheads to Southeastern Syria four weeks ago when the Red Death virus attack was stopped. The West in coordination with Russia and China are planning devastating sanctions like we've never seen. It will lead to our countries' demise. We had to act. So at 3 am this morning, we launched the three nuclear missiles at the United States designed to explode two hundred miles above the U.S. causing an EMP event that will knock out every electrical device in the country. This will decimate America, the country will fall into riots but at the same time North Korea has launched twelve of their nuclear ICBMs at the United States, South Korea and Japan. I believe we will be successful in causing a third world war from which the Muslim people, more specifically Iran will emerge victorious."

There are rumblings among the Mullahs, but General Aziz continues. "The ICBMs were launched from Syria and no doubt the Americans know that, but they don't know if it was us, the Russians or our brothers in al-Qaeda. That indecision is all we need to be successful."

The supreme leader slowly rises from his seat. He is an old man and knows his time to rule is short. "My brothers, we are at a crossroads in the history of our great country. This is our time to rule. It is our destiny from Allah. Allah 'arbar! Allah 'arbar! Allah 'arbar!"

All of Mullahs and the military present including General Aziz chant the famous God is Greater slogan. Aziz is not that religious, just power hungry. He wants the military to rule Iran and all of the Middle East. If Iran can survive this crisis, then he plans another revolution one in which his Revolutionary Guards will take power and he, General Aziz and his son will rule Iran and most of the Middle East will an iron fist.

www.ingramcontent.com/pod-product-compliance
Lightning Source LLC
Chambersburg PA
CBHW070753280626
47162CB00016B/202